THE ACT OF ROGER MURGATROYD

Gilbert Adair has published novels, essays, translations, children's books and poetry. He is the acclaimed author of *The Postmodernist Always Rings Twice*, and has also written screenplays, including *The Dreamers* – from his own novel – for Bernardo Bertolucci. A sequel to *The Act of Roger Murgatroyd* – *A Mysterious Affair of Style* – is forthcoming from Faber.

The Act of Roger Murgatroyd

An Entertainment

GILBERT ADAIR

faber and faber

First published in 2006
by Faber and Faber Limited
3 Queen Square London WC1N 3AU
This paperback edition first published in 2007

Typeset in Sabon by Faber and Faber Limited
Printed in England by Mackays of Chatham plc, Chatham, Kent

A CIP record for this book
is available from the British Library

ISBN 978–0–571–22638–2

2 4 6 8 10 9 7 5 3 1

For Michael Maar

The real world is nothing but the
sum total of paths leading nowhere.
RAOUL RUIZ

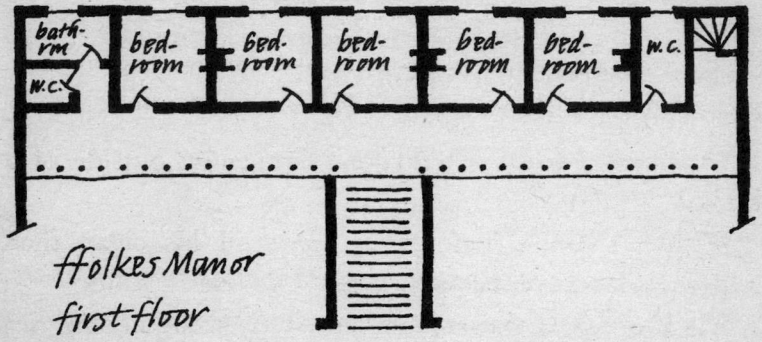

bath-rm

W.C.

bedroom

bedroom

bedroom

bedroom

bedroom

W.C.

ffolkes Manor
first floor

Chapter One

'Sort of thing you can't imagine happening outside of a book!'

With a shaking hand the Colonel lit his cigar, then added, 'D**n it all, Evadne, it could be one of yours!'

'Hah!' snorted the lady in question, straightening her pince-nez, which were sitting askew on the bridge of her nose. 'That only proves what I suspected all along.'

'What d'you mean?'

'That you were fibbing when you told me how much you enjoyed my stuff.'

'Fibbing? Well, of all the –'

'If you'd actually read my novels, Roger ffolkes, instead of just pretending to have read them, you'd know I never touch locked rooms. I leave them to John Dickson Carr.'

The Colonel was patently calculating how best to bluster his way out of the fix he'd got himself into when his daughter Selina, who until that instant had been seated beside her mother on the sofa, her face buried in her hands, suddenly startled both of them by shouting, 'Oh, for God's sake stop it, you two! You're being absolutely horrid, behaving just as though we were playing a game of Murder! Ray is lying dead' – she made a histrionic gesture in the vague direction of the attic – 'shot through the heart! Don't you even care!'

These last four words were spoken in audible capital letters: DON'T YOU EVEN CARE! It's true that, when Selina decided to study art instead of going on the stage, she may have chosen the wrong calling, but on this occasion nobody could have doubted her sincerity. She had only just ceased sobbing, all of half-an-hour after the body had been discovered. And though he and his wife had done what they could to comfort her, the Colonel, in the heat and confusion of that discovery, had already forgotten the strength of his daughter's feelings for the victim. He was now wearing a rather sheepish expression on his ruddy-complexioned features.

'Sorry, my sweet, sorry. I'm being awfully callous. It's just – well, it's just that this murder is so extraordinary I still haven't got over it!' He put an arm round her shoulder. 'Forgive me, forgive me.'

Then, typically, his mind started wandering again.

'Never known a locked-room murder to happen in real life,' he muttered to himself. 'Might be worth writing to *The Times*.'

'Ohhh, father!'

While the Colonel's wife continued ineffectually to pat her daughter on the knees, Donald, the American boy Selina had met at art school, hovered solicitously over her. He was, though, too bashful to do what he was surely pining to do, which was to cradle her in his arms. (That's Donald Duckworth, by the way, an unfortunate name, but his parents couldn't have anticipated that when they christened him back in 1915.)

In truth, the Colonel was by no means the sole offender. Though it's fair to say everybody present sympathised with Selina, some vocally, some silently, there could be no getting around the fact that, of the house-party, only she truly mourned the dead man. Even if their minds hadn't been monopolised by the astounding trappings of the crime, the others, without exception, had their own individual reasons for not wasting too much time in formulating conventional expressions of regret over the departure from this world of Raymond Gentry. Nobody, in short, was prepared to shed crocodile tears, and only Selina ffolkes real ones.

So if, on that Boxing Day morning, an intruder were to have strayed into the wood-panelled drawing-room of ffolkes Manor – its ineradicably male aura, as pungent as the aroma of one of the Colonel's cigars, feminised by a row of delicate Royal Doulton figurines on the mantelpiece and the exquisite petit-point that covered the armchairs – he would certainly have sensed a pervasive atmosphere of shock and even fear. But he would also have been puzzled by the virtual absence of personal grief.

The grandfather clock had just struck quarter-past seven. The huddled servants were already in their uniforms, while the guests were still in their dressing-gowns – except, that is, for Cora Rutherford, the stage and screen actress, one of Mary ffolkes's oldest friends. She was wearing a gaudy purple-and-gold garment which she called a 'kimono' and claimed was a Paris 'exclusive'. And it was she who spoke next.

'Why doesn't one of you men *do* something?'

The Colonel looked up sharply.

'Take a hold on yourself, Cora,' he cautioned her. 'This is no time to go wobbly.'

'Oh, for heaven's sake, Roger, you silly man!' she replied in her habitual tone of cordial contempt. 'My nerves are of stronger steel than yours.'

As though to demonstrate, she took a slim shagreen cigarette-case from one of her kimono pockets, drew out a cigarette, inserted it into an elongated ebony holder, lit it and dragged the smoke deep into her lungs, all with fingers as steady as the Colonel's had been shaky.

'All I meant,' she went on calmly, 'was that we just can't sit here with a dead body directly over our heads. We've got to take action.'

'Yes, but what?' answered the Colonel. 'Farrar has tried the 'phone – how many times, Farrar?'

4

'About half-a-dozen, sir.'

'Right. The lines are down and they're probably going to stay down for some while to come. And as you can perfectly well hear for yourself, the blizzard that brought them down is still raging outside. We have to face the facts. We're snowed in. Completely cut off – at least until this storm blows itself out. The nearest police station is more than thirty miles away and the only road that leads to it must be impassable.'

With a furtive glance at Selina, he concluded:

'And, after all, it's not as though – well, I mean to say, our Christmas get-together is utterly ruined and all that, and it's extremely unpleasant for all of us, but it's not as though the body's about to – about to walk away. I'm afraid we're just going to have to sit it out for as long as it takes.'

It was then that, from the fireside armchair in which she was ensconced, snug and shapeless in her woollen dressing-gown, Evadne Mount, the novelist we've already been introduced to, said to the Colonel with a hint of urgency in her mannish voice, 'You know, Roger, I wonder if we can actually afford to do that.'

'Do what?'

'Sit it out, as you say.'

The Colonel shot her a quizzical look.

'And why not?'

'Well, let's just consider what has happened here. Half-an-hour ago the body of Raymond Gentry was found dead in the attic. You, Roger, had to break down the door to get to him, a door that was locked on the inside with its key still in the keyhole. As if that weren't enough, the room's one and only window was barred. So, to all intents and purposes, nobody could have entered the attic – yet somebody did – and, once inside, who knows how, nobody could have got back out again – yet there's no denying that somebody also succeeded in doing just that.

'Now, as I've already told you, Roger, I don't do locked-room murders. I've written nine novels and three plays – my latest, *The Wrong Voice*, is in its fourth triumphant year in the West End as we speak – beat that, Agatha Christie! – and not one of them has featured a murder committed inside a locked room. So I can't pretend to have the foggiest notion how this murder was done.

'But,' she went on, pausing for a second or two, clearly holding back so that her next statement would have the greatest possible effect on her listeners, '*I do know who did it*.'

And, indeed, the effect was devastating. The drawing-room went deathly quiet. A few seconds elapsed when time seemed suspended. The servants stopped their nervous shuffling. Cora Rutherford's immaculately manicured fingers stopped dancing a pirouette on the transparent rim of her glass ashtray. Even the grandfather clock stopped ticking – or else tick-tocked on tiptoe.

The silence was finally, bathetically, brought to an end by an eruption of nasal wailing from the butter-fingered kitchen-maid Adelaide, adenoidal Addie, the other maids called her, who would burst into tears at the drop of a hat – or at least of a china teacup. With a loud 'Wheeesht, girl!', however, Mrs Varley, the cook, put an end to that, and everybody turned again to face Evadne Mount.

It was the Colonel who posed the inevitable question.

'Oh, you do, do you? So tell us. Who did it?'

'One of us.'

Strangely, none of the indignant protestations she might have assumed would follow such a dramatic assertion were forthcoming. On the contrary, it was as though its logic had impressed everybody, instantly and simultaneously, as irrefutable.

'I know that this house is situated right on the edge of Dartmoor,' she continued, 'and probably fantasies of escaped convicts have been flitting through all of your brains. And, yes, it's true that, with the 'phone lines down, we can't know for sure that some escaped convict isn't roaming about the countryside. As far as I'm concerned, though, it's not on. Like the White Queen, I'm capable of believing as many as six impossible things before breakfast – well, let's say *after* breakfast,' she corrected herself, 'I'm nothing till I've had my coffee. And, as an avid reader of my dear friend John Dickson Carr's whodunits, I'm also capable of believing that somebody managed to materialise

7

then dematerialise inside that locked attic room, killing Raymond Gentry in the meantime, and all without supernatural intervention. Great Gods, I have to believe it, since it happened!

'But nobody will ever make me believe that a convict escaped from his cell in Dartmoor, escaped from the most escape-proof prison in the country, made his away across the moors in a howling snowstorm, broke into this house without any of us hearing him, lured the wretched Gentry into the attic, did away with him, got out again leaving the door and window intact, and sneaked back into the storm! No – there, in life *and* in fiction, I draw the line. Whichever way you look at it, the murder has to be what the police call an inside job.'

Again there was silence, while again her words insidiously sank in. Even Selina lifted her tear-stained face from her hands to watch how everybody else was reacting. And again it was the Colonel, standing with his legs akimbo in front of the huge blazing fire, in a pose uncannily reminiscent of the actor Charles Laughton as Henry VIII, who spoke.

'Well, Evadne, that's a red-hot potato you've tossed into our laps, I must say.'

'I had to be blunt,' she answered unapologetically. 'It was you yourself who told us we must face the facts.'

'What you've just offered us is a theory, not a fact.'

'Maybe so. But if anybody else' – her eyes scanned the

room – 'if anybody else can draw a more plausible conclusion from the evidence before us, I'd be glad to hear it.'

Mary ffolkes, who hadn't said a word until then, suddenly turned to her and cried, 'Oh, Evie, you've got to be mistaken, you've just got to be! If it were true, it – it would be too gruesome to contemplate!'

'I'm sorry, old girl, but it's precisely because it's gruesome that we have to contemplate it. That's why I said we can't afford to hang around till the storm breaks. The very idea of us all sitting here wondering which of us . . . Good heavens, I don't have to spell it out, do I? I know what havoc this kind of mutual suspicion can cause.

'It was the theme of my first novel, *The Mystery of the Green Penguin*, you remember, in which a woman becomes so obsessed with the idea that her next-door neighbour is slowly poisoning her crippled husband that her own husband, driven to distraction by her compulsive spying and snooping and sleuthing, eventually runs amok and splits her head open with a piece of antique Benares brassware. And, of course, the neighbour turns out to be totally innocent.

'Now, I'm not suggesting anything like that is liable to happen here. But something's got to be done. And fast.'

From the other end of the drawing-room, where he stood stiffly alongside his fellow staff members, Chitty, the Colonel's butler, a man who even at such an ungodly hour contrived to uphold a butlerish gravitas, took one step forward, clenched his fist, raised it to his lips and gave a self-consciously theatrical cough. It was the sort of sound that, in their stage directions, playwrights tend to convey as 'ahem' and you could actually hear the two syllables 'a' and 'hem' in Chitty's cough.

'Yes, Chitty,' said the Colonel, 'what is it?'

'If I may be so bold, sir,' said Chitty ponderously, 'it did occur to me that – well, that –'

'Yes, yes, speak up, man!'

'Well, sir. Chief-Inspector Trubshawe, sir.'

The Colonel's face brightened up at once.

'Why, I do believe you've got something there! Trubshawe, of course!'

'Trubshawe? I know that name,' said Henry Rolfe, the local GP. 'Isn't he the retired Scotland Yard man? Moved down here two or three months ago?'

'That's right. A widower. Bit of a recluse. I invited him to join the party – you know, just to be neighbourly. Said he preferred to spend Christmas alone. But he's an affable enough cove once you get talking to him, and he *was* one of the top chaps at the Yard. Good thinking, Chitty.'

'Thank you, sir,' murmured Chitty with evident satisfaction, before noiselessly resuming his place.

'The thing is,' the Colonel went on, 'Trubshawe's cottage is six or seven miles along the Postbridge Road. Next to the level-crossing. Even in this storm, it might be feasible for somebody to drive there and bring him back.'

'Colonel?'

'Yes, Farrar?'

'Won't that be an imposition? At this hour. And at Christmas, too. He *is* retired, after all.'

'A policeman never really retires, not even for the night,' demurred the Colonel. 'For all I know, he might welcome some excitement. Must be bored rigid with no one but a blind old Labrador to talk to all day long.'

He at once started from his immobility and turned to each of the men who were standing, sitting or slouching in the room.

'Any of you ready to give it a go?'

'I will,' said the Doctor before the others had a chance to speak. 'My old crock can stand up to the worst weather. Fact is, she's used to it.'

'Let me come with you,' Don just as quickly seconded him.

'Thanks. I'll need some muscular assistance if she stalls.'

'If it's muscles you want, Doctor,' said Don, stealing a hopeful glance at Selina as he only half-jokily pumped up his biceps, 'then I'm your man!'

'Good, good. Well, let's get going if we're going.'

Henry Rolfe then leaned over the armchair in which his wife Madge sat, her unstockinged legs folded underneath her like those of a cat, and kissed her demurely on the forehead.

'Now, darling,' he said, 'I don't want you to be anxious about me. I'll be fine.'

Bearing up with fetching fortitude, Madge Rolfe, who always looked as though the major anxiety of her life was how long she might have to wait for some lovelorn lounge lizard to light her next cigarette, offered him no more than a wan smile in return for his kiss.

As he strode out of the room followed by Don, everybody wished them godspeed. Then, clapping his hands in quite the Oriental manner, mustering as much grim joviality as could be regarded as decent under the circumstances, the Colonel asked, 'Would anybody care to join me in a spot of breakfast?'

Chapter Two

It was a few minutes short of nine o'clock that same morning when a motor-car was heard pulling up in the forecourt outside the french window and a swift peek between the drawing-room's heavy velveteen curtains confirmed it to be Dr Rolfe's. It transpired (as the house-party was to hear it described to them) that the outward journey in particular had been a nightmarish experience. By the Doctor's account, his Rover had lurched perilously out of one deep snowdrift into another and poor Don seems to have spent more of the trip pushing the car than being driven in it. They had, though, finally made it to Trubshawe's cottage. Luckily, he was already up, nursing a mug of hot chocolate by the fire – perhaps also nursing a lonely memory or two – while Tobermory, his ancient Labrador, dozed at his slippered feet.

The Chief-Inspector first had to get over his natural surprise at finding a pair of strangers on his doorstep not merely on an icy December morn but on Boxing Day to boot.

Having digested that, he was to be surprised all over again when informed of the reason for their call. Once a policeman, however, always a policeman: he accepted without hesitation to return with them to ffolkes Manor. In fact, the Colonel may have been right when he predicted that Trubshawe would actually welcome an injection of excitement in what must have become a somewhat anti-climactic existence after four decades of sterling service at the Yard. Don reported having observed an exhilarated glint in his eyes as well as a coiled and almost cat-like alacrity in his gestures when he and Rolfe gave him a brief rundown of the morning's bizarre events.

Inside the gloomy hallway the three of them proceeded to divest themselves of their overcoats, scarves and gloves. Then, as the Chief-Inspector briskly dusted the snow from his walrus moustache, Tobermory, who couldn't be left behind on his own, since at this stage nobody knew for certain just how long it might be before his master got home again, treated his bulgy old frame to an unexpectedly vigorous shake before trotting into the drawing-room and, giving its occupants an incurious once-over, collapsed in front of the fireplace and promptly closed his rheumy eyes.

The company, it has to be said, had become more than a little fretful in the intervening couple of hours. Selina ffolkes had taken to her bed, or at least to her bedroom, minutes after the Doctor's departure and, with the exception of Chitty, whose idea it had been to fetch the Chief-Inspector and whom it would have been churlish to deprive of the spectacle of his arrival, the servants – the cook, the two housemaids, the kitchen-maid and the gardener-cum-chauffeur-cum-handyman – had all been sent back down to the kitchen, since the only contribution the three maids especially had had to make to the crisis was a nervous twittering that looked unlikely to let up in the short term.

As for the ffolkeses' house-guests, not knowing whether they ought to go up to their rooms or wait on in the drawing-room, they had all chosen – all but Selina, that is – to stay put.

Maybe 'chosen' isn't the correct word. Though nobody, not even the Colonel, presumed to give an order as such, there was an unspoken feeling among the whole party that, mortifying as it was to have to sit about in their dressing-gowns, hair unkempt and make-up unapplied, it might be wiser if they all remained within reassuring sight of each other until this Trubshawe person turned up, assuming he ever did. Naturally, they all implicitly trusted their fellow guests and hosts, all of them old, dear, close friends. Still, you could almost hear them thinking, if Evie *is* right . . .

Time passing as slowly as it invariably does, though, when you're eager for it to fly, Madge Rolfe had proposed a rubber of bridge to while away what, for all anyone knew, could be several hours before her husband's return. And since Mary ffolkes had long since given up playing with her own choleric spouse, it was Madge herself who ended up partnering the Colonel, and Evadne Mount the Vicar.

But it had been a spineless sort of game, with a dispiriting absence of the squabbling they all secretly enjoyed. It was clear they felt it would have been both tactless and tasteless to indulge themselves in one of their ripsnorting, corset-cracking rows. So that, when the search-party turned up at last with the Chief-Inspector in tow, it was with unanimous and undisguised relief that they all downed their cards.

Flanked by Don and Rolfe, the burly ex-Scotland Yard policeman stepped into the spacious drawing-room, whose light and warmth, following directly on from the gloom of the narrow hallway, caused him momentarily to blink.

The Colonel walked a few paces forward to greet him.

'Ah, Trubshawe, so they got you here in one piece? Look, I'm really sorry, old chap, to have to drag you away from hearth and home on Boxing Day – and what a stinker of a Boxing Day it is, eh, what? But we've been at our wits' end – we just didn't know what . . .'

The Chief-Inspector took a grip of the Colonel's hand and gave it such a forceful shake the latter couldn't prevent himself from flinching. Then he scrutinised the half-dozen guests seated around the fireside – their tired, obscurely frightened eyes lent a semblance of animation by its glow – without letting his own shrewd eyes alight for more than a couple of seconds on any one of them.

'You needn't apologise,' he said, absent-mindedly tweaking one of his bushy eyebrows. 'I quite see how you had to turn wherever you could for help. Sounds like a dreadful business.'

'It is, it is. But do come right in, right up to the fire. Warm your hands.'

'Thanks. I will,' he answered, marching over to the fireside with a series of generic nods to the attendant womenfolk.

'Ladies,' he said lightly, all but dipping his fingertips into the flames.

Then, turning back to the Colonel, he added, 'I think, though, I ought to be taken at once to the scene of the crime.'

'You wouldn't prefer to be introduced first?'

'Well – no.'

He addressed the others.

'I don't wish to appear rude, ladies – gentlemen,' he nodded again, this time to both genders, 'but, in view of the extreme gravity of the case, first things first. The body, I think.'

'Yes, naturally you'll want to see the body,' said the Colonel. 'Yes, yes, if you'll just come with me. But, you know, it does feel a bit odd you haven't yet met –'

'The body first,' the Chief-Inspector insisted.

'As you say, then. It – I mean the body – it's still in the attic. We haven't touched anything, you'll see. We left it – we left him – exactly as we found him. If you'd just like to follow me.'

'Thank you. And perhaps you, Mr Duckworth, would join us? Since you were with the Colonel when he broke into the attic.'

'Oh yeah, sure thing,' averred Don. 'In the car I told you everything I know, but, sure, anything you say.'

'It might be helpful if Farrar also came with us,' the Colonel interjected. 'Take notes. What say you, Chief-Inspector? He's my secretary and general manager. Good chap to have around.'

'I don't have a problem with that. Though I tend to make my own notes' – he tapped his forehead – 'inside my head, don't you know. But yes, why not.'

The small party was then led off into the main hall, a draughty, well-proportioned, high-ceilinged space, though one that some already found lugubrious even without the baleful influence of the present tragedy. On its walls the Colonel had mounted the stuffed heads of every imaginable wild beast, from a magnificently antlered Highland stag and an enormous grey elephant from the Indian hill country to a hybrid flock of smaller and friskier creatures, all of them mementoes of his travels in happier times. At the top of the broad central staircase, which arched out in both directions to two banistered galleries, an Egyptian mummy stood erect in its garish gilt coffin and, when the Colonel escorted Trubshawe past it, and noticed the bemused interest the policeman momentarily took in it, he remarked:

'My wife's. Given her by some archaeologist cousin of

hers. He – how shall I put this? – he, um, salvaged it from a dig he was directing in Luxor in – let me see – must have been in '31.'

He then made one of his typically lame efforts to lighten an awkward situation.

'As I say, it's my wife's mummy. What you might call my mummy-in-law. Ha ha ha!'

'Most amusing,' said Trubshawe politely.

(To be honest, it was a joke which Roger ffolkes had made to absolutely every stranger who had ever crossed the threshold of his house and by now it was as old and creaky as the mummy itself.)

The Colonel turned into the right-hand gallery past two guest bedrooms connected by a shared, in-between bathroom, then went right again into a narrow corridor at the end of which a spiral staircase led up to the spartan stone corridor along which the servants were variously quartered. It was there that, like a skein of ribbon whose festive curlicues had been neatly ironed out, the spiral staircase straightened itself into a short flight of steps at the very top of which, opposite the last step, loomed the attic door.

Even before the Chief-Inspector had reached that last step, he could see that a heinous crime had been committed inside the room. Not only had the door been forced to give way but it was still jammed against some large, inert object which prevented it from being opened more than a crack, an object which was all too obviously a human body, lying on the floor in a pose as random as a throw of dice. And from under the door a trickle of congealing blood had formed a blot of incongruously vibrant colour against the landing's drab flagstones.

Trubshawe wasted no time on that blood. Gingerly, so as not to disturb the corpse more than he had to, but aggressively nevertheless, because he wouldn't otherwise have been able to get into the room at all, he shouldered the door open as far as it would go, stepped over the now visible remains of Raymond Gentry and entered the room.

The attic was of a stark, cell-like austerity, higher than it was long except where its ceiling sloped down to the halfway mark of the wall furthest away from where the Chief-Inspector was now standing. And it was sparely equipped, its furniture consisting, for all in all, of a badly chipped wooden table with its own rickety cane-bottomed chair and, in a corner, one sad and solitary armchair. The latter's fabric, which would once have been described as chintzy, had suffered so much wear and tear that yellowy-white stuffing protruded unappetisingly from all over its faded surface and the chintz itself had become so worn it was next to impossible to figure out what might have been its original pattern.

There was also, above and behind the armchair, the attic's one and only window, which was oblong and glassless and traversed vertically by a pair of parallel iron bars.

It was, though, the sight of the dead Raymond Gentry

which transfixed everyone's attention. Wearing the arresting combination of jet-black silk pyjamas and a bathrobe of a fluffy white towelling fabric, he lay stretched across the floor, his sickly, effeminate features warped out of shape by a grimace of indescribable horror. Seeping through his two hands, as they desperately clutched his own neck, rivulets of blood snaked about his long, tapering fingers like so many exotic ruby rings.

Hunkering down to inspect the body, Trubshawe carefully unbuttoned Gentry's ripped and seared pyjama jacket to examine the bullet wound, an act that made Don shrink back in revulsion.

Then he got to his feet, took a gnarled old pipe out of his pocket, shoved it unlit into his mouth and turned to the Colonel.

'I presume this,' he said gravely, 'is exactly how you found him?'

'Indeed it is. Nothing's been moved or even touched. Am I right, Don?'

'Say what?' mumbled the young American, still shaken by his brusque exposure to the grisly details of Gentry's wound.

'I said, this is exactly how we found him?'

'Yeah, that's right. Just as he is now. Pushed up against the door.'

'And already dead?' asked the Chief-Inspector.

'Oh yes,' said the Colonel. 'No doubt about that at all.

We did ask the Doctor to take a look at him, but he was well past saving. From what Rolfe told us, though, he'd only just been killed. Which makes sense, because of course I had heard the shot myself.'

'I see,' said Trubshawe thoughtfully. 'Now, on our drive back, Mr Duckworth gave me his version of how you two made the discovery. I'd like to run it past you, Colonel, if I may, to assure myself there's no discrepancy in your accounts.'

'Yes, of course. Go ahead.'

'Well, what I gathered from Mr Duckworth was that you were drawing a bath when you heard the firing of a shot.'

'A shot followed by a scream. A scream, Chief-Inspector, that positively froze my marrow, and I'm no stranger to screams.'

'A shot and a scream that you immediately knew could only have come from the attic. Have I got that right?'

'Yes, I heard them both overhead. That's how I realised they couldn't have come from the servants' quarters, you see, because they all sleep in adjacent rooms further along the corridor. The attic is the only room in the house located directly above our bedroom.'

'So you instantly rushed out of your bedroom –'

'Well, not quite instantly. I did have to slip on a few more clothes than I happened to be wearing at the time.'

'Slipping on some extra clothes, you rushed out of your bedroom into the gallery, then up these steps we've just climbed and –'

'If I may interrupt you again, Chief-Inspector?'

'Yes, Colonel?'

'So that we're all in agreement about everything, I think you should know it was as I was starting to climb the steps that I collided with Don, whose bedroom happens to be the closest to them.'

'Quite so. That chimes exactly with what Mr Duckworth told me. Then, if I understand aright, you both observed blood seeping under the doorway and decided you had to break into the room at once?'

'You got it,' said Don. 'The first, I dunno, three or four times we put our shoulders to the door, it just wouldn't budge. But, you can see for yourself, the wood's really old and damp, some parts of it are rotten through – here, look, if you pick at it with your finger it just flakes away – so, anyway, we did eventually manage to get it open. Even then, we could only squeeze into the room by clambering over Gentry's body.'

While Don was complementing the Colonel's story, the Chief-Inspector bent down to study the door more closely. Now he stood up and said:

'I note, too, that the door is locked from the inside and the key is still in the lock. Is that also how you found it?'

'Absolutely!' exclaimed the Colonel. 'That's what's so dashed extraordinary about this business. Window barred, door locked from the inside, key still dangling in the lock! I never heard of such a thing, as the Scotchman said of the Crucifixion.'

'And the attic was empty when you entered it?'

'Completely empty – except, of course, for Gentry here. I'm blamed if I know how he did it – the murderer, I mean – and assuming it's a he. As I was saying downstairs a couple of hours ago, it's the kind of murder you can only imagine being committed in a book. Ironic, really, when you think that one of our guests is Evadne Mount. The thriller writer, you know.'

'Yes,' said Trubshawe, 'Mr Duckworth already told me she was here. I was quite impressed.'

'A fan of her work, then, are you?' asked the Colonel.

'We-ell,' answered Trubshawe evasively, 'I don't know as I'd call myself a fan. She's never been known to be a fan of Scotland Yard. Inspector Plodder – that's the moniker I'd be saddled with if I was unlucky enough to turn up in one of her books. I'd be the chump who does all the spade-work, who takes all the pains. Then along saunters some smart-alec of an amateur 'tec and –'

A stentorian voice rang out behind him.

'If it's *my* amateur 'tec you're talking about, Chief-Inspector, do at least get the sex right. Smart-alexis, if you please, not smart-alec.'

On the threshold, wrapped in her dressing-gown, the quintessence of one of those dotty, indomitable Home Counties matrons who are as irreplaceable a feature of the soft and undulating English landscape as Bedouin tribeswomen are of the no less soft and undulating Sahara Desert, stood Evadne Mount.

'Smart-alexis?' repeated the Chief-Inspector, too taken aback for the moment to issue the stern rebuke he doubtless felt she deserved for having followed him uninvited into the attic.

'If, as you seem to imply, you've read my books,' she said, jabbing a pudgy finger at him, 'and whether or not you feel you can count yourself among my many fans, you really should know my detective's name.'

'Which is?'

'Baddeley. Alexis Baddeley.'

'Why, yes, yes, of course it is!' said Trubshawe. 'It all comes back to me. Alexis Baddeley. Single lady – formidable intellect – of, as they say, a certain age. It was she who solved the identical-twin fratricide in *Faber or Faber*, am I right?'

'You are indeed. It's funny. I'd always been wary of that whiskery old device of identical twins. So when I finally did employ it, I decided, in my trademark fashion, to stretch the conceit as far as it would go without snapping.

'You see,' she rattled on, now extending her discourse to include Don and the Colonel, 'the novel's main characters are a pair of identical twins, the Faber brothers, Kenneth and George. Not only do they look exactly alike, they dress exactly alike. They even communicate in a strange coded language that nobody else understands and play endless practical jokes, vicious, mean-spirited pranks, on their neighbours, who of course have never been able to tell them apart.'

'But I –'

'Strangest of all,' continued the novelist, paying no heed to Trubshawe's attempt to interrupt her, 'is that they themselves are always quarrelling – the reader soon learns that they actually despise each other – so that, when one of them is murdered, it stands to reason the other must have done it. But since the survivor of the two maintains a stubborn silence as to his identity, the dilemma facing Alexis Baddeley is: which is which? She has to exert all her formidable intellect, as you so kindly put it, Chief-Inspector, to discover whether it was Kenneth who murdered George or George who murdered Kenneth.'

'And which was it?' asked Trubshawe, his head literally spinning.

'You say you read the book,' Evadne Mount drily countered. 'You tell me.'

He stared at her, almost if not quite rudely, before remembering that now was not the time for literary reminiscences.

'Miss Mount, we haven't been introduced so I'll do the honours myself. My name is Trubshawe, Chief-Inspector Trubshawe. Or, I should say, *ex*-Chief-Inspector Trubshawe.'

'Pleased to meet you,' returned the novelist.

'And I you. Honoured, in fact. However, I really must insist that you go back downstairs at once and rejoin your fellow guests. This is no place for a lady.'

Evadne Mount glanced dispassionately at the recumbent form of Raymond Gentry.

'Fiddlesticks. I can't speak for my fellow ladies, but I'm quite capable of outstaring a dead body without swooning away like some helpless ninny. And it could be useful to me, as an author of whodunits, to observe the proper – what's Scotland Yard parlance for it? – process? – no, no, no, procedure, isn't it?

'Besides which, as Roger just remarked, this is the sort of crime which is supposed to happen only in books and it's by way of being a theory of mine that, even in life, there exist murder mysteries we writers are better qualified to solve than you policemen. Naturally I don't expect you to share that view, but you would agree, surely, that the more the merrier?'

'The more the merrier, you say?' mused the Chief-Inspector. 'Isn't that rather an unfortunate turn of phrase to use while standing a few feet away from a corpse? And now we're on the subject, Colonel, I have to tell you this. Though, on the one hand, I've certainly sensed the shock and horror any group of respectable citizens would experience on discovering that a brutal murder has been committed in their midst, it hasn't escaped my notice, on the other hand, that none of you is what might be called prostrate with grief at the death of this young man.'

To Trubshawe's observation the Colonel seemed at first to have no adequate response.

'Ah, well . . .' he mumbled. 'It's just . . . just . . . Well, frankly, I'm at a loss to know what to say.'

'After all, the poor chap was a guest of yours.'

'That's just it. He wasn't.'

'He wasn't?'

'No, I'm afraid not,' said the Colonel.

'Then what was he doing here?'

'The fact is, Trubshawe, I never met Raymond Gentry in my life before. Not till he arrived on Christmas Eve. He came down with my daughter Selina – and Don here. He was Selina's guest, not mine or my wife's. It was one of those last-minute changes of plan young people find so appealing, I suppose because it makes them feel they're being all very Bohemian and free-spirited.

'I worship my daughter, you understand, but she's like all her crowd these days. She means no harm, but at the same time she has no consideration of how inconvenient some "amusingly" spontaneous act of hers might turn out to be for the rest of us. When I was her age, I'd never have dreamt of foisting a stranger on my people at Christmastime, some young man who hadn't been invited and whom none of us knew from Adam.

'But there you are, that's the younger generation for you. The Chelsea set and all that. They're a law unto themselves, are they not, just as stuck in their ways as we are in ours. And if you even so much as hint that it might have been nice if they'd thought to ask you first, they write you off as some kind of hopelessly hidebound old fusspot.'

'She gave you no prior warning?'

'None at all.'

'And this Raymond Gentry, didn't he feel discomfort at finding himself among people who were unable or unwilling to conceal their resentment at his presence?'

The Colonel snorted.

'Gentry? Huh! I tell you, Trubshawe, I shouldn't be at all surprised to learn that the whole idea of his coming down here hadn't been mooted by Gentry himself.'

'Aha. I gather you don't – didn't – care overmuch for the young man?'

'Didn't care overmuch for him?' spluttered the Colonel. 'Gentry was as nasty a bit of goods as I've ever had the ill-fortune to encounter. Know what he did for a so-called living? He was, wait for it, a professional gossip columnist for that despicable rag, *The Trombone*. Now you can't sink much lower than that!

'Yes, yes, I realise the man is lying dead at our feet, but there were times I had half a mind to horsewhip him out of the house and frogmarch him down the front drive! And, when you think of it, if I'd had a whole mind to do it, the young whipper-snapper would be alive today!'

'Why, then, didn't you?' asked Trubshawe quietly.

'Why didn't I what?'

'Horsewhip him? Frogmarch him?'

'In a word, Selina. As I said, it was she who invited him

down and she did seem to have a pash on the fellow. Don't ask me why. Selina's always been something of a handful, and more so of late, but she's our only child and Mary and I dote on her. So I decided I'd just have to grin and bear it – *try* to grin and *try* to bear it. Bite the bullet instead of firing it, ha ha ha!

'That, incidentally, Chief-Inspector, in case you hadn't understood, was my way of telling you that, sorely tempted as I often have been these past twenty-four hours, I did not kill Raymond Gentry.'

On this declaration of innocence his interlocutor, whose crafty old eyes were already taking in the dingily sinister little room, made no comment.

'I don't suppose,' he said instead, 'there's any point in my asking you if there was a murder weapon left lying about?'

'Nothing either of us could see, no.'

Trubshawe stepped over to the table, pulled at its two drawers at once – he had to give one of them a violent jerk before it would consent to slide scratchily open – and found both to be empty.

'Queer . . .' he murmured.

'What is?'

'Oh, just that if the murderer had wanted the thing to look like a suicide, then all he had to do was leave his revolver in Gentry's hand – and given the infernal trouble he must have gone to over the locked door, barred window and all, that surely would have been an obvious ploy to distract us from the true nature of the crime. By removing the gun, he – or, of course, she – has actually succeeded in drawing our attention to the fact that it *was* murder.'

He crossed to the window and ran a finger aslant its scabby wooden frame. Then, with that powerful grip of his, he endeavoured to prise apart its two iron bars. Neither so much as wobbled.

Rubbing his now dust-covered palms together, he turned to the Colonel again.

'Servants above suspicion, are they?'

'Good heavens, yes. They've all been with us for years – or, in the case of the maids, months, which is about as much as you've any right to expect these days.'

He reflected a moment.

'There is Tomelty, of course.'

'Tomelty?'

'He's my chauffeur-cum-gardener-cum-general-thingum-abob. Irish. Bit too Irish for my liking. Fancies himself as a real devil, Tomelty does. But, to be honest, if he is a danger, it's only to the village girls. Mary and I suspect he's already responsible for having popped a bun or two into some local ovens, but no one was able to prove anything – all the mums kept mum, so to say – and I'm not the type of employer who'll sack a man on the basis of rumour and tittle-tattle. Especially as, for all his occasional Irish insolence, he's d**ned good at his job. He's certainly no murderer.'

'And Farrar?' Trubshawe then asked him. 'Do forgive my bluntness, Mr Farrar, but it's a question that's eventually got to be put to your employer and I might as well put it now.'

The Colonel vehemently shook his head.

'Nothing there for you to worry about. Farrar's been with me – how long has it been? Three years? Four?'

'Four, sir.'

'Yes, four years managing the estate and never so much as a shadow of impropriety. In any event, Trubshawe, this whole line of questioning, if you don't mind my saying so, is absurd. Not one of my employees could have had any motive for murdering Raymond Gentry, a man they barely met, let alone knew.'

'Am I to assume, then,' said the policeman, 'you share Miss Mount's view that the murderer must be a member of the house-party?'

'Oh, and who told you I ever said such a thing?' Evadne Mount brusquely asked.

'Why, I think it must have been Mr Duckworth here. Yes, that's who it was. He told me as Dr Rolfe was driving us back to the house.'

Don's face creased with embarrassment.

'It's true,' he said to the novelist. 'I did tell the Chief-Inspector everything I'd heard said in the drawing-room. I thought he oughta know.'

'Young man, you have nothing to apologise for,' she

replied in a kindly tone. 'I just like to keep tabs on who said what and to whom.'

Whereupon, tightening her robe about her with a shiver, she wandered off into the room and started cursorily to inspect its few wretched items of furniture.

For a moment or two Trubshawe observed her out of the corner of his eye before asking the Colonel:

'Did you by any chance take a look' – he pointed down at the body of Raymond Gentry – 'inside the pockets of his robe?'

'Certainly not. I already told you, Chief-Inspector, we touched nothing.'

Without further ado, Trubshawe bent down and inserted his hand first into the left, then the right pocket of Gentry's blood-stained bathrobe.

From the left pocket he came up empty-handed. But, from the right, he pulled out a single sheet of crumpled paper. He bent back up and, without addressing a word to anybody, impassively unfolded it.

On one side of the paper four or five lines, mostly just strings of capital letters, had been typed out. These, he took a few seconds to peruse.

'Nothing relevant to the case, I assume?' said the Colonel, trying in vain to squint at the text.

'On the contrary,' said Trubshawe. 'Something extremely relevant to the case. A major discovery, if I'm not mistaken.'

He folded the sheet up and slipped it into his own jacket pocket.

'Tell me, Colonel, did all your guests share your distaste for Gentry?'

'None of them could stand the horrible little tick. Why do you ask?'

'Oh, I have my reasons,' the Chief-Inspector replied non-committally.

'You know, Trubshawe . . .'

Once more it was Evadne Mount who had cut in.

'Yes?'

'Major discoveries are all very well,' she cavalierly remarked, 'but sometimes they turn out to be of less significance than minor oddities.'

'Minor oddities?'

Drawing the tip of her index finger along one of the attic's floorboards, she held it up for his inspection.

'Why,' he said, peering at her fingertip, 'I see nothing there.'

'That,' she said, 'is the minor oddity.'

Chapter Three

Downstairs in the drawing-room the ffolkeses' house-guests were looking more dishevelled than ever. Stale cigarette smoke hung in the air, two of the womenfolk, Mary ffolkes and Cynthia Wattis, the Vicar's wife, had nodded off, faded fashion magazines lying half-browsed on their laps, and even Chitty, who prided himself that his employers had never once had occasion to see him other than unbowed and upright, was starting to flag.

When the Colonel entered, however, followed by the rest of the small investigative party, they all wearily roused themselves, the women adjusting their hair, the men re-knotting the cords of their dressing-gowns, and waited expectantly to hear what the man from Scotland Yard had to say.

It was, however, Roger ffolkes who spoke first. Turning to the Chief-Inspector, he asked:

'Perhaps now you'd like me to introduce my guests?'

'Certainly,' said Trubshawe. 'Be my guest. Or rather, be my host, what?'

'Ha, very neat, yes,' said the Colonel with a half-hearted smile. 'Oh, and I trust you'll excuse our varying states of undress. We've all been caught a bit off-guard, you know.'

'Please, please . . . In my profession, ladies, gentlemen, I'm quite used to it. I remember once arresting a villain while he was taking his bath. Can you believe it, even though I'd begun to read him his rights – "You aren't obliged to say anything, but anything you do say, etc., etc." – he continued to sit there calmly soaping himself!

'When I protested, you know what his answer was, the cheeky blighter? "You do want me to come clean, don't you, Mr Trubshawe?"'

There was more mild laughter at this witticism. But since no one was really in the mood for jocular wordplay, the Colonel at once proceeded to the round of presentations.

'Well now, Trubshawe – cigarettes on the table beside you, by the way, so please do help yourself.'

'Thanks, but I'll stick to this if you don't mind,' answered the Chief-Inspector, waving his still-unlit pipe in the air.

'As you wish,' said the Colonel. 'Now, let's see. On the sofa near the fireplace, over there, that's Clem Wattis, our Vicar, and his wife, Cynthia. Next to Cynthia is Cora Rutherford, the well-known actress, who I'm sure needs no introduction, as they say. Then there's Madge Rolfe, the wife of Dr Rolfe, who's the gentleman standing to her left.'

'Colonel,' interrupted Trubshawe, 'Rolfe and I *have* met. You forget, it was he who drove over to my cottage with young Duckworth.'

'Ah, yes, yes, yes, course it was. Foolish of me. Frightful thing, old age. Now who else haven't you been introduced to yet? Oh yes, my wife Mary.'

'How d'you do, Mrs ffolkes?'

'How d'you do, Inspector Trubshawe?'

'Snap!' said the policeman, and they both smiled, as one does.

'And, of course, Chitty, my butler.'

'Chitty.'

'Sir.'

'As for my daughter Selina,' the Colonel went on, 'I'm afraid . . .'

'Yes?'

'She really was awfully attached to Gentry, so his murder has come as a tremendous shock to her. She's gone up to her room to rest. Naturally, if you insist on her being here, I can always –'

'That won't be necessary for the moment. Later – when she's better able to tell me what she knows. I think, too, it might be wise if your butler is excused.'

On hearing these words, Chitty gave the policeman a respectful nod and may even have said something equally respectful, except that, if he did, he said it so butlerishly *sotto voce* the Chief-Inspector was unlikely to have heard what it was. Then, without waiting to be requested to do so by the Colonel, he left the room.

After watching him go, Trubshawe turned to face the whole company.

'Well now, ladies and gentlemen,' he said, 'as you don't need to be told, this is a most terrible and mysterious crime you've got yourselves entangled in. I literally couldn't believe my ears when I was first told what had happened but, having been up to the attic and seen for myself, I have to believe them now. In effect, the murderer contrived to get in, kill Raymond Gentry, then get out again, apparently without opening either a door or a window. I don't mind admitting I'm dumbfounded.

'What I require, though, is for one of you to fill me in on the events that led up to the murder itself. Coming over here in the car, Dr Rolfe and Mr Duckworth did give me a sketchy account, but, what with stopping and starting and getting out to push and getting back in again, well – you'll excuse me, gents, I'm sure you understand what I'm saying – but what I need now is a more coherent version, one with a beginning, a middle and an end in that order. Would any of you,' he said, glancing at everybody in turn, 'care to volunteer? Just one, mind.'

There was a moment's silence, then Mary ffolkes began to say:

'Well, it does seem to me that . . .'

'Yes, Mrs ffolkes?'

'I was going to suggest Evie. She's the writer Evadne Mount, you know. And, well, it *is* her job to tell stories – indeed, just this sort of a story. So I thought . . .'

'Uh huh,' murmured Trubshawe, his fingers drumming a restless tattoo on the mantelpiece. 'Ye-es, I suppose she would be the obvious choice.'

You could see, however, that he was less than ecstatic at the prospect of even temporarily surrendering the reins to his redoubtable rival in matters of criminality.

Evadne Mount could see it too.

'Now look, Trubshawe,' she said pettishly, 'I'll be happy to oblige but, if you'd rather it weren't me, then all you have to do is say so. I don't easily take offence, you know,' she added with less conviction.

'Oh, but you're wrong, Miss Mount,' he tactfully replied. 'I'd be pleased, very pleased, if you were to give me a rundown of what occurred here yesterday. All I'd say – but I'm sure I really don't need to – is, well, just stick to the facts. Keep your imagination for your whodunits.'

'Now that *is* a remark I might be offended by,' said the novelist, 'if I were so minded. But because it's you, Trubshawe, and I've already taken a shine to you, I'm going to pretend I didn't hear it. So, yes, I'd be happy to give you an account of everything leading up to Gentry's murder. When would you like it?'

'No time like the present.'

Stepping away from the fireside, Trubshawe indicated

39

that place on the sofa next to where the Reverend Wattis was seated.

'Mind if I park myself here? Beside you?'

'Not at all,' answered the Vicar, shifting sideways to make room for the detective's generous frame.

'Now,' said the Chief-Inspector to Evadne Mount, 'if you would . . .'

Our party (she began) got going under the most promising of auspices. We all arrived fairly early on Christmas Eve – less, of course, Selina, Don and Raymond, who, as you've already been informed, Chief-Inspector, turned up a few hours after the rest of us. The Rolfes and the Wattises are locals, so they motored over from the village, while Cora and I, who've been close chums and near-neighbours for absolute yonks, travelled down from Town together, catching the 1.25 from Paddington.

Now Roger and Mary are, I've got to tell you, quite the perfect hosts. The house, we discovered, was stocked with every delicacy appropriate to the season, from oyster soup to roast turkey, from succulent Brussels sprouts to the *pièce de résistance*, a gigantic Christmas pud steeped in the finest French brandy. Naturally, given the time of year, our rooms were a trifle nippy – like so many in this part of the country, ffolkes Manor is an impossible house to heat properly – but we all had lovely warming pans slipped between our bed-sheets an hour or so before we retired. As for this very drawing-room, when we arrived – just in time for a glass of mulled claret or else, for those of us in need of a more powerful stimulant, a whisky-and-polly – it was glowing from a huge open fire that had already been regularly replenished during the day.

It's true, the weather had deteriorated badly and what had amounted at first to not much more than a few feathery flurries of snow was already half-way to degenerating into a full-blown storm – except that my own feeling, Chief-Inspector, is that such a storm, however awkward it makes life for the poor traveller, can only *intensify* the snugness of a cosy little gathering like ours. The way, you know, a frosting of snow on a window-pane has the same magical appeal for us Britishers as the sound of rain pelting down on the roof of a lamplit bedroom. I do feel, don't you, that freezing weather actually reinforces that sense of security, of comfort, of 'indoorness', that's so indispensable to the spirit and success of an old-fashioned British Christmas.

Anyway, as I always say, the ideal complement to good food and wine is good company, and that, I think I can safely assert, we were. Oh, I suppose 'the younger set' would have found us a touch fusty, a touch out-of-touch, so to speak. But since we ourselves are all confirmed fogeys and fuddy-duddies, why should we give two hoots what they think?

After supper things settled down nicely. Cora, who is, you should know, a wonderful raconteur – or ought that to be raconteuse? – was delighting me with some appallingly indiscreet anecdotes about the *unprintable*, as she wittily puts it, Suzanne Moiré, with whom she co-starred in Willie Maugham's *Our Betters*. The Colonel was showing Clem Wattis the latest acquisitions to his stamp album. And the Rolfes were telling Cynthia Wattis all about their recent cruise around the Greek islands. In other words, it was the sort of evening that sounds deadly dull when you attempt to describe it afterwards, but really, while it was unfolding, it was all most congenial.

And because the ffolkeses don't 'believe in' the wireless – Roger, in his eccentric English way, refuses to have a set in the house because he regards it as too 'fangled' – there was no deafening dance-band syncopation to drown out our inconsequential chatter. Instead, Mary, a gifted pianist, treated us to a medley of the type of tunes everybody really likes, even if they're not always prepared to admit it: Rachmaninoff's *Prelude*; a couple of Cyril Scott pieces, *Danse nègre* and *Lotus Land*, as she knows I have an unwholesome penchant for the more palatable modernists; a pot-pourri of waltzes and schottisches; and, for an encore, 'The Teddy Bears' Picnic'. Fearfully gay.

Well then, at about half-past ten, when we were just about to plunge into a game of Charades – Roger and I had decamped to the library to plot how best to do King Cophetua and the Beggar Maid – we heard a car pull up in the drive.

It was, as expected, Selina and Don – along with, though

in his case not at all as expected, Raymond Gentry. Don, I have to say, and I'm sure he won't contradict me, was already looking extremely disgruntled at finding himself in a crowd of three. Selina, and she surely wouldn't deny this either if she were here, was, I felt, rather callously oblivious of the all too flagrant fact that Don was in a huff. And Raymond – well, Raymond was Raymond.

As there exists no more satisfying sensation than being fair about someone you loathe, I'd love to be able to say lots of nice things about Raymond Gentry. Well, but I can't.

From the minute he entered the house he set everybody's teeth on edge. Roger and Mary were both conspicuously put out about his being here at all, neither having reckoned on being obliged to accommodate an extra last-minute guest – and a total stranger at that. But, well, they *are* parents, so they know better than any of us how easygoing young people can be about what, for our generation, are the most elementary courtesies and formalities. Even so, Raymond was special.

I remember, when the Colonel asked him to park his motor-car, a Hispano-Suiza, wouldn't you know, inside the garage alongside the Rolfes' and the Wattises', he actually yawned – I mean, he actually, literally yawned in Roger's face! – and said, with that unblushing effrontery of his that we came so to dread, 'Sorry, old man, but it's such a fag putting a car away at night. In the morning – if I can be bothered.' If I can be bothered!

We all heard him say that and, half-fascinated, half-horrified, we all watched him languidly drape himself over an armchair. Though she didn't directly take him to task, Selina, who must surely have begun to regret inviting him in the first place, did have the grace not to hide her shame. As for Don, he was already so bristly with resentment as to be beyond surprise. We most definitely had the impression that the drive down in the Hispano-Suiza had been a tense one.

How to sum up Raymond? Well, Trubshawe, now that you've seen him, even if attired only in a bathrobe and pyjamas – and of course deceased – you may already have an inkling as to why not one of us was convinced by what he condescended to tell us of himself. When Mary enquired about his people, he alluded airily – understandably airily, in my opinion – to the so-called 'Gentrys of Berkshire'. Then, when he was questioned about his education, he had the nerve to inform us that his extortionately expensive public school was so exclusive he was forbidden from naming it in public. Well, I mean to say! A public school that can't be named in public! And all this accompanied by such a sarcastic smirk you really didn't know if he was pulling your leg or not.

If you ask me, I don't believe there are any Gentrys in Berkshire. Matter of fact, I don't believe his name is – was – Gentry at all. 'Gentry' – what kind of a name is that? It's almost as though he had such a craving to belong to 'the gentry', as he would have called it, he thought he could make it happen simply by renaming himself after it. Or else – it was Cora who whispered this to me – or else it was he rather fancied the consonance of 'Gentry' and 'Gentile'. Gentry – Gentile? You follow me?

At any rate, there was something about him, *everything* about him, which rubbed us all up the wrong way, and my heart went out as much to Selina as to poor Don, for a fool could see that, observing him for the first time in her life among her nearest and dearest, she was discovering what a thoroughgoing bad lot he really was. It's like trying on an item of clothing in a shop, you know, where it looks marvellous, then trying it on again in natural light. We, her family and friends, we were the natural light, and Selina, it became screamingly obvious to all of us, no longer cared for what she saw.

Even I, Chief-Inspector, and I'm celebrated for my vivid and colourful characterisations, even I wouldn't know how to communicate the sheer ghastliness of the man! To say that he drawled isn't the half of it. His whole body drawled, if you take my meaning. When he walked, his feet drawled. When he gesticulated, his hands drawled. When he sat down, his boneless body seemed to drawl and drool all over the furniture.

He had been drinking all day – he'd draw a silver flask from his hip-pocket from time to time, mock-surreptitiously but actually in full, flaunted view of everybody – and he was constantly on the verge of downright Dago rudeness.

45

For example, he never openly complained of draughts in the house – and, as Mary is the first to admit, it *is* a draughty house, though for those of us who love it that's part of its charm – but he never stopped talking about his own *enchanting* service flat in Mayfair, with its gleaming oil-fired radiators and draught-proof devices. And he never said, or not in so many words, that he was bored rigid with our company, but he couldn't resist reminding us again and again that, if he'd stayed in London, he'd be spending the evening in a modish West End 'watering-hole'.

Some of you, of course, will remember that I set the opening chapter of *The Stroke of 12* in just such a watering-hole – the Yellow Cockatoo, I called it. My victim is stabbed in the back at midnight on New Year's Eve and not one of his fellow revellers hears him scream out because of all the chiming bells and the bursting balloons and the tooting horns and the communal singing of 'Auld Lang Syne'. For at least ten minutes after the crime is committed, his dead body remains propped up by the swaying, drunken, jam-packed crowd, allowing the murderer to slip away out of – ah well, I can see from your faces that this isn't the time to get into that.

To put it in a nutshell, Raymond was *wrong* – simply, hopelessly wrong.

He had on the wrong clothes. A salmon silk tie worn over the top of a striped pullover in sick-making pastelly shades, one that I grant you might have been just the thing for the *plage* at Juan-les-Pins but was utterly out-of-place in an English country house in December. And a pair of grey Oxford bags squashed ever so nonchalantly into Nile-green wellies. Would that we could all be that careless in our attire. Most of us, though, just don't have the time or patience.

He was tanned, *he* said, but anyone could see there was more than a touch of the tarbrush there. He said 'Dahling!' all the time, to all of us indiscriminately, and not even Cora does that. Can you imagine, I chanced to catch him brushing away a fly that had settled on the rim of his cocktail glass and I actually heard him say, 'Buzz off, dahling!' A fly! But then, with him everything had to be a superlative. When he burbled on incessantly about the finest this and the greatest that, you felt you were being sprayed by the spittle of exclamation marks. And he was the type of name-dropper who doesn't just drop names, he drops nicknames. His conversation was all Binkie and Larry and Gertie and Viv – half the time it was like listening to baby-talk.

Even when he agreed with you, it somehow grated, he exaggerated so! Farrar here totes his own little ashtray around – it's a tiny bronze urn with a lid that opens and closes – there it is, perched on the arm of the sofa. Well, when Raymond claimed to admire it and Farrar confessed that the one problem he had with it was winkling out the pile of cigarette butts at the end of the day, he actually shuddered and said, 'Oh, I do, *do* sympathise! How *atro-*

cious that must be!' Now I ask you. Atrocious? Removing a tangle of cigarette ends from an ashtray? You never knew if he was serious or not.

Oh, and he had this word. *Penetrating*. Tagore's poems were *penetrating*. Spengler's philosophy was *penetrating*. A *sole aux ortolans* at the Eiffel Tower was *penetrating*. And, incidentally, when I say the Eiffel Tower, I mean the restaurant in London, not the monument in Paris, a gaffe Mary made and for which she paid dearly. She also confused *The Rite of Spring* with *The Rustle of Spring*, a mistake anyone could have made, but did she suffer for it! Oh, he was wrong, wrong, wrong! Just not one of us, you know. I can't put it any other way.

Well, Trubshawe, I leave it to you to guess how frayed our tempers had got well before the evening was at an end. It was, though, the following day, yesterday, Christmas Day, that they started to rip apart. And since there'd been a deep snowfall overnight, Roger couldn't simply kick Raymond out, ordering him to drive straight back to Town in his blasted Hispano-Suiza, something we all knew he was dying to do, Selina's feelings notwithstanding.

He didn't come down to breakfast at all, which was unpardonably impolite of him, but it did at least give Selina an opportunity to offer belated amends and apologies all round for his conduct. If it hadn't been Christmas, I do believe there'd have been an unpleasant scene between her and her father. But, in the spirit of the season, the Colonel decided, and suggested we all decide likewise, to make the best of a difficult situation.

Then, when he actually did surface, still unshaven, still wearing his dressing-gown, at ten forty-five, and found that the breakfast things had been cleared away, he at once went down to the kitchen and insisted that Mrs Varley – she's the cook – he insisted that she prepare him some bacon and eggs, which he proceeded to wolf down, his plate sitting on his knees, the aroma wafting round the drawing-room, while the rest of us were trying to have a game of Canasta. Even after he'd finished, he continued to prattle on unapologetically through the game – I can't tell you how distracting that was – and chain-smoke his stinky mauve fags – Sobranies, I think they're called – and take revolt-ingly gurgly swigs from his hip flask.

And then, very gradually throughout the afternoon, that nasty tongue of his turned positively viperish.

Examples? It's hard to remember, for there were just too many of them. Oh yes – wait. When Madge, looking out of the french window at the snow that was still swirling about the house, mentioned how queer it made her feel, since no more than a couple of months had gone by since she'd been swimming in Greece, Raymond remarked, all innocence, that the phrase she used reminded him of Mrs Varley's cooking. When she asked him why, his answer was that his bacon and eggs, too, had been 'swimming in grease'!

Well, tee hee. And yes, you might think that all very droll

and delightful, except that, when you come right down to it, it was also, for our hosts, beastly and gratuitous. And, needless to say, simply not true. But, you see, he just couldn't resist being funny at other people's expense. He genuinely enjoyed hurting their feelings. Because he had, I'm certain, what Dr Freud calls an Inferiority Complex, he just couldn't help dragging everybody else down to his own abject level.

When Cynthia Wattis praised Garbo's acting in *Queen Christina*, which had made her weep buckets, and politely asked Raymond for his opinion, he instantly dismissed it – *not* impromptu, if I'm any judge – as 'Greta garbage'. Oh, I daresay it was a terribly smart thing to say and all, but it quite crushed poor Cynthia and, really, one wanted to slap him.

Or when Don spoke about his 'creativity' as a painter – I'm told he exhibited some very dramatic seascapes at the Art School end-of-term show – all Gentry could find to say was that, just as if you talk too much about suicide you'll never commit it, so if you talk too much about your creativity it's a fatal sign you haven't got any.

Not even Selina, whose responsibility he was in a way, was immune to his barbs. Since she knew how he detested the music her mother had been playing on the piano, she ventured to propose that she herself execute some Debussy, seeing as, even though he's modern, he's also surprisingly melodic.

'I'd really rather you didn't, Selina,' he drawled at her in his most grating voice. 'Debussy isn't as easy as he sounds, you know, and your pianism – well, let's just say "execute" might be all too apt a word. Better if you were to ruin some naice' – he really did pronounce it 'naice' – 'some naice little piece of cod-Debussy. Like Cyril Scott.'

Naturally, I bridled at this calumny of my favourite composer and I saw Don itching to biff Raymond one on the jaw. But Selina herself, spirited as always, was determined to put a brave face on it. 'Why, Ray,' she said, 'I played *Clair de lune* at Roy and Deirdre Daimler's anniversary do, and the Daimlers' tabby, Mrs Dalloway, who hates music, any music, so much she slinks away in disgust at the first note, perched on my knees and only stopped purring when I'd finished.'

'Did it not occur to you, my sweet faun,' was Raymond's reply, 'that she probably didn't realise it was supposed to *be* music?'

By the evening it had got worse, much worse. He'd been drinking pretty steadily during the day and because he mixed his own cocktails – he referred to them as Spanners or Screwdrivers, some-such silly name – and never offered one to anybody else, it was difficult keeping up with just how many he'd got down himself. But a whole new layer of malevolence had begun to transform his face into a mask of rancour and devilry. You could see he was just waiting to be affronted by what he considered to be our philistinism.

As a result, we didn't dare talk about all the latest books

and plays. We were afraid of being shot down by him, afraid of being told that the people *we* liked were hopelessly *vieux jeu*, as he would put it, afraid of being ridiculed for believing that Charles Morgan's *The Fountain* and Sutton Vane's *Outward Bound* were imperishable masterpieces. Proust, *naturally*, was the thing. Pirandello, *naturally*, was penetrating. You had to be a foreigner to be admired by Raymond Gentry. Unless, of course, you were born a Sitwell!

So, as I say, we were simply too intimidated to have the kind of gossipy chit-chat we might have expected to enjoy over dinner – which was our big mistake. For, you see, it left the floodgates open for Raymond himself. And that's when we discovered just how evil – I weigh the word, Trubshawe, I weigh the word – just how evil he really could be.

It began, as I recall, with Cora here, who can be relied on, as I know too well, to give as good as she gets. She'd been telling us all, with the verve for which she's become a byword, about playing the lead in Michael Arlen's *The Green Hat*, which was one of her biggest successes in the twenties. We were having a rollicking good laugh at her inexhaustible fund of anecdotes when Gentry, who'd seemed not to be paying attention at all, suddenly opined that *The Green Hat* was 'remembered only for having been forgotten', as he phrased it, and that Michael Arlen was 'irredeemably *passé*, not so much green hat as old hat, a real has-been!'

Well, did Cora let him have it! She said something

extremely funny, as a matter of fact, something that, for once, knocked the wind out of his sails. She said – you'll forgive me, Cora, if I fail to do justice to your impeccable timing – she said, '*A has-been!?*' – and I could see her gearing herself up for one of those epic cat-fights on which theatricals thrive. 'Why, you putrid little twerp,' she spat at him. 'At least has-been means was! You – you weren't, you aren't, and you never will be!'

Well! Raymond plainly wasn't used to being answered back, and his face was quite a picture. I think it true to say everybody in the room, maybe even Selina, exulted in his come-uppance.

Our exultation, unfortunately, turned out to be just a tiny bit premature. His eyes narrowing with malice, he at once turned on Cora and he said – he said – ah, well, you have to understand, Trubshawe, I – after all, Cora's an old crony of mine and – and – all things considered, you really can't expect me to repeat what he said. All you need to know is that he alluded to certain – to certain scurrilous rumours that have dogged her private life, rumours that have never been more than rumours, you understand, except that Gentry, who of course made his living out of scandal-mongering, proved to be unexpectedly well informed about how she obtained – no, no, I really can't pursue this line further.

I did decide, however, that I couldn't abandon my friend to her fate and I told Gentry in no uncertain terms that he must apologise for such an unwarranted slur on her character. And, to my very great surprise, he did. He actually did apologise forthwith, doubtless because he could see how distressed Selina was by his conduct. For the next hour or so, during most of dinner, he was as sullen as ever but at least he behaved himself, more or less.

It was while we were all tucking into Christmas pud that he started again with a vengeance – and, given the fool he'd been made to appear by Cora, I'm sure 'vengeance' is the right word. He couldn't forgive any of us for having witnessed the spectacle.

The first of his victims was Clem Wattis. He had been regaling us with his theories on the far-reaching consequences of the Treaty of Versailles when Raymond, tapping his lips in a feigned yawn, drawled across the table, 'Oh dear, Vicar, I'm afraid your Great War is in danger of becoming a Great Bore!'

Clem – as befits his calling – is someone utterly incapable of losing his temper. Indeed, according to Cynthia, he's so absent-minded his temper is just about the only thing he never does manage to lose. So it was, I suspect, more in sorrow than in anger that he replied to Gentry, 'I suppose, young man, you think you're awfully clever.'

'Not at all,' came the riposte, cool as the proverbial cucumber. 'It's only because I'm talking to you that I *appear* clever. Almost anyone would.'

Now even the Vicar's dander was up.

'Have you forgotten, you insolent young pup,' he

barked, 'it was to make the world safe for the likes of you that we fought the Great War in the first place? And this is the gratitude we get!'

Whereupon Gentry, he – well, he – what can I say? – he started to cast aspersions on – on the, well, on the exact extent and degree of the Vicar's wartime duties.

By then it was evident that nothing and nobody could stem the tide of his bile. He'd somehow got wind of the sordid secrets in each of our lives – every life, as you know, Trubshawe, even the most outwardly blameless, harbours its secrets, for there's the public life and the private life and then there exists the *secret* life – and each of us in turn came to feel what I can only call the lash of his vitriol.

And that's how it was that, thanks to a single gate-crashing guest, our merry little Christmas house-party was to become nothing less than a living nightmare.

You'll excuse me, I trust, if I decline to go into greater detail about the painful things we all had to hear about each other. All I'm prepared to say is that, when we turned in that night, there wasn't one of us who wouldn't have rejoiced if Raymond Gentry had been struck down by a thunderbolt.

Or, for that matter (she concluded), by a bullet.

Chapter Four

'*H'm, I get the picture . . .*'

Having digested the information that she had just been feeding to him, the Chief-Inspector then congratulated the novelist.

'Thank you for that, Miss Mount. Very pithily put, if I may say so. To be honest, I'm not much of a one for detective stories. They're too airy-fairy in my opinion, with not nearly enough of the hard slog, the sheer dogged legwork, that goes into bringing your typical murderer to book. But you do have a knack for boiling a complicated situation down to its essentials.'

'Well, thank *you*, Chief-Inspector,' she said beaming, 'it's really most magnanimous of you. More magnanimous, I fear, than I tend to be in my whodunits where you and your colleagues are concerned.'

'Oh, it's all good clean fun,' Trubshawe answered heartily. 'I hope we're big enough at the Yard to take your ragging of us in the spirit in which I'm certain it's intended.

But enough of these pleasant futilities. We've now got to decide what's to be done next.'

'I really don't see what there is we can do, Trubshawe,' said the Colonel. 'We're snowed in, as you're aware, and until the weather lifts, and the telephone wires are reconnected, we can't even inform any kind of official authority what's happened.'

'In that case, may I enquire why I'm here?'

This question appeared to leave the Colonel at a loss for words.

'Why you're here . . .? Ah well, it just seemed like the only – well, when you put it like that, I'm not – it was just that Chitty suggested . . .'

'Chitty?'

'Yes, he reminded me that you'd settled down in the area and proposed that – dash it all, man, I do have a dead body in my house! If I have a leaky pipe I send for the plumber and if I have a – a leaky corpse, well, naturally, I send for the police!'

'Probably what the Colonel means is that we all felt, at least until the local constabulary were able to reach us, that it would only be right and proper for a member of the police force to be in attendance, even if a retired member.'

'Thank you, Farrar,' said the Colonel gruffly. 'That *is* exactly what, in my clod-hopping manner, I was trying to say. Fact is, Trubshawe, once we'd taken the decision to have Rolfe and Don fetch you over, I don't suppose any of us really asked ourselves what precisely it was we were fetching you for. I hope you don't mind – I apologise again – it being Boxing Day . . .'

'No, no, no,' said Trubshawe, 'you did the right thing, and I would have been remiss in my duty – and, retired I may be, I still see it as my duty – if I'd declined to come.'

'Why, that's just what *I* said!' exclaimed the Colonel. 'Didn't I say a policeman never retires? Not even for the night.'

'Well, I don't know about that, but let it pass. The question is, am I here merely to lend a seal, or the semblance of a seal, of officialdom, or again, as you rightly say, of semi-officialdom, to the hours and p'raps even days that lie ahead of you all before you're able to re-establish communication with the outside world? Or do I myself do something about the situation in the meantime?'

The Colonel drew a doubtful finger along his unshaven chin.

'Do something?' he said. 'I don't get you. Do what?'

'You aren't going to arrest us all, are you?' squealed the Vicar's wife in a fluttery falsetto.

'Dear lady,' the Scotland Yard man smoothly replied, 'even if I wished to arrest you – which I assure you I don't – I couldn't. Remember, I'm retired. I no longer have any official position, which means, logically, I no longer have any official power. However . . .'

His voice trailed off in a trio of tantalising suspension points.

'However . . .?' echoed the Colonel.

Trubshawe noisily cleared his throat.

'Look, I realise what a dreadful ordeal this has been for all of you – and, between you and me, things are liable to get a good deal worse before they get any better. But it does strike me that a chance has presented itself which might allow us to clarify matters in the meantime.

'It was Don here who told me, in Dr Rolfe's motor, of the conversation you'd had in this very room a mere half-an-hour after he and the Colonel had discovered Raymond Gentry's body. He told me, in particular, of Miss Mount's insistence that you just couldn't afford to sit around the house for hours, conceivably even days, with a corpse in the attic and an atmosphere of festering suspicion in the drawing-room. For he also apprised me of her theory – that one of you must logically be the murderer – a theory which, ladies and gentlemen, I'm obliged to endorse.'

This last statement of his provoked a collective gasp, almost as though a new and unexpected accusation had been levelled at the party, even though all the Chief-Inspector had done was, of course, reiterate what Evadne Mount had said earlier. It was possibly because, on this occasion, the charge was being made not by a novelist famed for her morbid imagination, the kind of imagination you look for and long for when you settle down at the fireside with a whodunit, but by an individual whose diagnosis of the situation couldn't help but carry, even into his retirement, the ring of authority.

'Yes,' Trubshawe continued after a moment, 'I fear you'll have to forget any convenient notion that this murder might have been an outside job. I've seen Raymond Gentry's body. And I've seen the room in which he was done to death.

'And there's another thing. I also found, inside the pocket of his bathrobe, a piece of paper that clearly implicates him as a blackmailer – whether amateur or professional I couldn't yet say. I'd like you all to take a look at that paper.'

Whereupon he drew it out, flattened it with his fingers and spread it on to the table so that everybody could read it.

```
            REV - WAR
       CR + EM = COCA + LES
         HR - DEAD BABY
   MR - SORDID MISBEHAVIOR IN MC
```

No matter how enigmatic these words and symbols would have been to anybody else, they certainly seemed to make a meaningful impact on the various members of the ffolkeses' house-party who, one after the other, the colour draining from their features, could all be seen recoiling from a hasty perusal of the damning text.

Only Evadne Mount, either because she was of a more robust temperament than her fellow guests, or simply because of her congenital propensity to pry, continued to pore over the crumpled paper.

When she raised her head at last, Trubshawe noticed at once that she wore an expression of frowning perplexity.

'What is it, Miss Mount?' he quickly asked her.

'Well, I don't really know,' she mumbled almost plaintively.

'You don't know?'

'No, I don't. It's just that – well, I just can't help feeling that there's . . . there's, you know, something wrong with that piece of paper. But what?'

'I beg you to share with us whatever it is you have to say. You never know what could turn out to be important.'

She looked back down at the page of notes and studied it again for a few moments. Then she shook her head.

'No, sorry, Trubshawe, I don't know what it is that's troubling me, really I don't. It may come to me if I stop thinking about it.'

At first the Chief-Inspector seemed undecided whether or not to pursue the matter, then he asked Roger ffolkes:

'Colonel, do you by any chance recognise the typing?'

'Recognise the typing? How could I possibly recognise the typing? It's not as though it's handwriting.'

'Actually,' Trubshawe said patiently, 'it is in a way. No two typewriters, you see, ever produce an exactly identical typeface. What I mean is, do you happen to know on whose machine this was typed out?'

He handed the sheet of paper over to the Colonel, who gave it no more than a perfunctory inspection.

'Haven't a clue. Don't even know what I'm supposed to be looking for. Here, Farrar, you take a gander at it, will you? Perhaps you can see what the Inspector's on about.'

'Why, yes, Colonel.'

'What? You mean you can?'

'Yes, sir. It's – well, it was typed on your typewriter.'

'Mine?!'

'Definitely, sir. The one in the library. You see here – Chief-Inspector – this letter c? And this one again? The arc is broken – look, it has like a tiny space in the middle. Both of them. It's your typewriter all right, Colonel.'

'Well, I'm jiggered!'

'So,' ruminated the Chief-Inspector. 'That means these notes were typed inside this very house, probably at some time in the last thirty-six hours. Colonel, would Gentry have had access to your library?'

'Why, naturally he would. I don't keep parts of my house out of bounds to my guests, even the uninvited ones. Anyone in search of a book to read, or if he just fancied being on his own for a while, was free to wander into the library.'

Trubshawe folded the paper up again and stuffed it back in his pocket.

'Well,' he said, 'since it's clear there was no love lost

between any of you and the victim, and since this' – he patted his jacket pocket – 'is a significant part of what makes it clear, it's my belief that it would be a waste of time looking elsewhere for possible motives for his murder, at least before I've investigated those closer to home. By that I mean, here in ffolkes Manor.'

'Before you've investigated . . .' said Dr Rolfe. 'Are we to understand that you're suggesting you yourself conduct an investigation?'

'Yes, that is what I'm suggesting.'

'Here and now?'

'Yes, again.'

'Let me get this straight,' said the Colonel. 'You're proposing to – what? – question each of us in turn?'

'That's right. That *is* just how I was thinking of going about it.'

'Even though you're retired and have no authority to do so?'

'Look,' said Trubshawe. 'You do realise that, when the police eventually get here, you're all going to be subjected to some tough questioning. What I propose could almost be like a dress rehearsal. It's true, I'd have to be fairly tough myself. There wouldn't be much point to the exercise if I weren't. But because I wouldn't be interrogating you in an official capacity, and also, of course, because none of you would be on oath, well, if you began to think you really ought to have a lawyer present or else you simply found yourself getting a little hot under the collar, then there's nothing I could do or say to prevent you from refusing to answer.

'And if, by chance, though I must confess this strikes me as a very long shot indeed, if I arrive at the solution before the police arrive at the house, if I actually succeed in identifying Gentry's murderer, then the whole distasteful process will have taken place away from the prying eyes of the yellow press.

'For don't delude yourselves, you're in for some extremely unsavoury publicity. As I understand it, Gentry was a gossip columnist on a nationally syndicated scandal rag. Well, I can promise you, the public will juicily eat that up and come back asking for lots more of the same. By having the interrogation now, you may actually be sparing yourselves the worst.

'As for the alternative, you all know what that means. Sitting here, hour after hour, wondering which of you did it and when he – or she – is going to strike again.'

'Well,' muttered the Colonel, 'that does put a new complexion on things.'

He turned to face his guests.

'All right. I think it's only fair we be democratic about this. So let's hear what you all think of the Chief-Inspector's idea.'

For a while it seemed as though everyone was waiting for someone else to speak first, exactly as happens at many a public lecture, whose listeners, visibly aching to interrupt the lecturer with their own opinions, opinions just as passionately held as his, suddenly seem to be struck dumb when questions are thrown open to members of the audience.

It was, as ever, Evadne Mount who broke the silence.

'Since you lot seem too timid to speak up, I will. I'm all for it. Matter of fact, Trubshawe, I might even give you a helping hand. Only if you wanted me to, of course. But we whodunit writers have a few aces up our sleeves, you know, just as you coppers have.'

'No comment,' replied the Chief-Inspector in an amiably dismissive aside. 'But thank you anyway, Miss Mount, for taking the initiative. That's one in favour. Any other takers? Rolfe?'

'It *is* irregular, of course,' said the Doctor, 'but it certainly does seem to me preferable to doing nothing at all. I'm with you.'

'Good. That makes two.'

'However,' Rolfe continued, 'I would like to remind the undecideds' – he gave his friends a steady appraising glance – 'that the presence in this house of Raymond Gentry has reopened a number of wounds that many of you, many of *us*, believed and hoped had been closed for good. I fear the Chief-Inspector's questions are going to open up those wounds even wider. We've all got to be prepared for that, am I not right, Trubshawe?'

'Yes, Doctor, you are, and that was well put. As I said

before, I'm not in a position to oblige any of you to answer my questions. You won't be required to take any kind of oath, as you would in a courtroom. And if you should opt to lie to me, no action could be taken against you, which would not be the case during a proper police interrogation, where lying is a very serious offence indeed.

'Let me add, though, that if in your mind you're already planning to be, well, economic with the truth, then, frankly, I'd prefer we didn't waste our time by embarking on the experiment at all. You may like to think of it as a bit of a game, but, don't forget, there's not much point to any game, be it Ping-Pong or Mah-Jongg, if you refuse to abide by the rules.'

'Then may I make a rather controversial suggestion?'

'Please, Doctor, any suggestion, any sensible suggestion, is welcome.'

'We're all old friends here, aren't we?' said Rolfe. 'And with everything that's due to happen in the next few days whatever we elect to do now – the police trampling over our lives, the press snapping at our heels – our friendship is going to be put under a greater strain than it's ever known. Already, both Evie and Trubshawe have spoken about how easy it is to poison the atmosphere with no more than a few lethal droplets of suspicion. Luckily, we haven't had enough time yet to savour those droplets. But when the police do manage to get here, I guarantee there won't be one of us who hasn't hysterically accused his dearest friend of the murder of Raymond Gentry.

'So it does appear to me to make extremely good sense to let the Chief-Inspector conduct his interviews. But what I also propose is this. So that none of us starts worrying about just what helpful little clues the others might be dropping into his ear in private, he should question us all together.'

'All together?' retorted an incredulous Colonel. 'You mean, we all speak to Trubshawe in front of each other?'

'That's exactly what I mean. That we're all present when each of us is being questioned. If dirty linen is going to be aired in public, then let it really be aired in public. It won't be pleasant for any of us, I'll be bound, but at least we'll all be in the same boat. Otherwise, don't you see, questioning us individually behind closed doors could destroy our friendship just as surely as not questioning us at all.'

The Chief-Inspector was manifestly intrigued by this notion, but he was also perturbed by its unconventionality. For forty years he had stoutly upheld the Law not merely in its majesty but in its minutiae, in all its procedural codes, practices and orthodoxies, and, in the matter of being taught new tricks, he may have been an older dog even than Tobermory.

'We-ell, I really don't know,' he said. 'If you ask me, that sounds less like something we at the Yard would countenance than a scene from one of Miss Mount's novels.'

'Oh, rubbish!' the novelist interjected. 'If you're referring to the kind of scene I think you are, then you should know I reserve it exclusively for a book's climax. I mean the chapter in which the detective assembles all the suspects in the library then demonstrates, step by meticulous step, just how and why the murder was committed. Not the same thing at all.

'But I have to say,' she went on thoughtfully, 'I do believe Henry's idea is a good one. None of us will be able afterwards to accuse anyone of seeking to lay the blame elsewhere. Not that any of us would, of course. Then again, you never can tell, can you?'

'Well,' said Trubshawe, 'that's two in favour. Miss Rutherford?'

'I'm going to surprise you,' said the actress, 'but I'm for it. Surprise you, I say, because I've got more to lose than any of you.'

'Oh? And why is that, Cora?' asked the Colonel.

'Listen, darling, we now know we all have skeletons in our cupboards. I mean, what with that stinker Gentry spewing his rancid guts out last night, our dirty little secrets are practically in the public domain, right?'

'Er, well – yes, I suppose so, right.'

'But mine are a *star's* dirty little secrets. They're of interest to everyone. I tell you, there are muckraking journalists in Fleet Street who'd pay a small fortune to get the lowdown on my private life. However, I also know I didn't murder Raymond Gentry and I'm ready to answer Trubshawe's questions so long as I have his assurance that anything that turns out not to be relevant to the case stays within these four walls.'

'That goes without saying,' said Trubshawe.

'Nevertheless,' replied the actress, 'I'd like to hear it said. When someone like you says, "That goes without saying", he can always claim afterwards, perfectly honestly, that he never actually said it.'

The Chief-Inspector smiled wearily.

'I solemnly promise not to repeat anything I hear inside this room in the next few hours that proves to have no bearing on the solution to Gentry's murder. Satisfied?'

'Satisfied. Then I'm in.'

'Well,' said Trubshawe, 'we seem to be heading for a majority here. For the others, shall we take a vote? Remember, ladies and gentlemen, we can't proceed unless you're *all* prepared to participate. So who, among those of you who haven't yet spoken up, supports Dr Rolfe's proposal that I undertake an immediate interrogation at which all of you are present throughout?'

The second hand to be raised was Madge Rolfe's. Then Don shot up his arm. And then, to everyone's astonishment, Mary ffolkes more tentatively raised hers – to everyone's astonishment, because her friends had always known her to be the sort of wife who would wait until she had learned exactly what her husband's thoughts were on any given topic before daring to air a view of her own.

It was obvious that the Colonel himself was taken aback, for he gave her a sharp glance before (reluctantly?) raising his own arm.

Then there was silence.

Trubshawe finally turned towards the Vicar, who was seated next to his wife, a pained expression on his almost anaemically pale features.

'Well, Vicar,' he said. 'As you see, Miss Mount, Miss Rutherford, Farrar, Mrs Rolfe, Don and now both the Colonel and his wife – they've all agreed to be questioned. That leaves just you and your good lady.'

'Yes, I realise that,' said the Vicar vexedly. 'I, uh – well, you see, I – I – I really don't think it's –'

'You do understand, don't you, that if you refuse, we can't conduct the investigation at all?'

'Yes, you *have* made that point, Inspector.'

'You'll all have to sit about waiting for the police to turn up, wondering which of you did it, why they did it and whether they'll do it again. Is that really what you want?'

'No, no, of course it's not, but I shan't – I shan't be bullied, you know. I'm a free agent and – well, it does seem – I'm sure Cynthia feels the same way, don't you, my –'

'Oh, for cripes' sake, Clem!' Cora Rutherford ejaculated. 'We're all in this together! And, frankly – I'd never say this except under circumstances as exceptional as these – but, frankly, you really have the least to lose! I would wager, from what Gentry hinted at last night, that most of us have already rumbled your Terrible Secret. And it's going to come out anyway, whether you like it or not.'

'She does have a point, Reverend,' said Trubshawe softly.

The Vicar gazed helplessly at his wife, whose twinkly-eyed decency and pragmatism, precisely the modest English virtues one would expect to find in the helpmeet to a man of the Anglican cloth, were of scant assistance to him in a dilemma of this order. Then he gulped – you could almost hear him gulp – and said:

'Oh, very well. But I do insist that – that –'

'Yes?'

'Oh, well, no, nothing. Yes, yes, I agree.'

'Good,' said Trubshawe, rubbing his hands in anticipation. He looked at his watch.

'Ten-fifteen. You've all been up now for over two hours. May I suggest you repair to your bedrooms, freshen up and get dressed. Then we'll all come together in, let's say, twenty minutes – inside the library.

'And what,' he appended to what he'd already stated, 'what *does* go without saying is that none of you take it upon yourself to go wandering up to the attic. Not, you understand, that I don't trust you. Except that, if Miss Mount is right, and I think she is, there's at least one person in this room whom none of you can afford to trust. You get what I mean?'

They all got what he meant.

'So, Colonel,' he said, 'would you like to show me the way?'

They were already deep in conversation as they entered the library, Tobermory plodding faithfully behind them.

'I must say I began to think that Vicar chappie was going to scupper the whole scheme,' the Chief-Inspector could be heard saying.

'Yes, he's something of a fusspot all right,' answered the Colonel. 'But he's also a nice well-meaning old bird and all he needed was a poke in the ribs.'

'I believe I'll start the ball rolling with him, just so he'll have no time to change his mind.'

'I say, Trubshawe, this *is* a rum affair and no mistake.'

'That's true enough,' said the policeman. 'I never in my career came across such an outrageous crime. It's like something out of one of Evadne Mount's – whatyamacallums? – whodunits.'

'Don't let her hear you say that. Said exactly the same thing myself and had my head snapped off for it.'

'Really? I'd have thought she'd take it as a compliment.'

'Oh, you know what people are like. You pay them the wrong kind of compliment and they react as though they've never been so insulted in all their lives. Alexis Baddeley, I'll have you know, won't be doing with locked-room murders.'

'Is that so?' replied a bemused Trubshawe. 'Choosy about the kind of murders she solves, is she? Wish I could have been.'

'I've no patience with Evie's stuff myself, but Mary tells me that, apart from locked rooms, you'll find the whole trumpery bag of tricks. You know, a secret passage that only the murderer has a key to. A clock and a mirror facing each other at the scene of the crime, meaning the dial was read in reverse. Some black sheep of a family shipped off to South Africa and supposed to have died there, except that nobody's certain he really did. All the usual whodunit hoo-hah. Load of codswallop, if you ask me.'

'Well, we won't have to go looking for anything of that kind in this case, I'm sure.'

'No – except that, as it happens, ffolkes Manor does have its own secret passage. It's a former Priest's Hole, you know, located in a panel behind one of these walls. I should show it to you some time.'

'Thanks. I'd like that. For the moment, though, I can't see how it could possibly be relevant to Gentry's murder. From what you told me, there was such a loathing of him among your guests, it seems to me that all I've got to do is find out the individual reasons for that loathing and, of course, who got there first.'

During the latter part of their conversation, the Colonel had begun to grow slightly fidgety and his agitation at last caught Trubshawe's eye.

'Something the matter, Colonel?'

'Ah well, Trubshawe . . . yes. Yes, I have to say there is.'

'What is it?'

'*Well*' – he took a deep breath – 'you *are* planning to question all of us, am I right?'

'Right.'

'Which means me too, I suppose?'

'Well, naturally, Colonel. I really don't know how, in all fairness, if your guests are prepared to submit to the ordeal, I can leave you out. The others simply wouldn't have it.'

'No, no, of course not. It's just that, like Cora, I *know* I didn't murder Raymond Gentry and there are certain facts I've kept from Mary all these years, facts – from my past, you know – facts that would break her heart if they were suddenly to emerge at this late date. So I thought . . .'

'Yes?'

'I thought, if I were to give you those facts now, in private, just the two of us, you could – well, you could keep them out of the questioning.'

The Chief-Inspector had started shaking his head even before the Colonel finished speaking.

'I'm sorry, Colonel, but there you're asking too much of me. We've got to have a level playing-field, don't you agree?'

'Oh yes, quite. Quite. It's only that the secrets – secret, I should say – the secret I'm thinking of is a rather special one. In view of the very serious consequences it could have for me, it just can't be compared with the Vicar's petty fibs or Evie's peccadilloes, whatever they could possibly have been.'

'Still, you really can't expect me to give you privileged treatment. Not the done thing. Not cricket.'

'I understand . . .'

It was clear, however, whether he understood or not, that the Colonel was still unwilling to give up.

'Then what about this?' he suggested. 'What if I tell you now what it is I'm talking about and, when you interrogate me, if you judge, as I'm sure you will, that it's got nothing to do with the murder, you won't force me to bring it up?'

The policeman pondered for a few seconds.

'Colonel,' he finally agreed, 'I'll do what I can. But I make no promises. Understood?'

'Understood.'

There was a brief silence. Then:

'So? What is it you have to tell me?'

'Well, Trubshawe, I haven't always been the pattern of a model citizen. When I was young, scarcely more than a nipper, I got into a whole series of scrapes. Nothing close to murder or anything like that, but – well, it won't serve any purpose my reciting all my crimes to you – it's a lengthy list – I mean, it *was* a lengthy list – all of this happened a long time ago. But the fact is that in this country I have a criminal record.'

'Aha.'

'Aha, indeed. Caught you out there, didn't I? I mean, to look at me now, who'd ever suspect such a thing? But there you are. The police, naturally, have a set of my fingerprints and, if this business explodes in our faces, it would be extremely disagreeable for me, innocent as I am. And for poor Mary, of course, who's even more innocent. Not to mention Selina.'

'I see . . .' said Trubshawe, who visibly hadn't expected such a revelation. 'So the Yard actually knows your name?'

'H'm?'

'I said, the Yard knows your name?'

'Well, in fact, no.'

'But they must do, man, if, as you say, you have a criminal record.'

'No, they don't. Because Roger ffolkes isn't my real name.'

'What?'

'Don't you see, I had to change my name. After I'd – well, after I'd paid my debt to society, I left to make my fortune in America and, when I returned, I couldn't take the risk of one of my former accomplices tracking me down. I'd done jolly well for myself in the States and I felt I deserved a new life. So, surely forgivably, I gave myself a new identity.'

'Then what *is* your real name?'

'It's Roger all right – just not Roger ffolkes.'

'Roger what?'

'Well . . .'

At this point, the Colonel slowly and almost conspiratorially began casting glances around the room, even though there was no one in it but himself and the Chief-Inspector.

Then, just as he was about to speak, there was a knock at the door.

'Er, yes, who is it?'

'It's Farrar, sir.'

'Ah, Farrar. Come in, will you?'

'Sorry to interrupt you, sir, but you should know – you and Mr Trubshawe – that your guests are already on their way downstairs.'

'I see. Well, thank you. Ready for them, are you, Trubshawe?'

'Yes, Colonel, I am. But you were going to –'

'We'll speak about that later, shall we? When we manage to have a private moment together.'

'Just as you say, sir, just as you say.'

Chapter Five

In ones and twos, confidently and timidly, the ffolkeses' guests trooped into the library, its walls lined ceiling-high with identically bound volumes which, as most of them were not merely unread but unopened, made the shelving appear as though it were supporting row after row of cigar-boxes.

Only Selina, still too distressed to make a re-appearance, was missing. But, in the twenty minutes which had elapsed since the others had retired to their rooms, they had all made themselves as presentable as they could for the trial they knew lay ahead of them.

Clem Wattis, to be sure, still looked very much the English Vicar incarnate, with his dog-eared dog-collar and raggedy ill-fitting cardigan, its leather elbow-patches so threadbare they themselves seemed in urgent need of patching. The Doctor, for his part, had gone for a prudently countrified look – checked sports jacket, impeccably creased corduroy trousers and tan suede shoes. As for Don, his canary-yellow V-necked jumper and tartan bow-tie instantly identified him as your typically modern American college student.

Evadne Mount, meanwhile, was wearing one of her yolk-of-egg tweed outfits, along with a pair of singularly unbecoming suet-coloured stockings and shoes so sensible, as they say, you felt like consulting them on whether you should cash in your shares in Amalgamated Copper. From her wardrobe Mary ffolkes had selected a flower-patterned taffeta dress that was unabashedly unfashionable but probably pricier than it looked. Madge Rolfe sported a stylishly plain frock of pale red crushed-velvet, a frock that, even if one had never set eyes on it before, one might have guessed had been worn more than once too often. And the Vicar's wife had on a shabby brown cotton skirt with, over its matching blouse, a woollen cardigan nearly as shapeless as her husband's.

Then there was Cora Rutherford. Like all of her thespian ilk, she was always 'on', even in deepest Dartmoor. She had decked herself out in a tailored suit in pleated grey tweed and a high-collared silk shirt, around which she'd negligently flung a chic fox-fur throw. Though her eyes were lavish with mascara, and her lips with cyclamen, her only jewellery was a pair of virtually invisible pearl earrings. The actress herself – the message came across loud and clear – was the jewel.

They were all requested to take seats around the Chief-Inspector, who stood in the centre of the room in front of a massive mahogany desk on top of which sat two of Roger ffolkes's embossed stamp albums, an extra-large magnifying-glass, the typewriter on which Gentry's notes had been typed out and, of all unlikely, unlovely artefacts, one of those 'humorous' ashtrays on whose rim a diminutive top-hatted toper unsteadily supports himself against a lamppost.

When everybody was settled, the Colonel mutely signalled to the detective to assume command.

'Well now,' said the Chief-Inspector, 'I'd first like to thank you all for being so prompt. Each of you knows why you're here, so the only thing that remains is for me to decide the order in which you're questioned.'

He reflectively scanned the party as though he hadn't already made up his mind who his first victim would be.

'Perhaps I might call on you, Vicar,' he said at last, 'to open the batting?'

The Vicar almost leapt out of his chair.

'Me!' he exclaimed. 'Why . . . why me?'

'Well, somebody has to go first, you know,' said Trubshawe with an only just perceptible twinkle in his eye.

'Yes, but I . . .'

'Yes?'

'Well, it does seem unfair to pick on . . . to . . .'

'Of course, if you'd rather not, perhaps you yourself would nominate one of your friends to take your place?'

'Oh, but that's also unfair! Oh, calamity!' groaned the Vicar, who looked as though he were about to burst into tears.

'Come now, Mr Wattis,' said his tormentor gently but firmly, 'aren't you being a little childish? I promise I'll do my utmost to make it all as painless as possible.'

Aware not only from the Chief-Inspector's rebuke but also from the way his friends were staring at him that he had let himself be shown in a rather unattractive light, the Vicar now hastened to retrieve his composure.

'Oh well . . . in that case, Mr Trub – I mean, Inspector Trub – that's to say, *Chief*-Inspector Trub. Trubshawe! I suppose if you really think . . .'

'Yes, Vicar, I do. I really do,' the policeman nimbly cut in. 'However –' he began to add.

'Yes? You say however?' the Vicar once more interrupted him, and this time his already squeaky voice came perilously close to cracking.

'However, I say – in the light of Miss Mount's account of last night's events, an account with which, I noted, not one of you present – you yourself included, Vicar – chose to take issue, I feel duty-bound to advise you that the phrase "as painless as possible" shouldn't be construed to mean that our conversation will be totally, ah, pain-free. You do realise I'm going to have to ask you some very probing – indeed, some very personal – questions?'

'Oh dear, I – I just don't know whether –'

'Questions,' pursued Trubshawe, who was no longer prepared to be put off his stride by the clergyman's inter-jections, 'that, had I been assigned to this case in an official capacity, I would be asking you teat-a-teat, as the Frogs say, in the privacy of your own home or in a police station. But since everyone, you again included, fell in with the Doctor's proposal that my interrogation, which, I repeat, is wholly informal –'

Now it was Cora Rutherford's turn to interrupt.

'Oh, for heaven's sake, Trubshawe, we know all that!' she snapped. 'Do stop blethering, will you!'

'Patience, dear lady, patience,' Trubshawe calmly retorted. 'When it comes, as it will, to your own turn, you may not be quite so desirous to have things rushed. The fact is that my presence is extremely irregular, and I wish to make sure you all understand that no one is actually, legally, obliged to undergo questioning here and now.'

'But, I tell you, we do understand!'

'Also,' he went on unperturbed, 'that, if you do agree to be questioned, then, notwithstanding the fact that you aren't under oath, there's simply no point to the exercise if you end by telling me less than the unvarnished truth – or at least what you sincerely believe to be the unvarnished truth. Aren't I right? You do see what I'm driving at, Vicar?'

Clem Wattis bristled at what he clearly felt was a slander on his character.

'Well, really! I must protest – I really must lodge a protest, Chief-Inspector. You appear to be singling me out in an offensively gratuitous fashion!'

'Please, please, Mr Wattis, let me assure you. No offence was intended. If I put it to you in particular, it's only because you're the one who's going to set the ball rolling.'

The Vicar was now so flustered that beads of sweat glistened atop his bald head and his owlish horn-rimmed glasses were starting to cloud over.

'Oh well, if you – if you insist. After all, as a man of the cloth, I'm bound to tell the truth anyway. I mean, I'm bound by a higher authority than yours.'

'Yes, yes, of course, I quite understand. So shall we . . .?'

'Uh huh,' said the Vicar unhappily.

'Good,' said the Chief-Inspector. 'Now – I'd like to start by inviting you to relate your own experience of the Christmas dinner party. The way Miss Mount described it – that, for you, was substantially accurate, was it?'

Clem Wattis shot a quick, helpless glance at his wife. She said nothing, but, with nervously rocking little nods of her head, appeared to be encouraging him to speak up. It couldn't have been easy for her, however, knowing as she did what was in store for him, and her lips were pursed so tight you felt that, if she were to relax them, her whole face would unravel.

'Well, Inspector – oh dear, I keep getting it wrong, don't I? – I mean, Chief-Inspector –'

'That's quite all right, Reverend. As I say, I'm retired, so my rank is only a courtesy. Please go on.'

'Well, Evadne certainly – she certainly "caught" Raymond

Gentry. I mean, I know one should never speak ill of the dead – indeed, a man of my vocation shouldn't speak ill even of the living – but I am only human, after all, I don't pretend to be saintlier than any of my flock, and I cannot deny I took an instant dislike to that young man. There, I've said it!'

'An instant dislike, eh? Mostly, I suppose, for the same reasons as Miss Mount?'

'Absolutely. So sad, too. Our little gathering was just getting going when he turned up with Selina. Then the atmosphere became quite inspissated.'

Trubshawe blinked.

'Did it now? Can you give me a "for instance"?'

'I can give you many "for instances". Right from the start Gentry insisted on letting us know that he was among us only because poor, benighted Selina wanted him to meet her people.

'Now, no one could be fonder than I am of Selina ffolkes, but she has, I fear – and I've had occasion to say so to her face, so I'm not telling tales out of school – she has never been too fastidious in her choice of male companions.'

Then, realising that Don was glaring at him, he added a hurriedly improvised postscript:

'Er . . . that's to say, not until now.'

Mopping his brow with a handkerchief which had been discreetly handed to him by his ever-watchful wife, he sought to get back on track.

'Gentry simply couldn't resist driving home to us how much more amusing – no, no, no, not amusing, *penetrating* – that was the word – Evadne hit it on the nose, he used that word "penetrating" so often it, well, it penetrated right into my brain, giving me quite a migraine, something I –'

'Vicar,' said Trubshawe, 'if you would . . .'

'What?'

' . . . stick to the point?'

'Well, I'm sorry, Inspector,' said the Vicar querulously, 'but, as you'll see, this *is* the point. If his prattle hadn't given me one of my splitting headaches, along the whole right side of my face, I might have been able to adopt a more benevolent, more truly Christian, attitude towards him. I might have tried harder to feign interest in his addle-pated talk about the "crowd" he moved in, all those vegetarians, Egyptologists, fakirs, Cubists, Russian dancers, Christian Scientists, amateur photographers, Theosophists and goodness knows what else! Now there's a "for instance" for you.'

'What is?'

'Theosophists. Evie omitted to mention how much Gentry went on about conducting séances at the Planchette, making contact with Those Who Have Passed Over, you know, all that silly spiritualistic hanky-panky. In his foetid little mind he realised that, as an Anglican clergyman, I couldn't possibly approve of such pagan foofaraw, so he taunted me and taunted me and I could see him, with a sly, lethal glint in his eye, simply waiting for me to rise to the bait.'

'And did you?'

'Inspector, I must tell you that even in this agreeable little backwater of ours I've been buttonholed by potty-mouthed disbelievers before, and I find that the only way to handle them is to refuse to descend to their level. So I said to him, "I know what you're up to, young man. I can put two and two together."'

'What was his answer to that?'

'Oh, he was awfully clever – as usual. "Yes," he said, in that nasal whinny of his which drove us all to distraction, "you can put *two* and *two* together – and come up with something *too, too* ridiculous!"'

'I see . . .' said the Chief-Inspector, suppressing a smile. 'So you think he was being deliberately rude to you?'

'I don't think, I know. He never let a chance go by to mock my most deeply held beliefs. When the Colonel passed some blameless remark about the Great War – you remember, Roger – about how we'd stemmed the tide against the Hun, I observed that being born British meant that one had drawn first prize in the Lottery of Life. Gentry being incapable of offering any plausible argument against that, he simply scoffed. And I mean scoffed!

'You know, Inspector, until I met him I never really knew the meaning of that word. I mean to say, I know what it looks like, what it physically looks like, when somebody sneers, for example, or frowns or scowls. But scoffs? Well, Raymond Gentry truly, *physically*, did scoff. He made an *extremely* indecent noise by blowing saliva through his lips. Obscene little bubbles were actually visible between his front teeth. Ah, I see you don't believe me, but – Evie? Aren't I speaking the truth?'

'Why, yes, Clem, I never thought of it like that,' said Evadne Mount. 'Yet you're right. Gentry really did give a new meaning to the word "scoff". I assure you, Trubshawe, Clem's made quite an insightful remark there.'

'Why, thank you, Evie,' said the Vicar, unaccustomed to compliments from somebody generally so parsimonious with them.

'And it's a remark, if I'm not mistaken,' said Trubshawe, 'that brings us to the very crux of the matter.'

'The crux, you say?'

'I mean the War. You just referred to the Great War.'

The Vicar blanched. Here it was. Here and now was what he dreaded most. If ever a face was an open book, it was his at that instant.

'You'll recall, Vicar,' the policeman continued, 'that the first line of Gentry's notes read: REV – WAR. And, later, Miss Mount made mention of what she called aspersions, aspersions that Gentry cast on your war record. Isn't that so?'

'Er . . . yes,' said the Vicar, 'that – that is correct.'

A few seconds elapsed during which neither he nor Trubshawe nor anybody else spoke. Like a group of miscreant schoolboys who, waiting in a morose huddle to be punished by their headmaster, anxiously scrutinise the features of the first boy to emerge from his study for any external clues as to the nature of that punishment, the ffolkeses and their guests were probably thinking as much of their own future plight as of the Vicar's present one.

'Would you care to elucidate?' Trubshawe finally asked.

'Well, I – I – I don't really see how . . .'

'Come now, sir, we did all agree, did we not? The unvarnished truth? So shall we have it?'

The wretched clergyman, at whom seemingly not even his wife could for the moment bear to look, realised there was no longer any escape.

'Farrar?'

'Yes, Vicar?'

'I wonder if – if I might have a glass of water? My throat seems a little tight. Constricted, somehow.'

'Why, certainly, Vicar.'

'Thank you.'

A moment later, having taken a few modest sips, he was ready to continue – or as ready as he'd ever be.

'Well, you know, I – I took up my post here in 1919 – in January, was it? Or February – oh well, I don't suppose it really matters.'

'No, it really doesn't,' said the Chief-Inspector drily. 'Just go on.'

'Anyway, it was in one or other of the early months of 1919, so not too long after the end of the War, and my predecessor in the parish had been a young man, relatively young, but nevertheless much liked, I might almost say much loved, by his parishioners. All the more so because he'd been killed in action – during one of the last Big Pushes. I ought to explain, too, that he'd been so keen to do his bit for King and Country he'd actually concealed the fact that he was a clergyman and enlisted as a common soldier. Then he was posted to the front, where he died quite the hero's death. He was mentioned in dispatches, you know, and there was vague talk of a posthumous George Cross.

'In any event, when I arrived here to take up my living in 1919, I found that his presence, if I may put it that way, was still very, very powerful. Not that there was any resentment against me, I hasten to add – well, not to start with – it was just that the locals hadn't forgotten the shining example of his courage. I fear I must have struck them as something of a letdown by comparison.

'That would certainly explain why, when Cynthia and I moved in, the parish was at first a trifle standoffish, a trifle "sniffy". There was, in particular, a Mrs de Cazalis. She's our local *grande dame* and she'd evidently been very "in" with my predecessor. Harker, the village's odd-job man, had a nickname for her – Vicar's Pet. You know, like the kind of schoolchild who gets ragged for being Teacher's Pet?

'Well, it soon became clear that she expected things to go on just as they had before. My predecessor had been a bachelor, you see, and whilst you might expect that to have counted as a point against him, it had in reality turned out to be the reverse. All the local ladies – now, Inspector, I wouldn't like to suggest that they were *all* busybodies – but all the local ladies who *participated*, don't you know, who organised our Charity Sales and Mystery Tours and Chara-banc Outings for the Old Folk, well, they were absolutely in seventh heaven that there was no interfering vicar's wife to run these things, which is traditionally the case.

'Hence it was, at least in the first few months, a rather lonely life for us. It's a lonely part of the country, anyway, and we had problems making new friends, as we tend to do. So, without thinking of the possible consequences, Cynthia eventually elected to busy herself with all the usual chores of a vicar's wife and, I'm afraid, only succeeded in putting a few noses out of joint. There was even, at last, a sort of showdown – is that what it's called? – a showdown in the Vicarage.

'I can still see them all sitting in our little front room, rattling their teacups in their laps, and after some pointed comments on the very *exceptional* calibre of my predeces-sor, on his heroism, all of that, Mrs de Cazalis turned to me and enquired, bold as brass, "And what did *you* do in the Great War, Vicar?" The italics, needless to say, were hers.'

There was a pregnant pause, and it was the Chief-Inspec-tor, the only one of the Vicar's listeners not to know his story's dénouement, who nudged him into continuing.

'You understand, Inspector,' said the Vicar, 'I really didn't mean to tell a lie. I didn't. It was almost as though – well, as though I wasn't *stealing* the truth – which is what I always think a lie is, you know, a stolen truth – but, as it were, embezzling it.'

This original concept clearly intrigued the policeman.

'Embezzling the truth? I confess I . . .'

'As though I'd temporarily stolen somebody else's truth to get myself out of a hole, but fully intended to replace it once the crisis was over.

'Alas,' he sighed, 'like so many embezzlers before me, I was to discover that there never does arrive that convenient moment when you're able to return what you've stolen. Before you could say Jack Robinson, I'd gone on stealing other truths that didn't belong to me, until I found myself – oh dear God forgive me! – I found myself living a permanent lie.'

The poor man now really was on the verge of tears, and his wife would have attempted to offer him comfort, except that she must have realised that at such a point any display of affectionate solidarity on her part would have done for him.

'Mr Wattis,' said Trubshawe, 'I know how difficult this is for you, but I have to ask. What *was* this "truth" which you – you embezzled? That you too had been a war hero, p'raps?'

The Vicar was aghast at such a calumny.

'No, no, no, no, no! The very idea, Inspector! I would never, *never* have presumed . . . By lying as I did, it wasn't at all my intention to puff myself up. I simply hoped to take those prying old – I mean, the ladies of the Church Committee, down a peg or two.

'I recall a schoolmaster friend of ours – I'm thinking of Grenfell, dear,' he said to his wife, 'who once admitted to me that he, the very gentlest of souls, would be a regular martinet with his charges at the start of every new term, actually going so far as caning them for the most piffling of offences, even as it went against the grain, because he believed that, if he gave them so excessive a demonstration of his authority straight off, he'd never have to use his cane again. Well, that in a sense was what I was also trying to do. I allowed myself to tell one little untruth right at the beginning – merely to impose *my* authority, so to speak – and I trusted I'd never have to tell another.'

'Yes – yes,' replied Trubshawe, 'I can see how that might have worked. But I have to put it to you again – what was the lie?'

'The lie?' said the Vicar sadly. 'The lie was that, throughout the War, I'd been an Army padre in Flanders. Nothing grand, you understand, no heroics, no mention in dispatches. I just left my parishioners with the impression – not much more than an impression, I assure you – that I'd, well . . .'

'I get you. You claimed you'd seen action in Europe.

Instead of which . . .?'

The Vicar almost literally hung his head.

'Instead of which, I'd been a company clerk in Aldershot. I hadn't yet been ordained and, in addition, I was declared unfit for active service. My feet, you know.'

'Your feet?' said the Chief-Inspector.

'They're flat, I'm afraid. I was born with flat feet.'

'Aha. I see. Well, Vicar,' said Trubshawe benignly, 'I have to say it strikes me as a pretty forgivable fib. Not much there for anybody to make a song-and-dance about, surely?'

'No,' said the Vicar, 'perhaps not. If that had been all there was to it.'

'There was more to it, then?'

'Well, I fear it all rather got out of control. You're familiar, I'm certain, with the old rhyme "Oh, what a tangled web we weave when first we practise to deceive"? Once I'd told the original lie, there I was, caught in my own web. Even though I played down any notion that I might have been a hero, I daresay I sinned by omission when I let the inference stand.

'The consequence was that these ladies of the parish took it for granted that I was being disarmingly modest about my experience and started pestering me about everything I'd seen and done at the front. Oh, don't misunderstand me, I feel sure their curiosity in this regard was utterly irreproachable, except – except in the case of Mrs de Cazalis herself, whom I confess I did come to suspect – it was most un-Christian of me, I know – but I did come to suspect her of harbouring, alas, all too well-founded doubts about the probity of my character and even of hoping to trip me up. Then it all came to a head with the matter of the organ.'

'The organ?'

'The church organ. When I arrived in the parish, it was in dire need of repair, as many church organs were in the aftermath of the War, and as always there was simply no money to pay for it. So, following innumerable committee meetings, with all the internecine bickerings which would appear to be part and parcel of these meetings, and whose endless ramifications and recriminations I'll spare you, we decided to hold a Grand Charity Fête.

'It had Tombola, Morris Dancing around the Maypole, a Punch-and-Judy show for the tots, a Pin-the-Nail-on-the-Donkey's-Tail stall for the older children and an entertainment which we, the members of the Church Committee, got up ourselves. We invited some jolly Pierrots and Harlequins over from the Postbridge concert-party, the Fol-de-Rols. The girls of St Cecilia's performed a series of tasteful Tableaux Vivants. Mr Hawkins from the Post Office charmed us all with his famous bird-call impressions. And his eldest son Georgie – well, Georgie, as I recall, did some sort of an act with gaily coloured hoops. I never did know quite what was supposed to happen to those hoops, as we had next to no time for rehearsals, but Georgie surely didn't mean for them all to bound off the stage in every direction at once. Anyway, it got the biggest laugh of the day, which I suppose was the main thing.'

'Mr Wattis,' the Chief-Inspector nipped in quickly, 'sorry, but where exactly is this business of the Fête going? And what has it to do with Raymond Gentry?'

There was a snort from the Colonel.

'Really, Trubshawe!' he cried. 'Why must you badger the poor fellow so! You asked him for his story and that's just what he's giving you. It's a deuced uncomfortable spot you've put him on, you know, but he's doing his level best. Go on, Clem, and take your own time. Whatever courage you did or did not show in the War, you're certainly making up for it now. You're an example to us all.'

'Very kind of you to put it that way, Roger,' said the Vicar, visibly touched by his friend's unsolicited words of support. In fact, with the relief of having got over the worst, there had now come a new confidence in his voice.

'The thing is, Inspector,' he went on, 'I was expected, as Vicar, to contribute some little thing of my own to the show. And, as I couldn't sing, or juggle, or do bird-call impressions, or anything of the kind, it was finally proposed – by the perfidious Mrs de Cazalis, surprise surprise – that I deliver a public talk about my wartime experiences.'

'H'm. Quite a can of worms you'd opened up.'

'I simply couldn't say no, particularly as it was to benefit the church, and the other ladies of the committee excitedly backed her up, and I felt well and truly trapped. Cynthia will confirm how I agonised long and hard over how I might extricate myself. I tell you, Inspector – all of you – it got to the point where I even contemplated resigning from my living as the only decent thing to do, but – well, that would undoubtedly also have meant quitting the Church, which would have been a frightful cross to bear for the rest of my life. As well as something I could ill-afford.

'Anyway, the upshot was, I agreed to give the talk.

'There was absolutely no question, as I already said, of inventing stories of my own so-called courage, but I realised I would have to offer a detailed summary of conditions at the front. So I read every single book on the war I could lay my hands on, until I became quite an expert on the subject – history manuals, personal memoirs, whatever there was, I read it and made copious notes. And, you understand, I couldn't even borrow these books from the circulating library, as I suspected it would soon dawn on the snooping Mrs de Cazalis what I was up to. So I had to buy them, putting a real strain on our purse-strings, given that Cynthia and I are as poor as a pair of church-mice.

'But even if what I had to say wouldn't be, couldn't be, *my* truth, I wanted it to be, at some level, *the* truth. You do understand? That was very important to me.'

'What happened?'

The Vicar seemed briefly in danger of once more losing his composure, but he swiftly rallied.

'It was a fiasco!'

'Really? But why? If, as you say, you'd done your homework?'

'The fact is, I'm simply no good at lying. I was convincing, more or less, when I gave my audience a general outline of the situation in Flanders. But when I started to talk in the first person – about *my* visiting the trenches, *my* consoling the walking wounded, *my* holding a service in a half-ruined village chapel with the distant rumble of Big Bertha shaking the rafters – well, Inspector, I quite went to pieces. I stumbled over my words, I was hazy on details, I got my dates all mixed up, I lost the place in the notes I'd made, I hemmed and hawed and then hemmed all over again. I was clueless, clueless!'

'I'm truly sorry, Reverend. You didn't deserve that for one minor lapse.'

'Oh, it all happened a very long time ago. Yet, you know, I still wake up in a sweat at the memory of it. No, no, no, why should I pretend any longer? Not in a sweat. I wake up screaming. Do you hear? I, the sweet old Vicar, dear old Clem Wattis who wouldn't harm a fly – *I wake up screaming in the middle of the night!* Oh, my poor Cynthia, what I've forced you to put up with!'

His wife's eyes looked into his with infinite love and compassion.

'Where was I?' he finally asked himself. 'Oh yes. Well, I could already hear a smattering of titters from the audience and I could see, in the very front row, Mrs de Cazalis savouring every minute of her triumph.

'And then I came in my notes to the word "Ypres".'

'I beg your pardon,' said the Chief-Inspector. 'What word?'

'Ypres. The Belgian town, you know. I had blithely jotted down the name without thinking I'd actually have to pronounce it when I gave my talk, and I got so tangled in my pronunciation it emerged from my mouth like a – forgive the vulgarity, but I'm afraid there *is* no other word – like a belch.

'I'd also misspelled it, which didn't help. It's an old failing of mine, spelling. I can't spell for toffee. Matter of fact,' he added with an unexpected dash of self-deprecating humour, 'I can't even spell "toffee".'

Everyone smiled at this *mot*, but smiled at it as much for its having relaxed the tension as for its own moot quality as wit.

'Well,' he bravely went on, 'the titters started gradually shading into outright guffaws, and, as for Mrs de Cazalis, the gloating expression on her flushed fat face left me in no doubt that she regarded it as game, set and match to her. It was the worst moment of my life.

'Nor did it end there. For months afterwards in the village I was the target of all sorts of derisive little digs and *doubles entendres*, and the greengrocer's barrow-boy would career past me on his bike yelling not "Yippee!" but

"Ypree!" It was touch and go whether we'd simply pack our things and slip away in the night. But Cynthia, bless her, urged me to stand fast.

'And, you know, she was right. For even though I genuinely believed I could never live down such a humiliation this side of Kingdom Come, time after all does pass. It does heal wounds, precisely as they say it does.

'Oh, once in a while I'd overhear some remark I felt I'd eavesdropped on – eavesdropped even though it was addressed to me. Somebody might say that when we're burdened with troubles we just have to "soldier on", you know, the sort of thing people come out with when they've nothing better to say, and I'd blush inwardly – and sometimes outwardly – at what I took to be an allusion to me. Again, though, Cynthia would persuade me I was being overly sensitive, and most likely she was right.'

'How long did this period last?'

'How long? Several months, I suppose. And then, I repeat, it all began to die down. Even though I never ceased to suffer in private, publicly it came to be so much water under the bridge, and my wife and I lived on for many years in the village as contentedly as we were able.

'That is,' he added after a lengthy pause, 'until Raymond Gentry entered our lives.'

'Tell me,' asked Trubshawe, 'what exactly was it he said?'

'It wasn't what he said,' answered the Vicar. 'It was what he implied with all his feline, sibilant little insinuations about the War. I realise he's lying dead upstairs, a bullet through his heart, but, as Evie rightly said, there was something un-English about him. Not foreign exactly, but, you know, oily and underhand, like many of his unfortunate race. No one who wasn't already aware of the background to my story would have grasped what he was getting at, but I knew that he knew, and he knew that I knew that he knew, and this loathsome complicity between us, with everyone else looking on and listening on, became quite intolerable.'

'How do you imagine he found out?'

'Ah well, now there you do raise an interesting question, Inspector,' said the Vicar. 'As a professional snitch, Gentry could of course be expected to know the – the, eh, dirt about the private lives of the ffolkeses' starrier acquaintances, like Evie here and Cora. But the local Vicar? The local Doctor? Now who could have passed on to him that kind of information? I hate to be hurtful to Roger and Mary, dear, dear friends who invite Cynthia and me down here for Christmas every year when I doubt anybody else in the locality would, but I fear the prime suspect has to be Selina.'

'When Miss ffolkes is ready to join us,' Trubshawe intervened judiciously, 'you may be sure I'll ask her whatever questions I consider to be relevant to her relationship with the deceased. But for now, Vicar, I have to ask you the hardest one of all.'

'Yes?'

'Did you kill Raymond Gentry?'

The Vicar almost choked with incredulity.

'What! Is that a joke question?'

'Not at all.'

'You're asking me *seriously* if I . . . ?'

'Now look,' replied the Chief-Inspector soberly. 'Why do you think I've been putting you through all this unpleasantness, if not because you are, along with everybody else present, a suspect? I thought that was a given.'

'Well, yes, of course I understand that to be the case, but do be serious, man. Can you really be asking me if I'm the kind of person who kills just anybody and everybody who happens to do me wrong? Do I look like a murderer?'

'Ah, Vicar, if murderers looked like murderers, if every burglar went around wearing a domino mask and a striped jumper and toting a bulging sack over his shoulder with the word "Swag" stencilled on it that he'd purchased from some burglars' emporium, how easy our job would be!'

'Oh, very well, yes, I do see what you mean,' said Wattis resignedly. 'Point taken.'

'And so – the answer to my question?'

'The answer to your question, Inspector, is no. No, I did not kill Raymond Gentry. I may have felt like it – I know everybody else did and, as I say, I've never made any claim to be better than my fellow men. But I certainly did not act on whatever evil impulse he might have provoked in me.

Actually,' he added, 'in some respects I have reason to be grateful to him.'

'Grateful?' exclaimed the Colonel. 'Good Lord, Clem, how on earth can you be grateful to such a swine for causing you the pain he did?'

'Yes, Roger, it's true, he did cause me pain – but, oddly, he also brought me relief from that pain. I've finally got the thing off my chest. I've finally been compelled to yank it, kicking and screaming, into the open air and, honestly, I think I feel the better for it. I feel as though I've been purged. I may have been a liar, and God is my witness that I've paid for my lie many times over. But I never was, as God also knows, a coward. It's true, I didn't see any action in the War, like my glorious predecessor, but neither did thousands of others like me with flat feet and short sight and fallen arches, and it wasn't their fault just as it wasn't mine. When all is said and done, I had a perfectly respectable War and have absolutely nothing to be ashamed of. "They also serve . . .", you know.'

'Hear hear!' cried the Colonel.

'Good for you, Vicar,' the Chief-Inspector nodded in agreement. 'And thank you for being so co-operative. Now let me put one last question to you and then you're free.'

'Please.'

'Did you leave your bedroom at all during the night?'

'Yes, I did,' was the surprising answer. 'Several times, in fact.'

'Several times!? Why?'

The Vicar threw back his head and laughed – he actually laughed aloud.

'Well,' said Trubshawe, 'I may be getting dim, but I fail to understand what's suddenly so funny.'

'Oh, Inspector, now that I've crashed through the barrier of embarrassment, I'm willing – as only half-an-hour ago it would have been unthinkable for me – I'm willing to give you a brutally straight answer to that question. If I left my bedroom several times during the night, it was because I had to reply to several Calls of Nature. When you reach my age, Nature can become quite . . . quite pressing. Especially after the sort of blowout we had at dinner.'

'I see. And roughly when, may I ask, was the last time?'

'Actually, I can answer that one not roughly but precisely. Nature, at least in my current experience, tends to be a creature of routine. It was five-thirty.'

'And did you see anything suspicious? Or even just untoward?'

'No, nothing at all. I woke up, got up – yet again – trotted along the corridor and . . .'

Whereupon, abruptly falling silent, he started to frown in an effort of remembrance.

'So you *did* see something?'

'N-o-o-o,' murmured the Vicar when he answered at last. 'No, I didn't *see* anything.'

'But you stopped as though –'

'It wasn't what I saw, it was what I *heard*. How very odd. With everything that's happened since, it completely slipped my mind.'

'What did you hear?'

'As I was returning from – from my last Call of Nature, I heard voices raised in anger, an argument, a real argy-bargy, between a man and a woman, quite a violent one too. I couldn't distinguish what was being said, all of it taking place behind closed doors, you understand, but it certainly sounded as though it must have been alarmingly loud inside the room itself.'

'Inside which room?' asked Trubshawe.

'Oh, as to that,' replied the Vicar, 'there can be no doubt at all. It came from the attic. Yes, it most definitely came from the attic.'

Chapter Six

'An argument inside the attic at five-thirty in the morning, eh?' grunted the Chief-Inspector. 'Between a man and a woman? The plot thickens . . .' he added satirically.

Tugging at one of his moustache's nicotine-stained fringes, he then asked the Vicar:

'You didn't recognise either voice, I suppose?'

'I'm afraid not. I say again, Mr Trubshawe, I didn't actually hear the argument itself – who was arguing and what it was about. I heard only that there *was* an argument.'

'And naturally you didn't get any sense of how old they were?'

'How old who were?'

'The man and woman you heard arguing?'

'No, no, no. I *was* half-asleep, you know, which is why I've only just remembered that I heard it at all.'

'I see. Well, thanks for that, Vicar,' said the policeman. 'You've been extremely helpful.'

He turned his attention to the five women present.

'Now, ladies,' he said, 'you've just heard what the Vicar has had to say. So may I enquire if any of you went to the attic, for whatever reason, you understand – for, even though it's highly improbable, it's nevertheless not impossible that the argument overheard by the Vicar and the subsequent murder of Gentry are unconnected. I repeat, did any of you, for whatever reason, go up into the attic at approximately five-thirty this morning?'

It was, unexpectedly, the Vicar himself who answered first.

'Not,' he said without any too apparent asperity in his voice, 'that my word, my word of honour, is likely to carry as much weight with you as it might previously have done, Inspector, given what I've just confessed to, but I would like to vouch for Mrs Wattis. She was sound asleep when I crawled out of bed at five-thirty and she was sound asleep when I climbed back into it no more than seven or eight minutes later. You may believe me or not as you will.'

'My dear Vicar,' Trubshawe diplomatically replied, 'I'm not here either to believe or disbelieve you. You or anybody else, for that matter. I'm here to listen to what you all have to tell me in the hope of uncovering some clue as to how and why and by whom the crime was committed. As I've already had cause to remind you, I did not volunteer to come to ffolkes Manor.'

'Please be patient with us, Trubshawe,' said the Colonel. 'We're all of us still on edge. Evadne may find it hard to conceal her glee at being directly implicated in the kind of whodunit she's only ever lived by proxy – don't deny it, Evie dear, it's written all over your face – but I can assure you that, for the rest of us, knowing we're suspects in a real-life murder mystery is no laughing matter.

'As for vouching for our better halves, as Clem has just done, well, I fear I for one cannot oblige. As per usual, I was snoring my head off at five-thirty and Mary could have danced the hoochie-koochie in front of the wardrobe mirror for all I'd have been aware of it.

'She and I, though, have been man and wife for nigh on twenty-six years, twenty-six cloudless years, and it's on *that* evidence that I'm prepared to vouch for her. It probably won't be enough for a police officer like you, but it's more than enough for me.'

He laid his hand on his wife's shoulder and let her clasp it in her own.

An unmoved Trubshawe, meanwhile, addressed the Doctor.

'Rolfe? Sound asleep at five-thirty, I suppose?'

'Afraid so. Both of us – I mean, both Madge and I – we tend to sleep through the night. It's just one of those quirky habits we've fallen into. Pity, really. If I'd known what was about to happen, I'd have struggled to stay awake. But, there you are, no one gave us any advance warning.'

'If you don't mind, Doctor,' said the Chief-Inspector with a sigh, 'we can all live without the heavy sarcasm. These questions have to be asked. Miss Mount, you will vouch for yourself, I suppose?'

'If you mean by that, was I in bed, was I in bed by myself, and was I sound asleep at five-thirty in the morning, the answer is yes on all counts.'

The Chief-Inspector sighed again.

'And you, Miss Rutherford?'

'Me? I've never even heard of five-thirty in the morning!'

'H'm,' said Trubshawe, 'that leaves just Miss Selina. Naturally, I'll wait till she's sufficiently recovered before putting any questions to her. And please don't look so anxious, Mrs ffolkes, I'll be diplomacy itself. I know how to handle these tricky situations. Heaven knows I've had enough practice.'

With an unwavering gaze, he looked at each of the occupants of the drawing-room in turn until, slowly doubling back, his eyes settled at last on Cora Rutherford.

'Perhaps, Miss Rutherford,' he said, 'you wouldn't mind going next?'

'Delighted,' said the actress.

Now, it should be said that, whether she really was the coyly generic age she claimed for herself – 'Not quite the Bright Young Thing I used to be, darling!' – Cora Rutherford was by no stretch of the imagination a leathery old filly. She still had a trim figure, possibly too trim to have survived the years more or less intact without artificial enhancement, and though it wasn't easy to tell beneath the waxy make-up which fossilised her face in a permanent *moue* of pinched hoity-toitiness, that face did seem to be genuinely unwrinkled.

'I swear,' she announced, 'to tell the truth, the whole truth and nothing but the truth. And then some!' she huskily added with a flamboyant flourish of her cigarette-holder.

'Very well,' said Trubshawe. 'Then can I please hear your own first-person account of the run-in you had last night with Raymond Gentry?'

'Certainly,' she answered, a tiny smoke-ring drifting over her head like a halo in search of a saint. 'As you're doubtless sick to the back-teeth of hearing, Gentry took the absolute pip. He was a beast, a rotter of the first water, a self-infatuated, sallow-complexioned little climber, with his artistic hair and his scarlet lips and his T. S. this and his D. H. that and his eternal boasting and bragging about his acquaintance with the Maharani of Rajasthan or the Oom of Oompapah or some other equally improbable pasha or pashette.

'But there was one particular story he told of which it so happened that I had heard a distinctively different version from the horse's mouth. As ever, he was bending our ears back with tales of all the famous people he had met and he mentioned that he'd once had a cocktail at Claridge's with Molnar – the Hungarian playwright, you know, entrancing man, as witty as a barrel of monkeys. Well, it turns out that I know Ferenc – Ferenc Molnar, that is – I know him really rather well – I starred in his play *Olympia*, you recall, Evie? – and long before I ever had the ill-fortune to encounter Gentry, he himself had told me what actually occurred.

'One evening Gentry had accosted him in the bar at Claridge's and asked if he'd consent to be interviewed for that filthy rag of his. Ferenc naturally refused – he could smell a slice of phoney-baloney a mile off – and when Gentry continued to badger him, he simply turned on his heels and stalked out. As he was leaving the bar, though, he chanced to look back and what do you suppose he saw? The preposterous Gentry was furtively finishing off his – I mean Ferenc's – cocktail!

'So when I heard him talk about "having a cocktail with Molnar", I just laughed in his face. In fact, I haven't laughed so much since Minnie Battenberg got her knickers in a twist – literally her knickers and literally in a twist – on the opening night of *Up in Mabel's Room*!

'I can't stand male gossips anyway,' she continued. 'In my experience, and I've had plenty, they're all nancy boys. Frankly, when Gentry first sashayed into the drawing-room, I immediately pegged him for a pansy and I wondered what in heaven's name poor Selina could be getting out of it. You know who he reminded me of, Evie?'

'No, who?'

'The villain in that story of yours that was so naughty you had to have it published in France.'

'*The Case of the Family Jewels*?'

'That's the one. Such a scream! But, of course, it wasn't a book Evie could ever have hoped to bring out in stuffy old Blighty. It all took place in Portofino, as I recall.'

'That's right,' said the novelist. 'I set the scene among a –'

'I fancy it's my turn, ducks,' said Cora Rutherford waspishly, loath to let herself be upstaged even by the author of the book in question. 'It revolved around a group of British aristos partying at a beach-side villa and what was so awfully ingenious was that the crime was solved before any of them actually realised it had been committed. Old Lady – Lady – Lady Beltham, was it, who's hosting the party has left this priceless heirloom lying about her boudoir just itching to be pinched, a heavy, multi-stringed pearl choker – you know, the kind of thing Queen Mary always wears. She's also procured for herself a brand-new *hombre* young enough to be her son – or even grandson – in the book he's named just Boy – and it's obvious to everybody but *la* Beltham herself that he's the worst type of leech. All the more so because there's no doubt whatever from his manners and mannerisms that he's, you know, iffy? Of the Uranian persuasion, as the Oscar Wilde set used to call it, and camp as all-get-out. So, of course, everyone suspects the only reason he's canoodling with the besotted old crone is that he can't wait to get his greedy, grubby little paws on the pearl choker.

'Really, Miss Ruther –' the Chief-Inspector began to say in an endeavour to stem the flow.

'Which is when her nephew – Lady Beltham's nephew and the heir to the heirloom – engages a private detective and introduces him to his aunt as a former school pal so he can fit in with the house-party. I say "him" because, for once, this detective isn't Alexis Baddeley but a fey young laddie – Elias Lindstrom, I think his name was – who, we are led to understand, is also a Uranian.

'Well, one morning everyone's lounging on the beach when Boy emerges from the villa, disrobes and, watched by his clucking sugar-mummy, wades into the ocean in a pair of resplendent figure-hugging bathing-trunks. And it's at that moment that Lindstrom realises he's just stolen the choker.

The twist is that he himself – Lindstrom, I mean – has already indulged in a little bout of bedroom hanky-panky with Boy, just in the line of business, you understand, and when he catches sight of the really rather impressive bulge in his trunks, a bulge that bears no relation to what he . . . . Well, I don't have to draw a picture, do I? He knows there has to be something else in there besides the family jewels. So when Boy wades back out of the ocean, the detective, without so much as a by-your-leave, yanks his trunks down to his ankles – and out pops the pearl choker!

'Anyway, to return to last night – yes, yes, Trubshawe, I *am* getting there – to return to last night, Gentry reminded me of that sleazy young bounder and, to repeat, I simply couldn't fathom what lay behind his interest in Selina, not to mention hers in him. But when I showed him up over the bogus Molnar business, I realised at once I'd made an enemy for life.

'What I didn't realise, though, was how quickly he'd go on the offensive. For some people, you know, an enemy's blood is like a fine vintage wine. It has to be savoured, swilled about the palate, all that wine-bore guff and stuff. Not Gentry. He immediately went for the jugular.'

'What did he say?' asked Trubshawe.

'The first thing he said – I mean, insinuated – the first thing he insinuated was that, professionally, I was on the skids because – because –'

At this point, just as the Chief-Inspector had predicted, the actress seemed to find herself suddenly as tongue-tied as the Vicar before her. For all her brazen self-possession, airing in public what was, even for her, an unpalatable home truth was patently turning out to be not as easy as she had expected.

'Oh, well,' she finally sighed, 'here goes nothing. He insinuated that I was on the skids because of my increasing and, so he implied, incapacitating dependency on certain – on certain substances.'

'Drugs?'

'Cocaine, if you must know.'

The horrified silence with which this last statement was met derived less from the revelation that Cora Rutherford was a dope fiend – as Evadne Mount had already hinted, such a rumour had been circulating for years – than from the cool defiance with which she acknowledged it as a fact of her life.

'And was what he insinuated true?'

'To that, Chief-Inspector, my answer would be yes, no and certainly not.'

'Explain, dear lady.'

'Yes, I do take cocaine. No, I am not incapacitated. And certainly not, as far as my career being on the skids is concerned. I've just ended a ten-week run at the Haymarket, playing Ginevra in *The Jest* by Sem Benelli, a dramatist whose plays, it goes without saying, will be staged as long as theatres exist to stage them in. I'm currently in talks with Hitch – Hitch? Alfred Hitchcock? The famous film director? No? You've really never heard of him?? None of you??? Lawks almighty! Well, anyhow, I'm in talks with Hitch about playing Alexis Baddeley in a forthcoming picture version of Evadne's *Death Be My Deadline*. A character role for me, of course. I'm going to need lashings of slap'.

'Miss Rutherford, did Raymond Gentry actually threaten to expose your – your –'

'My addiction?'

'Yes, your addiction. Did he threaten to write it up in *The Trombone*?'

'No, not in so many words. Just as the article itself, had he had the time and opportunity to write it, wouldn't have been in so many words, if you follow me. But it was all too obvious what he intended to do. By debunking his Molnar story, I'd made him look an ass in front of Selina and he was determined to take his revenge.

'Oh, he wouldn't have dared to use the word "cocaine" in print – that would have been positively actionable, since he couldn't have proved a thing – but his readers all understand the *Trombone* code and he would have left no doubt in their minds what he was talking about.'

'Yet,' said the Chief-Inspector, 'if rumours of your dependency had been circulating for years, as we heard from Miss Mount, surely it wouldn't have made too much of a difference if some what-you-call coded piece were to be published in *The Trombone*?'

'You'd think so, wouldn't you? These things, though, never work like that. So long as rumours just "circulate", as you put it, they can't do too much harm, because so many stories circulate, true and false alike. It's when they get into print, even as rumours, and they become news – that's when they become dangerous.'

'Yes, I believe I get what you're saying.'

'And it wasn't only the drugs. There was also –'

At that point she fell silent again.

Trubshawe waited a few seconds before pressing her.

'There was also what?'

'I – well, it's really not for me to bring up the – the other thing.'

'Please, Miss Rutherford, as far as I'm aware you've dealt an honest hand so far. I insist you let me know everything that could be relevant to the situation you're all in.'

The actress continued to remain mute.

'Could your reluctance to go on,' he then asked her, 'have something to do with' – he once more pulled Gentry's page of notes out of his pocket and read aloud what he suspected must be the operative line: '"CR + EM = COCA + LES"?'

'Ye-es – yes, it could,' answered Cora Rutherford after a moment of hesitation. 'The problem, Trubshawe, is that another person's privacy is involved. I feel it would be –'

'Oh, Cora, just tell the man,' Evadne Mount brusquely interrupted her. 'It's bound to come out. Eventually.'

'You really mean that, Evie?' said the actress. 'After all, can we be certain he was referring to – you know what?'

'Course he was, the obnoxious little toad. What else could it have been? But if we have Trubshawe's word that none of this will leak beyond these four walls, then I'm willing to be as outspoken as you were.'

'I've already given you that word.'

Now the moment had come for the novelist to take up the story.

'Well, you see, Chief-Inspector, Cora and I – we've been best friends since the year dot. When we were both still in our twenties, she was a struggling young actress and I an aspiring young writer. For a couple of years we actually shared a flat in Bloomsbury, quite the weeest flat you ever saw.'

'Wee!' said the actress. 'Wee wasn't the word! You literally couldn't have swung a cat.'

'A cat?' said the novelist. 'You couldn't have swung a mouse!'

Suddenly assailed by memories of a dim, unknowable past to which they alone were privy, both women fell to giggling like the two gawky, galumphing young gals they probably once were. There was something almost poignant about the spectacle.

'Anyway,' Evadne Mount continued, wiping a nostalgic tear from her eye, 'I was writing my very first book and –'

'Ah no!' the Chief-Inspector shouted her down. 'Here I really must insist! Now is not – I repeat, *not* – the time or place for another one of your hyper-ingenious plots.'

'Oh, don't get yourself into such a tizz! This is one novel whose plot I wouldn't dare to relate in detail. At least, not in front of the Vicar.'

'Eh? What's that you say?' interjected the policeman, now clearly intrigued in spite of himself. 'So, eh, so tell me, exactly what kind of a novel was it?'

'That's just it. It wasn't a whodunit. In those days my ambition was to be a great literary genius. The model for the book was *The Well of Loneliness* – Radclyffe Hall, you know. Its title – I blush to think of it now – but its title was *The Urinal of Futility* and it was all about a virginal young woman who has just graduated from Somerville, about her painful reconciliation with her own' – here the novelist's

voice dropped to a whisper – 'her own h-o-m-o-s-e-x-a-l –
no, wait, there's something wrong there, h-o-m-o-s-e-x-*u*-a-
l-i-t-y' – then, having at last managed to spell out the
offending word, she at once raised her voice again to its
natural booming resonance, just as though she'd turned up
the volume switch on a wireless – 'and her intimate relationship with a – with a – well, let's just say it was autobiographical and be done with it.

'Yes, Clem, you heard me. It was autobiographical. And,
yes, I know how terribly delicate your susceptibilities are,
but there's no call for you to look so scandalised. I'm not
the only one of us on whom life has played a sneaky, underhand trick. You have flat feet, after all.'

'Evie, please!' the Vicar tut-tutted. 'I cannot concur with
such an idea – that flat feet and what you suffered from –
and I hope I may use the past tense – are to any degree com-
parable.'

'This is all very interesting, Miss Mount,' Trubshawe
intervened, 'but I must be getting dense again, for I simply
cannot figure out what it has to do with Miss Rutherford.'

'Judas to Judas, man,' cried the novelist, 'it's positively
shrieking at you!'

'Is it? Yet I still –'

'Look. Cora and I were both, as I say, in our early twenties and she was ravishing and, incredible as it may seem to
you, I wasn't actually too bad-looking myself – certainly
not the tweedy panda you have in front of you now – and

we were lonely and we shared a minuscule flat which had just one great big bed and – well, to quote Cora, would you like me to draw a picture?'

'No!' shuddered the Chief-Inspector. 'I'm afraid you already have.'

'In any event,' was Evadne Mount's brisk rejoinder, 'nothing was ultimately to come of it for either of us. Indeed, as readers of *Kine Weekly* well know, Cora has had no fewer than three husbands. It *is* three, isn't it, Cora darling?'

'Four, darling, if you count the Count.'

'I never count the Count.'

'Neither do I,' chuckled Cora.

'As for me, I chose to channel my emotional energies into my books, by which I mean my whodunits. *The Urinal of Futility was* published – privately – but I've never let it be reprinted and I've always left it out of my entry in *Who's Who*. Its author is not *Who* I am any longer nor *Who* I've been for many years. It was a road not taken, as they say. And thank God too, I say. My readers are all very nice people, I'm sure, but it's my experience that, once you get beyond the pleasantries, the how-d'you-dos and lovely-to-see-yous, it's these same very nice people who tend to spout the most horrendously bigoted opinions.'

'Yes, yes,' said Trubshawe impatiently, 'but could we get back to Gentry, please?'

'Oh well, there's not much more to say. Precisely the same thing happened to us as happened to poor Clem.

Having somehow got wind of our mutual past, Cora's and mine, Gentry started to taunt us both across the dinner-table. And all in so sly and subtle a fashion that, as Cora has told you, only she and I could have known what he was talking about.'

'How did the subject come up?'

'Really, it was so puerile I can barely remember.'

'"Lady of Spain", Evie?' the actress prompted her. 'You might mention that.'

'"Lady of Spain"?' repeated a bemused Trubshawe.

The novelist winced at the memory.

'Yes, it was that silly. Selina happened to be seated at the piano and she asked if any of us had a request. When Cynthia suggested "Lady of Spain" – you know, "Lady of Spain, I adore you, tra la la la, I implore you!" – Gentry instantly treated Cora and me to one of his sniggery stares and proposed that, for our benefit, the song be titled not "Lady of Spain" but "Ladies of Lisbon".'

Now Trubshawe looked downright baffled.

'Ladies of Lisbon? I don't understand. Lisbon's in Portugal, not Spain.'

Once again both actress and novelist burst into gales of uncontrollable laughter. Once again a glimpse, so fleeting as to be almost imperceptible, was afforded of two fun-loving young women who, eons before, had shared a small cold flat and a big warm bed in Bloomsbury. Then, as rapidly as they had emerged, the ghosts of their younger, gayer selves beat a discreet retreat into the past where they belonged, just as a matching pair of blushes lit up Trubshawe's cheeks. It had taken a few seconds, but he had, finally, got it.

'I see – yes, yes, I do see,' he mumbled, audibly mortified.

'Your word, mind?' said Cora Rutherford. 'You gave us your word?'

'Oh yes. I gave you my word and I assure you I'll keep it. Queer, that is, giving something you end up also keeping, but you know what I mean. You can trust me, ladies.

'And now,' he concluded, 'I have, of course, that one direct question of mine to put to you both. Miss Rutherford, Miss Mount, did either of you murder Raymond Gentry?'

'You first,' said Cora Rutherford to Evadne Mount.

'No, no, I insist, you first,' said Evadne Mount to Cora Rutherford.

'Age before beauty,' said Cora Rutherford.

'My sentiments entirely,' said Evadne Mount. 'Which is why you've obviously got to go first.'

'Curses! Why must you always have the last word, you hideous old bag?' said Cora Rutherford with a boxy shrug of her padded shoulders.

She faced up to the Chief-Inspector.

'No, I did not murder Raymond Gentry. Though, to be candid with you, Trubshawe, I wish I had. It's profoundly satisfying to me, as it is to everybody else in this room, I'm sure, that the monster is no more. But it would have been even more satisfying to know that it was I who had had the pluck – the pluck or the luck – to put him out of his misery. I mean, of course, out of *our* misery.'

'Snap!' cried Evadne Mount.

Chapter Seven

The Rolfes, whose turn it was next, had in reality two stories to tell, not one, and it was the Doctor who narrated the
first and his wife the second. Since, in their case, the Chief-
Inspector's interpolations were relatively few and far
between and, until the very end of Madge Rolfe's account,
were mostly routine and pedestrian, and since neither husband nor wife saw fit to question the other on a matter of
interpretation, or interrupt on a matter of fact, it will make
better sense to edit out all extraneous comments.

Well now (said the Doctor, caressing his moustache, so neat
and pencil-thin it scarcely seemed to belong to the same
species as Trubshawe's hirsute excrescence), Madge and I
settled down here, as many of you are aware, some seven
years ago. Most conveniently for us, old Dr Butterworth in
Postbridge was on the point of retiring. He'd put his practice

up for sale, I bought it off him, and I also bought the charmingly dilapidated cottage which went with it and in which we've been living ever since.

In Postbridge, of course, I'm nothing but a common-or-garden GP. Most of my work seems to involve colic, corns and chilblains. I never see a serious case, I mean an interesting study, from one twelvemonth to the next. I am what you might describe as a human placebo. And I've long suspected that my bedside manner, which those of you who think me something of a cold fish may be surprised to learn I can turn on and off at will like a bathroom tap, has a markedly more remedial effect on my patients than anything I ever prescribe for them.

It wasn't always thus. I trained as a paediatric surgeon and, even though I say so myself, it was becoming pretty clear that I was destined, if not perhaps for greatness, then let's say for real eminence. I published several admired papers in the *Lancet* on the pathology of parturition – that's childbearing to you – and at St Theodore's was considered very much the coming man.

In those halcyon days Madge and I were, I suppose, as content as we've ever been or are ever likely to be again. We had a circle of attractive, clever acquaintances, even a cluster of famous or semi-famous ones, and we lived in a minute mews house in Notting Hill. Hardly a fashionable area, I grant you, but for those of us who couldn't afford Kensington it was a nice enough place in which to live, to entertain our friends and, above all, to envisage bringing up a family.

Bringing up a family. Ah now, there was the terrible, tragic irony of our lives. It may be hard for you to credit this, you who've only come to know her in recent years, but all Madge ever wanted was to have lots of children. Even among my own patients, I've known few women with such a strong maternal instinct. And it was that maternal instinct of hers that made our plight so horribly ironic. For, you see, we – I should say, I – *I* couldn't have children. Even though I was raised alongside half-a-dozen brothers and sisters, I myself am . . . well, I'm sterile.

So now you know. On us, too, life played, to borrow Evadne's phrase, a sneaky, underhand trick. There I was, a distinguished paediatric surgeon, aiding and abetting healthy young wives every day of my professional life to bring bonnie babes into the world, and I was incapable of giving my own wife the sprogs she so desperately desired.

Our marriage was undone by that failure of mine. It was haunted by the children we never had. It was almost as though we *had* had them and they'd died – as though, don't you see, they'd died on us even before they'd had a chance to be born. They lived with us, those unborn children of ours, they lived with us like little ghosts, like little baby ghosts, in our nice little house in Notting Hill.

My apologies. I haven't let many people see me like this. Not even Madge, when I think of it. I tend to reserve my bedside manner exclusively for my patients.

Anyway – to continue. Naturally, we discussed the possibility of adoption. I have to say, though, we were seriously discouraged by the experience of some neighbours of ours. They were childless too, and they adopted a little orphaned boy, hardly more than an infant, whose parents had both been decapitated in a motor-car accident. But what they weren't told – not, at least, until the problem had got out of hand – was that the tot's father had been an illiterate navvy and his mother a gin-swigging, half-gypsy slattern. In short, they were as common as dirt and, as was inevitable, that bad blood had been inherited by their wretched offspring.

By the age of fifteen he was getting all the local schoolgirls into trouble, he was repeatedly hauled up before the magistrates' court for petty, and not so petty, pilfering and he was obstinately incapable of holding down any of the jobs his decent and despairing foster-parents had found for him. He ended on the gallows, needless to say.

So, you see, no matter how careful you are, you can never, *never* be sure what kind of child you're adopting. Breeding *will* out – as a doctor, no one knows better than I that that is one of the most inflexible of all biological laws. And considering how far down the road to self-destruction our marriage had already travelled, Madge and I simply couldn't take the risk.

Then something happened which seemed heaven-sent to help us patch up our relationship. I had an aunt, a maiden lady who'd been living out her last years in Farnborough. She'd been Lady-in-Waiting to the exiled Empress Eugénie, who, on her death, left her a legacy of five thousand pounds, a legacy that was virtually intact when she herself passed on. I was her only living relative and, even though Madge and I had never what you might call cultivated her – to our eternal shame, we'd never once bothered ourselves to visit her and her little court of decrepit royal hangers-on – it was into our laps that the windfall, um, fell.

Five thousand pounds was a tidy sum in those days and while we were pondering what to do with it, I received the offer of a post as resident surgeon at the Cedars of Babylon Hospital in Ottawa, Canada. It was, so we both imagined, the miracle we'd been praying for and I accepted without hesitation.

Alas! As Thomas Carlyle, I believe, eloquently expressed it, 'Here or Nowhere, and Now or Never, Immigrant, is thy America.' Our roots were here, and uprooting ourselves ultimately changed nothing. I had my work to occupy me, of course, but poor Madge found the Canadians almost as chilly as their climate.

My colleagues, for instance. They'd invite us to dinner – just the once – then drop us. Not, I venture to suggest, because they didn't care for us, or anything of that sort, only because they believed that, having once had us over, they'd done their duty by us. It was as though, you know, we were nothing more than acquaintances in transit, friends of friends, merely passing through. They'd established their own little social circles and our invasive presence must have skewed the symmetry. It would be wrong to say they treated us as interlopers. It was just that there was no room, no vacant space in their lives, left for us.

The effect on our marriage was devastating. Night after night, we'd have nothing to do but scream at one another – sometimes silently, if you know what I mean, sometimes in a whisper and sometimes, too, at the tops of our voices. And that's when I started drinking.

Not that I was ever an alcoholic. I really wasn't. But every evening, as I prepared to go home, I realised I was going to need a dose of Dutch courage in order to face my own wife. No, no, that's unfair, what I've just said. Madge wasn't at all to blame. It wasn't my wife I couldn't face, it was our marriage – or what remained of it.

Anyway, I began drinking and, worse, I went on drinking. If the city of Ottawa had nothing else to offer, it did boast a generous selection of friendly bars and I was soon propping up most of them.

Till, one day, the inevitable happened. I had to perform a Caesarean. To start with, it all looked quite unproblematic, no trickier than any other. But it turned out to require rather more drastic abdominal surgery than anyone could have foreseen and – well, to cut a long story short, I was obliged to sacrifice the baby in order to save the mother's life.

Again I swear I made no mistake. Every paediatric surgeon in the world would have found himself in the same predicament I did, would have been faced with the same dilemma and would unquestionably – I repeat, unquestionably – have arrived at the same decision. These things happen. And they can happen to the most eminent of medical men.

The father, a Mountie, was naturally distraught at losing his son, though he was also deeply grateful to me for having returned his wife to him more or less in one piece. But then, you know, most ordinary people hold a doctor, any doctor, in such awe it goes against their instincts ever to query whether so heroic a personage, as they perceive him, could possibly have been negligent.

So it could all have passed off without any adverse reflection on me had not some nosy nurse gone straight to the Dean of the hospital to complain that, when tying on my mask, she'd smelt Scotch whisky on my breath.

Naturally, I was called into the Dean's office where I made the point, quite calmly, that there'd been no imprudence on my part. The anaesthetist, I said, would assuredly support me in my contention that nothing more could have been done to save the child. And he did just that, except that, under the Dean's unexpectedly pugnacious questioning, he also confessed that he, too, had had the impression, apparently from some alleged slurring of my voice, that I'd been drinking. And not, he added, for the first time.

And not for the first time. Those were the words that did for me. The Dean went off the deep end. He ordered me there and then never to darken the hospital's door again. Initially, I fought back. I protested that I couldn't be, that I shouldn't be, dismissed on an anaesthetist's word, but he refused to hear me out and, frankly, my heart was no longer in it. If I'd decided to pursue the case, it would have provoked a scandal not only for the hospital but also for me personally and I didn't know whether a marriage already as rocky as ours could have survived all the ensuing publicity.

That, you might think, was the end of it. But no – it was neither the end nor, in a way, the worst. I have no idea who blabbed – the nurse, I daresay – but, well, there are secrets which are impossible to keep, in spite of the Hippocratic oath, and it eventually came to the ears of the Mountie and his wife that I'd been 'dead drunk', can you believe, in the operating-theatre.

They wrote letter after letter to the hospital's Board of Trustees. They started to plague us with threatening telephone calls. And even though they didn't know our home address, his being a policeman meant of course that he would have had no problem digging it out. You'll understand, then, why Madge and I chose not to hang around.

We immediately packed our bags, fled to New York – 'fled', I'm afraid, is the *mot juste* – and booked passage on the first ship, the *Zenobia*, bound for Europe. Six days later we disembarked in Le Havre, that very evening found us in Paris and the following day we were Southward bound on the Blue Train.

From which point (he concluded in the same clipped and concise tone as he'd delivered his whole speech) the story becomes more Madge's than mine. So, if I may, I'll pass the baton to her.

Throughout her husband's confessional, Madge Rolfe's eyes had been so intently trained upon him you had the sense she was not just watching him, watching his face, but actually watching his *lips*, watching them formulate those words and phrases which might damn them for ever in the eyes of the only 'set' to which the two of them could any longer aspire to belong. Now at last she turned away from him towards those who had been watching and listening to him almost as intently as she had.

She cleared her throat. Then she lit a cigarette – an actress through and through, albeit an actress who'd never trodden the boards, she was using both lighter and cigarette precisely as a professional would, as Cora Ruther-ford herself would have done. For her they were, supreme-ly, a couple of handy theatrical props, ones that would permit her to stall for a moment or two while she mentally rehearsed her lines and re-gathered her forces.

She sat frowning prettily for a few seconds more, then commenced her own account of their shared past.

You have all heard Henry (she said) dissect our marital

problems. You've heard him *operate* on them, with a steadier hand than he operated on that poor woman in Ottawa. Yes, yes, Henry, I know, you weren't 'dead drunk', I know that. But I also know that, if you weren't drunk, you *were* drinking, and I think, if you're honest with yourself, you'll admit that perhaps after all you weren't in a fit state to perform that operation.

What was it Socrates said? That a doctor can't make a mistake because, the instant he does make a mistake, he ceases to be a doctor. Well, let's just say that, for a few instants in the operating-theatre, you ceased to be a doctor.

Perhaps, too, according to the same logic, I was never truly unfaithful to you because, the instant I started going around with other men, I ceased to be your wife. Oh, and please don't pretend to be surprised or shocked, my dears, you all knew *that* was coming. You all saw Gentry's notes and I can't imagine you haven't already worked out for yourselves who he meant by 'MR'.

Henry, though, was right. If our marriage collapsed, it was for the simple, stupid reason that the only thing I ever really wanted out of life was children and we couldn't have them. I assure you all, the pain involved in giving birth is nothing, *nothing*, to the pain of *not* giving birth. It's funny. I remember how terribly upset I was when he told me about that baby dying on the operating-table and for a long time I wondered why – until it finally dawned on me that his death had had the effect of making me feel childless all over again . . .

In any event, after the scandal and the sacking and the scary 'phone calls and the flight back to Europe, we fetched up in the South of France with Auntie's five thousand pounds still in our pockets. And, there, we did what most of you would have done. We did our darnedest to spend it.

We started running with a crowd of English expats in Monte – the usual Riviera riff-raff. There was John Fitzpatrick and Patrick Fitzjohn – those were the only names they'd answer to – Eddie and Henrietta Arbuthnot, 'Plum' Duff Something-or-Other and his boyfriend Dickie – and now I come to think of it, there may have been more than one of those Dickies, wasn't it so, Henry, I seem to remember that Plum referred to all his boyfriends as Dickie? – and life was a perpetual whirlwind of breakneck drives along the Grande Corniche, hair-raising sessions at the Casino, balmy nights under the sheltering palms – Plum used to call it 'moonbathing' – and weekend jaunts across the frontier to San Remo and Ventimiglia. Oh, it was *such* fun and we were, of course, perfectly miserable.

Then I met Raymond Gentry.

Yes, it's true. I see the surprise on your faces, especially on yours, Chief-Inspector, but it's all too true. I already knew Ray before he turned up here on Christmas Eve.

But I insist you understand that I never knew him Biblically, as they say, even if in those days that was the only meaning the word 'Biblical' had in my life. Frankly, like Cora, I had him down as a pansy. Or a eunuch. And with his cocktails and his cravats and his cut-glass accent, I felt he was just too perfect an Englishman to be the real McCoy. I assumed he must be some sort of Central European Jew with ideas above his station, though he was too slippery an operator to let anything be proved against him. And I was broad-minded. Lord knows, I was broad-minded.

In any event, the Gentry I met in those years was one of those prettified young men who hired themselves out to escort rich old hags to the Casino and the Carnival while pocketing a few extra bob for themselves along the way. And if I was certainly no hag – though, had Henry and I hung around the Riviera long enough, I'd surely have got there in the end – that was the service he provided for me. While Henry drank away the nights alone in our hotel room, I was looking for somebody – ideally, somebody not too threatening – to accompany me up and down the Croisette. And no more than that.

It's true, at the beginning he did pay me fumbling court. Once, I recall, he even copied out a poem by Rupert Brooke, altered a couple of names so that it would apply to us, and presented it to me tucked into a corsage of orchids. But it was all really for form's sake, more of a face-saving exercise than anything else. We both knew where we stood with each other.

Then, one evening, at a party given by the Murphys, Gerald and Sara, at the Hôtel Welcome in Villefranche, he introduced me to an acquaintance of his, Maxime Pavesco.

I never did know what Maxime's nationality was. He wasn't Rumanian, even though his name appeared to suggest he was and he did claim to be a close personal friend of Princess Marie. Nor was he Greek or Spanish or Corsican. I actually took him for an Albanian. I always say, if someone doesn't come from anywhere else, then he must come from Albania.

Now I know what you're all thinking. How could an Englishwoman like me sink so low as to consort with an Albanian? Well, to be honest with you, I'd have gone out with a Hindoo if he'd had a clean collar and a presentable dinner-jacket.

And Maxime, you see, was just so handsome, so very silky and smoky and seductive. So very, *very* un-English. When we were on the town together, he made me feel desirable all over again. When I saw how other men envied him, just as I could see other women envying me, I no longer felt as though, well, as though I was on my way to becoming a dowdy back number.

Oh, don't imagine I had any illusions about him. He was a parasite and a sponger and, when he was in one of his moods, he could be a cad. Yet, I can't deny it, I was proud to be seen with him.

What I came to realise only later, because that contemptible little Ray Gentry had naturally never breathed a word to me, was that I was making an utter fool of myself. Maxime, *my* Maxime, had already done the round of every lonely, wealthy, middle-aged woman on the Riviera, every not-so-merry widow and not-so-gay divorcee who'd lost, or was prepared to lose, whatever pride in herself she'd once possessed. He was recommended by one to the next like a manicurist or a fortune-teller. If I was second-hand goods, then Maxime was off the slush pile.

It was I, of course, who always picked up the tab. In restaurants I'd slip a few hundred francs into Maxime's pocket so he could pay the bill and save face – also save a few francs for himself, for I never saw any change. Then, gradually, he no longer cared about saving his face. When he was losing at the roulette tables, and he never did anything *but* lose, he'd brazenly hold out his hand to me for an immediate supply of new funds. Sometimes he'd even stick his fingers into my handbag and draw out a fat wad of notes for himself. And all this in full view of everybody else.

I myself was already so far gone I, too, had ceased caring. I didn't care a jot when he and I would drop into some fashionable men's boutique on the Promenade des Anglais and, without worrying whether he might be heard by the shop assistant who was serving us, he'd start wheedling with me to buy him a Lanvin safari suit. I didn't care that he was nothing but a scheming gold-digger. I knew he was and it meant nothing to me. Or I pretended it meant nothing to me . . .

Then it happened, the cruellest irony of all. I discovered I was expecting his child. I, who had for so long hoped to have not just one but lots and lots of children with Henry, there I was, pregnant by an Albanian gigolo!

Well, as I'm sure you understand, no matter how strong my maternal instinct, there was never any question of having and keeping such a child. Which was when, all very neatly, all very conveniently, Ray Gentry popped up again in my life.

I suppose Maxime had told him about the plight I'd got myself into. Or else – or else from the beginning the whole business had been a set-up job between the two of them. Whichever it was, Ray just chanced to know of a China-woman in Toulon who would perform a nearly painless operation – I recall the relish, the malevolent relish, with which he enunciated that word *nearly* – for a few francs. How few, I asked him. Twenty, he replied. Twenty francs? I repeated. I was relieved but also disbelieving. No, was his answer, twenty thousand.

That's right. Twenty thousand francs. It was blackmail pure and simple, though Raymond naturally never used the word nor any euphemism for it. Nor did he even hint that, if I were to refuse to pay up, he'd start spreading the dirt all along the Côte d'Azur – as smoothly as marmalade on toast. He didn't have to drop any hints. We both knew exactly what he was up to.

So now it was my turn to be the bearer of bad news to Henry. We were a sorry pair all right, he and I. And maybe – maybe we each of us had to drink our poison to the very dregs before we could face ourselves again.

Without, I have to say, a single word of reproach, Henry gave me what I needed. I went to Toulon and had my insides skewered by a cackling Chinese witch, skewered so crudely – yes, I see from your faces you're ahead of me – skewered so crudely that, even if I still wanted children, I couldn't have any. Though, as it happens, all I do want (now she turned to gaze straight into her husband's eyes), all I do want, for the very first time in my life, is what I already have.

Well (she went on after a long reflective pause), there was just enough left of his aunt's legacy for Henry to buy Butterworth's practice and, seven years ago, we settled down here and eventually gathered a little set of friends around us – Roger and Mary, the Vicar and his wife, Mr Withers, our local librarian, Miss Read the postmistress, and a handful of others.

Ours is a dull existence, I suppose, but we don't mind – well, not much. To be honest, we've had all the fun and excitement we'll ever demand of this world. Beyond a certain age, that phrase that people toss about so casually, 'a waste of time', well, it starts to acquire a real meaning, doesn't it, a real weight. You realise you've been wasting something you're fated to have less and less of. You've been dipping into your capital. You forget you've got a leasehold on life, not a freehold.

She sat for a moment without speaking, without even lighting up one of her Player's, before continuing:

Then abruptly, on Christmas Eve, with Ray Gentry's arrival at ffolkes Manor, our past was dragged out of the closet that we'd hoped it had been consigned to for ever. You've read those notes, Chief-Inspector. So I leave you to imagine just how he set about torturing us both. It shouldn't be too difficult.

Trubshawe, who had said next to nothing during their linked testimony, now took a quiet moment to thank them both. Then he asked Henry Rolfe:

'Dr Rolfe, did you kill Raymond Gentry?'

'No, I didn't,' replied the Doctor, adding, 'Don't you see, Trubshawe, I had no cause to.'

'No cause, you say?' said the Chief-Inspector. 'What about jealousy?'

'Jealousy? I tell you, there was no reason for me to be jealous of Gentry. After all, his role in the affair was only that of go-between. When Madge told me about the necessity of a – of an operation, she never once mentioned his name and I always assumed, until just five minutes ago, that her blackmailer had been Pavesco himself. Him I might well have wanted to murder, but he disappeared from circulation almost at once, probably after splitting up the spoils with Gentry. Last thing we heard, he'd been sighted in Anacapri in the company of a flashy South American Jewess.

'So, as I say, I had absolutely no knowledge of Raymond Gentry's existence until he drove down here with Selina and Don.'

'Well, thank you again for your testimony.'

The Chief-Inspector now turned to Madge Rolfe.

'Mrs Rolfe, I know I've already given you, along with the other ladies, a chance to answer this question, but I'll ask it once more if you don't mind. Was it you who quarrelled with Gentry in the attic?'

'No, it wasn't. There was nothing I had to say to him, either in public or in private.'

'Did you murder him?'

'No again. And shall I tell you why you ought to believe me?'

'Yes, indeed, why don't you?'

'Because if I *had* murdered Gentry I wouldn't have shot him. I wouldn't have stabbed him. I wouldn't have poisoned him. I'd have done it – had God given me the strength – I'd have done it with my own two bare hands. I wouldn't have wanted anything – not a gun, not a knife, not a drop of cyanide, not even a piece of string – I wouldn't have wanted *anything*, do you hear, to come between me and the pain I inflicted on the rat!'

It was only when she'd finished speaking that everyone realised Selina ffolkes had been standing on the threshold of the library during the whole of her tirade.

Chapter Eight

For a moment the atmosphere was just too electric for anyone to react.

Then Mary ffolkes hurriedly rose from her chair and, followed by Don and the Colonel, rushed over to the door.

'Oh, my darling Selina!' she cried, sweeping her daughter up in her arms and asking so many anxiously commiserative questions at once it was hard to tell where one ended and the next began. 'Are you all right?' and 'You really feel you should have got up so soon?' and 'You've had a dreadful, *dreadful* shock, you know – would you like me to have Mrs Varley prepare you a cold compress or a nice cup of camomile tea?'

To all of which Selina offered a series of unexpectedly self-controlled responses, whether it was 'Yes, Mummy, I'm quite all right' or 'Yes, yes, I'm all recovered now' or 'No thank you, Mummy, I really don't need a cold compress. Or a cup of camomile tea.'

Don also fussed and fretted around her, cooing, 'You

poor kid! Oh, you poor, poor kid!' over and over again. But even if his hand ached to establish a consoling contact with her shoulder or tenderly disentangle a stray wisp of hair from one of her pale cheeks, it was again noticeable that it continued to hover a few inches from her without ever daring to settle.

In the meantime, making sympathetic tut-tutting noises with his tongue, the Colonel helped shepherd her into the library under the watchful eyes of his guests. Giving up his own chair for her to sit on, he asked:

'Is there anything *I* can get you?'

'No thank you, Daddy, I have everything I need.'

She slowly ran her eyes around the room.

'But . . . but what's going on?'

'Ah, yes . . .' replied the Colonel. 'It's true, something *has* been going on here. I want you to listen very carefully, my love. We have a policeman among us – don't you remember, it was Chitty who came up with the suggestion – and, well, here he is, Chief-Inspector Trubshawe from Scotland Yard.'

'Miss Selina,' said Trubshawe with an avuncular nod of his head.

Appearing to display little surprise at his presence, Selina acknowledged it with a wan smile.

'The Chief-Inspector,' explained her father, 'lives quite near us – close to the level-crossing – and he very kindly agreed to come here – it was Rolfe and your friend Don, you know, who went and fetched him – and he agreed to come over and see what could be done about this horrible situation.'

'I understand,' said Selina composedly.

'The thing is, he's been asking us all about what we know of – the murder. It's completely off-the-record, you understand, just till the storm passes and the police – I mean, the official police – get here. But we've all been taking turns at answering his questions and,' he concluded, 'well, if you still don't feel up to it, I'm sure he'd –'

'No, no,' Selina gently interrupted him, 'I really am quite well.'

Her blonde curls rolling over her unlined forehead like the crest of a wave about to unfurl itself on a virgin beach, she actually now produced a proper smile, sweet and dimply, one that almost made you forget how curiously devoid of emotion were her clear, china-blue eyes, eyes no longer blemished by the copious tears they had doubtless been shedding. Wearing a green cashmere jumper and a foulard dress that might have been labelled 'country practical' if it didn't so perfectly fit her own perfect figure, she was as pretty as the proverbial picture.

'You see,' she explained, 'I haven't just been resting, I've been thinking. Thinking about everything I've seen and heard here in the past two days. Not just Raymond's – Raymond's death, but everything that led up to it. It's been ever so long since I've had time to think for myself, to think *about* myself, about my friends and my family and even' – she captured all of the ffolkeses' guests in her limpid gaze – 'even my family's friends. And I see things very differently now.

'So, Mr Trubshawe, if you wish to question me, I'm ready. And I promise I won't break down or anything silly like that. I've done all the weeping I intend to do.'

'Oh, gee, Selina, you're swell!' cried Don, adoration radiating from his eyes. 'You just don't know how I've – how we've all been missing you! Really missing you!'

This effusion, for some inexplicable reason, provoked an outburst from Evadne Mount so resoundingly loud it caused the whole company to jump.

'Great Gods!' she bellowed. 'I've been blind as a bat! Of course! That's it!'

Everybody, Selina included, turned to stare at her, causing the novelist to blush furiously.

'Sorry, sorry, sorry! What I meant was,' she started to mumble, visibly struggling to find a plausible excuse for her extraordinary interjection, 'what I meant was, yes, naturally, we've all been missing you! Yes, indeedy!'

A few more seconds elapsed in silence, for this was exceptionally odd behaviour even from somebody as eccentric as the novelist was universally deemed to be. Then Trubshawe turned towards Selina.

'Well, Miss,' he declared, 'I can't deny it would be extremely helpful to me if you did agree to answer my questions. But, really, your father's right. If you still feel shaky, understandably so under the circumstances, it can all be postponed until the local police arrive.'

'No, no,' insisted Selina. 'I rather think I do want to talk about it. What I wouldn't mind, though, is a cigarette.'

Madge Rolfe leaned forward to proffer her packet of Player's, while Don, a non-smoker, did his own bit by grabbing off the Colonel's desk a bulbous silver cigarette-lighter in the shape of Aladdin's lamp and holding it up expectantly to Selina's lips.

She took one of Madge's cigarettes, gracefully accepted a light from Don and faced the Chief-Inspector.

'What exactly is it you want to know?'

'Well now,' he began diffidently, 'I gather you got here late on Christmas Eve in the company of Mr Duckworth and the victim, Raymond Gentry?'

'That's right. I was originally due to take the train down with Don alone. Then Ray, who has a car' – she calmly corrected herself – 'who *had* a car, a Hispano-Suiza, happened to say to me he thought it might be amusing for once to experience an old-fashioned family Christmas in the country and suggested driving us both down.'

'He hadn't been invited?'

'No – but, you see, that was Ray. If he got an idea in his head, he wasn't going to let himself be stopped from carrying it out by what he would call petty-bourgeois propriety. You know, what's done and what's not done.'

'And despite the fact that your parents hadn't invited him and weren't expecting him, you saw no reason to demur?'

For the first time since she had entered the library, Selina looked a little ill-at-ease.

'It was just Ray's style. He had rather a commanding personality, you know, and he always seemed to end up getting his own way. He'd make you feel dreadfully strait-laced if you raised any objection to one of his madcap schemes.'

'So you were quite relaxed about his coming down here unannounced?'

'No, I can't honestly say I was. I *am* a little strait-laced, you know – I still am – and, as a matter of fact, I did propose first telephoning Mummy and Daddy. But Ray said that giving them advance warning would only spoil the surprise of it all and that it'd be lots more fun if he were simply to turn up.'

'And how did Don feel about that?'

Selina sneaked a guilty glance at the young American.

'Oh well, as you can imagine, he was just a teensy bit put out. He *had* been properly invited and – well, you know, two's company, three's a crowd, and all that.'

'But that didn't bother you either?' Trubshawe put to her.

Selina abruptly drew back and, by the time she was ready to reply, her lips had closed in a thin line.

'Yes it did. I told you, Chief-Inspector, I don't mind you questioning me, but I do mind you putting words in my mouth. I've already admitted I was bothered by Ray coming down here uninvited and I was also concerned for Don's feelings. He's somebody I'm very, very fond of' – that repeated 'very', as nobody could fail to notice, caused a scarlet-faced Don to gaze at her in even more than his usual rapture – 'but, as I say, Ray had a very strong character and if he wanted something he generally got it. Anybody who knows him – who *knew* him – will tell you the same thing.'

'Miss ffolkes,' Trubshawe then asked, 'how long did *you* know Raymond Gentry?'

Selina reflected for a moment or two.

'Oh, just a few weeks. I met him at the Kafka Klub.'

The Chief-Inspector's eyebrows uplifted.

'Sorry – you met him where?'

'The Kafka Klub. You don't know it? It's in the King's Road in Chelsea. It's *the* hang-out for all the fashionable young writers and artists.'

'Go on.'

'Well, Ray and I were introduced to each other at the Kafka and we got to talking about Art and Life and Philosophy and the Sex Drive and he knew everything and everybody and he wrote free verse and he understood the symbolism of Hauptmann and Maeterlinck and he told me he was one of only seven people in the whole of England who'd read *The Communist Manifesto* in the original Russian. And, you see, I was nothing but a timid little dormouse from Dartmoor and I'd never met anybody like him before and, well, do you wonder I was swept off my feet?'

'N-o-o,' replied Trubshawe, 'I don't suppose I do. But, you know, Miss, I can't pretend to be as familiar as the late Mr Gentry apparently was with the likes of – of those two foreign fellows you just mentioned – but even I, dull old Inspector Plodder,' he said, a steely ring insidiously entering his voice, 'even I know enough to know that Karl Marx was German not Russian and consequently wrote *The Communist Manifesto* not in Russian but in German. That's just by-the-by, of course.'

Selina ffolkes blinked like a frightened faun.

'And while we're about it, darling,' Cora Rutherford muttered under her breath, 'did you never stop to think that his verse was free because he couldn't find anyone to pay for it?'

Now Selina seemed so close to tears the actress at once took pity on her.

'Sorry to be such a cat, my sweet,' she said. 'Just couldn't help myself.'

'Look, Miss,' Trubshawe said, 'I fancy what Miss Rutherford here and I were trying to do in our clumsy ways was demonstrate that Raymond Gentry wasn't really worthy of somebody like you. Not a very nice person, now, was he?'

'No,' cried Selina, her eyes suddenly ablaze, 'no, maybe he wasn't! But he was alive, don't you see, he was clever and he was fun and he widened my horizons! Oh, I realise how silly and childish it must sound to you but, compared to Ray's world, everything in my own life seemed so shrivelled and dried up! Before I met him, all I'd ever known was this house and the village and the countryside around it. Well, I wanted something better out of life! I told myself I was free, white and twenty-one and I wanted everything that was going in this crazy world – furs and fine wines and wild, extravagant parties! And I didn't want it some day – I wanted it now! Was that so very wrong of me?'

Her voice dropped an octave.

'No, don't answer, anybody,' she said contritely. 'It *was* wrong, I know. Now I know.'

'How,' enquired Trubshawe softly, 'do you know?'

Selina stubbed out her cigarette, on which she had taken no more than a couple of jerky puffs.

'Mr Trubshawe, if you've been questioning my family and their friends, then you must already have been told how intolerably rude and disrespectful Ray was to all of them from the moment we arrived. I watched him with mounting horror – watched how he couldn't resist needling them and making them squirm. It was as though it was in his blood. What I had remembered as so gay and amusing and penetrating in the Kafka Klub now struck me as just stupidly arrogant and cruel.

'That was one of his pet words, you know, "penetrating". I used to think it was priceless the way he used it about everything. Down here, though, I realised for the first time what a hollow, shallow, meaningless word it was, the sort of word only a know-all like Ray would ever dream of using, a word whose sole purpose was to make other people feel small. Every time I heard him – here, here in this house, in my home, in front of my parents and their friends, *my* friends, my *true* friends – every time I heard him describe somebody or something as penetrating I wanted to scream!

'I was seeing him as he really was and I couldn't wait for Christmas to be all over so he'd drive back to Town, alone this time, and I'd never have to set eyes – or ears – on him again!'

She turned towards her parents, who had been listening avidly to her.

'It's true – Mummy – Daddy. I am so terribly, terribly sorry for what I've put you through, but I swear that even before – before what happened to him, I'd made up my mind to break things off. Before it went further . . . before it went too far . . .'

'Oh, Selina, my darling,' cried Mary ffolkes, giving her a smothering hug, 'I just knew you'd eventually see what an awful person he was!'

'I did. But it was Don who really showed me what Ray was worth.'

'Don?' echoed the Chief-Inspector. 'What did he have to do with it?'

'Well, as I told you, Don was unhappy from the very beginning, from the drive down here, with Raymond taking over all the arrangements as he did, and I could see him silently suffering Ray's presence and just dying to give him what-for. Then when Ray, who got disgustingly drunk – that's another side of him I used to find charming, if you can believe it – when Ray began needling even me, about my piano-playing, Don leapt up and actually threatened –'

Intuitively divining Trubshawe's reaction to that last word, Selina abruptly clammed up.

'I – I don't mean –' she finally began to stammer. 'It's just that, compared to Ray, Don was – you know – he was so – so virile – so . . .'

The Chief-Inspector doggedly pursued his advantage.

'What did Don threaten to do to Raymond Gentry?' he almost barked at her.

'What?'

'What was it Don threatened to do?'

'*I threatened to kill him.*'

Trubshawe wheeled about to confront the young American who had just spoken.

'What did you say?'

'You heard what I said. I threatened to kill him.'

'Oh, Don,' said Selina in a whisper, 'I oughtn't to have spoken. I really didn't mean to –'

'Aw, shoot. He'd have found out on his own.'

'So you threatened to kill him, did you?' said Trubshawe.

'Now that *is* interesting. Interesting for a reason that should be obvious to us all, but also interesting because it's something Miss Mount omitted to include in her account of last night's events.'

'Yeah,' said Don, glancing at the novelist, 'I noticed that too.'

'Heavens!' protested Evadne Mount. 'It ought to be perfectly plain why I didn't mention it. People never stop threatening to kill other people – why, I've heard four-year-olds threaten to kill their parents – and in pretty much every case, in 99.9 per cent of cases, I'll wager, it doesn't mean a thing. But the police, naturally, would have pounced on such a threat and, don't forget, Trubshawe, I hadn't seen you in action yet. You might have been just the kind of copper who's always willing to jump to the first and most obvious conclusion.'

'Yes,' Trubshawe had to agree, 'I might at that,' and he added, 'especially as this particular threat happens to belong to the remaining 0.1 per cent where the threatened individual *does* actually end by getting himself killed.'

'I grant you that,' the novelist grudgingly conceded. 'But anybody can see that Don didn't kill Gentry.'

'He might not have done in one of your whodunits, but we're in the real world here.'

He turned back to Don.

'Am I to take it you really meant to kill Gentry?'

'It's what I *felt* like doing,' replied Don cagily. 'But I didn't.'

'Then why did you threaten him?'

'Listen, Mr Trubshawe, you never knew the creep. He was a complete . . . well, in mixed company I can't say what he was a complete . . . but you've heard everyone else tell you what *they* thought of him.

'With me it began earlier – when Selina telephoned to say he'd be joining us for Christmas. Everything had been hunky-dory up to then between Selina and me and I was beginning to think – to hope . . . Then there I was, squashed into the rumble seat of his Hispano-Suiza watching Selina give him "my hero" looks. I was one pretty browned-off guy, I can tell you.

'And when we eventually got down here, the three of us, and straight away Gentry started driving everyone nuts, I found it tough work just holding myself back.'

'But, at least to begin with, you did? Hold yourself back, I mean.'

'I reckoned it was none of my beeswax.'

Trubshawe frowned perplexedly.

'None of your what?'

'My business. It was when he got fresh with Selina herself I just couldn't see straight.'

'And what exactly did you do about it?'

'I grabbed him by the scruff of the neck and ordered him to lay off.'

'H'm. Stirring stuff all right, if not quite the death threat you admitted to, was it?'

'No . . . but that wasn't all.'

'Oh yes?'

'Yeah. He began making remarks about my parents – I'm an orphan, you see, I never knew my real mom and dad, and Gentry began to say – well, you won't get me in a thousand years to repeat what he said but I warned him if he ever told any of his filthy lies again – or ever harmed a hair on Selina's head – I'd kill him.'

'And you meant it?'

'Sure I meant it! And I'd have done it too. But what can I say? I'm in the same boat as everyone else in this room. Some lucky stiff got there first. I don't know who he was and, even if I did, I wouldn't tell you because, by bumping off a louse like Raymond Gentry, he did me – me and the world both – a favour!'

As Selina now treated Don to exactly the same 'my hero' look he'd just been alluding to, the Chief-Inspector shifted to another tack.

'Miss Selina, while you were resting upstairs in your room, I was listening to your parents' guests talk about the way Raymond Gentry taunted them by dropping all kinds of evil hints about certain regrettable incidents in their respective pasts. But even though he was a professional gossip, as I understand, he couldn't have been made privy from his usual sources to the more, shall we say, *local* of these secrets, and we've all been rather wondering who could have passed them on to him.'

'Yes . . .?' she said, a faint tremor detectable in her voice.

'Well?' he queried her.

'Well what, Inspector?'

'I think you know what, Miss. It *was* you, wasn't it? It was from you he got that information?'

There was a lengthy pause while Selina gazed helplessly into the faces of her parents' guests.

'Come now, Miss. You'd be better off telling me the truth. Everyone else has.'

'Well, you see,' she said, so faintly you had to strain to hear her, 'when it was agreed that Ray would drive us down, he asked me what kind of a crowd he'd be mixing with. You understand, he hated anybody who wasn't, in his eyes, "amusing", he got bored so awfully easy, so I just couldn't say, you know, there'd be the local Vicar and his wife, the local Doctor and his wife. They just wouldn't have sounded amusing enough for him. So I – well, I found myself trying to make them more – more interesting to him and I suppose I did let slip some of the local gossip. I didn't mean any harm and, if I'd known what he intended to do with it, I swear I wouldn't have breathed a word.

'Oh, will you ever find it in yourselves to forgive me?' she cried disconsolately to everyone present.

'Yes, I can see how you might be feeling pretty rotten about your indiscretions now,' said the Chief-Inspector before anyone had a chance to reply. 'But the idea that, after you'd known him only a few weeks, this man had become so important to you,

you were prepared to divulge your friends' most intimate secrets to him? I must say, that does surprise me.'

'But they weren't secret! It was wrong of me, I know, but most of what I told Ray – Dr Rolfe's operation in Canada, the Vicar and the War – it was common knowledge in Postbridge village. If you really want to know everything about everybody around here, all you have to do is pass the time of day with the postmistress or the librarian.

'As for Evie, you've only got to look at her to guess what the skeleton in her closet must be.'

'Well, thank you for that, my dear,' the novelist acidly cut in. 'I think I'm speaking for all of us when I express my gratitude to you for being so bracingly outspoken!'

'Oh, I'm getting all muddled!' said Selina, who was indeed beginning to sound as fluttery as her mother tended to do in a crisis. 'I love you all dearly, I do, I do. But what I'm trying to get the Chief-Inspector to understand is that I didn't tell Ray anything he couldn't have found out for himself after spending an hour or two in the village.'

'Miss Selina,' Trubshawe then demanded questioningly, 'did you have a rendezvous with Raymond Gentry last night – or rather, early this morning – in the attic?'

Selina gasped. This was one question she hadn't been expecting.

'Why . . . how did you know that?'

'You were heard,' replied Trubshawe bluntly. 'It seems you and he had a violent altercation. At about five-thirty.'

It took her a few moments before she was able to answer.

'Yes, it's true. I did meet him in the attic.'

'Why don't you describe what happened?'

'I simply couldn't sleep last night. I couldn't stop brooding about what a complete stinker Ray had been, I just couldn't get it out of my head. I wanted to bring everything to an end between him and me but I didn't want to leave the unpleasant business of breaking up till next morning – this morning – when the whole household would be up and about.

'So, at around five, I slipped on a dressing-gown and tiptoed along to his bedroom. I tapped on his door again and again – I didn't dare knock too loudly for fear of waking the others – and he eventually opened it. He was in a beastly temper – hungover, I guess – and he started remonstrating with me for getting him up at such a godawful hour, as he put it. I told him we had to talk and suggested we go to the attic, which was never used and where we wouldn't be overheard. After lots of mumbling and grumbling and fumbling about, he agreed.'

'So then you did both go upstairs to the attic?' asked Trubshawe.

'Yes.'

'Which you found unlocked?'

'Oh yes. It's never locked.'

'I see. Go on.'

'Inside the attic I let him know what I thought of him and how he'd only shown himself up by being so horrid to my friends. Then I insisted he drive back to Town the very next morning. I mean, today.'

'What was his reaction?'

'He laughed at me.'

'Laughed at you?'

'Yes – a horrible kind of devilish laugh it was. In fact, as I realise now, it was just the same wicked laugh he'd always had – you know, wicked in the witty sense of the word, or so I used to kid myself. But now that it was directed against me, it brought home for the first time how it must have felt to his victims.

'Well, he just went on ridiculing me and Mummy and Daddy and their friends and their values and their traditions and he even began sneering at how pathetically dreary and boring life in the English countryside was. He said it was all warm beer and dog lovers and old maids cycling to Communion through the early morning mist . . .'

'And what was your answer to that?' asked Trubshawe.

'I shouted back at him and it all got louder and louder until I thought if I stayed in that room another instant my head would explode. It wasn't only the sound of Ray's voice I couldn't bear any longer, it was the sound of my own. So I turned on my heels and ran back to my room.'

'And then?'

'Ten minutes later I heard Raymond walk along the corridor. He was whistling, he was actually whistling, as though . . . It was "The Sheik of Araby", I remember.'

'Oh, the swine!' said Don through gritted teeth.

'And there I stayed, inside my bedroom, crying myself to sleep, until I was woken up by . . .'

She faltered, unable to go on.

'By the discovery of the body . . . I know,' murmured Trubshawe. 'Tell me, what were your feelings about that?'

'Oh, terrible, terrible! I actually felt guilty! It was almost as though I were in some way the cause of his death. Ray *had* been a close friend, after all, and however badly he'd behaved he surely didn't deserve that . . . Oh, I don't know what I'm saying any longer . . . I'm so – so dreadfully confused . . .'

'You may be confused, Miss,' said the Chief-Inspector after giving her a few seconds to pull herself together, 'but above all you've been brave, very, very brave. And I'd like to thank you for that. Not,' he added, shaking his head, 'that what you've had to say has brought us much closer to a solution, but that would appear to be the nature of the beast. The nature of the case, I mean,' he explained, lest anyone were mystified by his metaphor. 'Thank you again. For you the ordeal's over.'

Then, as Mary ffolkes started to fuss around her daughter again, the Chief-Inspector, who was clearly a man who didn't believe in wasting time, immediately turned to her husband.

'Colonel?'

'Yes, Trubshawe?'

'Now that Miss Selina has told me everything she knows, I believe it's your turn to walk over the hot coals.'

'My turn to . . . Oh yes, of course, of course,' Roger ffolkes quickly replied.

For a few seconds, though, he fiddled uneasily with his cigar's cellophane wrapper, before finally saying:

'There's just one thing, Trubshawe. We do seem to have been at this for hours already. I wonder if the others think the way I do, that maybe we might take a short break. It's very draining on us all, you know, being interrogated in this way, and I'm sure my guests would like to have a bit of a lie-down in their bedrooms. As for me, I haven't had my constitutional today and I really need to stretch my legs.'

'In *this* weather, Colonel?'

'In all weathers, sir, in all weathers. Isn't that so, Mary?'

'Oh yes, that's quite right, Inspector. Roger won't let a day go by without his constitutional.'

'We-ell,' said Trubshawe uncertainly, 'p'raps a break wouldn't be such a bad idea at that. Though a short one, mind.'

On hearing the Chief-Inspector's acquiescence – which for him, of course, implied a stay of execution, however short-lived – the Colonel instantly became his breezy self once again.

'Oh, absolutely!' he genially replied. 'Absolutely! All I want is a lungful of good fresh wintry air. Half an hour, no more, there and back, I promise.'

'Actually, Colonel,' added Trubshawe, 'if you *do* intend going for a walk, I wonder if you wouldn't mind taking Tober along with you. The poor old boy needs his constitutional too.'

'Not at all, not at all,' said the Colonel. 'But will he follow me?'

'Oh yes. Follow anybody for a walk, Tober will. Even a villain, ha ha! Hey, Tober, won't you, though? Walkies! Walkies!'

No sooner had the Chief-Inspector pronounced the magic word than the Labrador, who had been lying slumped at his master's feet, dragged himself up to his own feet with such surprising energy you might have thought his furiously wagging tail was acting as a kind of hydraulic lever.

'There's a good boy,' said the Colonel, tickling the dog's sticky-wet muzzle and starting to lead him out of the library. 'Going for walkies, are we, you and me? Eh? Eh, Tobermory?'

Just as he reached the doorway, however, he turned round.

'Farrar?'

'Yes, Colonel?'

'Whilst I'm out, you might pop down to the kitchen for a while. Make sure the servants are all right.'

'Yes, of course, sir.'

'And Farrar?'

'Yes?'

'Have Iris serve tea in the drawing-room. I imagine everybody's dying for a quick cuppa before they go up to their rooms.'

'Will do.'

Chapter Nine

'Cracking piece of bacon, is this, Mrs Varley.'

'Well, thank *you*, Mr Chitty. Your appreciation is much appreciated, I'm sure. Can I tempt you to some more cold turkey?'

'Don't mind if I do, Mrs Varley.'

'Addie!' cried Mrs Varley.

There was no response.

'Addie!!!'

Little Addie, little adenoidal Addie, wiping her two grimy little hands on her apron, came running in from the coal-house.

'Did you call me, mum?'

Mrs Varley spluttered in disbelief.

'Did I call you? she says! Who else was I calling? Stop yer twittering and cut Mr Chitty another slice of turkey. And make sure it's nice and thick.'

'Yes, mum. Right away, mum.'

'Oh no, my lass, not right away. You'll wash yer hands

first. And proper, mind. They're positive caked with muck.'

'Yes, mum.'

As Addie hurried over to the sink, Tomelty, the ffolkeses' Irish gardener and general handyman, lit up a Senior Service, gave his scarlet braces a devil-may-care snap and ran his fingers through his wavy, dreamy, Brylcreemy, jet-black hair. Something of a self-fancying Don Juan, the terror of the village girls, with his gleaming white teeth and smouldering five o'clock shadow, he was slouching at the far end of the kitchen table from Chitty, his Senior Service in one corner of his mouth, his trademark sneer in the other.

Watching the butler sup his steaming tea, he commented amiably, 'Well, Mr Chitty, this 'ere murder business don't appear to 'ave done your appetite no 'arm.'

'Ah, Tomelty,' replied Chitty, extracting with repulsive gentility a sliver of bacon which had got lodged between two of his front teeth, 'must keep our peckers up, you know.'

There was a pause.

'You're very quiet, Mr Farrar,' someone said.

'Sorry, what?'

'What do *you* think?'

'About what?'

'Who's going to be the murderer's next victim?'

'Tomelty!' Chitty snapped at him. 'Just you watch that tongue of yours! I won't have you scaring the womenfolk with sly talk of murder. Not whilst I'm master in this kitchen.'

Chitty had been a boxing referee for some years before entering domestic service and seldom let his inferiors forget it.

'No talk o' murder? Fat chance!' exclaimed the chauffeur. 'Nothin' this int'r'stin' 'as 'appened at ffolkes Manor since I began workin' 'ere. And you think you can stop us talkin' about it? You've gone funny in the 'ead, you 'ave. Aren't I right, Mr Farrar?'

'Ye-es. Whatever else can be said about it, Gentry's murder is certainly interesting.'

'I'm surprised at you, Mr Farrar, you so well educated!' said Mrs Varley. 'Interesting? What word is that to use about a guest found with a bullet in his brains?'

'Heart, surely?'

'Heart – brains – what's the difference? A man's been shot dead. I can think of a lot of words for that, but interesting wouldn't come top of the list.'

'And I can think of a lot o' words for Raymond Gentry,' said Tomelty, 'and int'r'stin' wouldn't come top o' that list neither.'

'We-ell, that's true enough,' said Mrs Varley, recalling just how recently it was she had been furious with the late gossip columnist. 'Slimy is more like it.'

'Now, now, Mrs Varley,' said Chitty. 'As you yourself just said, the poor man's lying dead upstairs. A little Christian charity is called for.'

'Poor man!' said Mrs Varley, warming to her theme. 'The gall, the unmitigated gall, asking for bacon and eggs at eleven in the morning! Where did he think he was? The bleedin' Savoy hotel! He had a right bleedin' nerve, if I may say so. Pardon my French, Mr Chitty.'

Chitty, who clearly shared the sentiment – for he too had found himself at the receiving end of more than one of Gentry's sallies – felt nevertheless that it had been ill-expressed.

'Language, Mrs Varley, language . . .'

'I'm sorry, Mr Chitty, but you're not above denying, I'm sure, he was an all-round bad lot who deserved everything that was coming to him.'

'Oh, I don't know as how I'd go that far . . .'

Addie, meanwhile, whose squashed little features could just conceivably have been appealing had she known how to make herself up and pinned back her hair so that it wasn't always dripping into her eyes, came over to the table with an extra-thick slice of turkey and prodded it on to Chitty's empty plate with the blunt edge of a large bread knife.

'Coo!' she said to nobody in particular. 'I wouldn't 'alf like to foxtrot to one o' them Savoy bands like you 'ear on the wireless. Better than the Christy Minstrels you get on Southend pier.'

'Well, you never will, so forget it,' replied Mrs Varley. 'Go and bring the rest of the coal in.'

'Yes, mum.'

She skittered off, nearly colliding with Iris, the upstairs maid and one of flame-haired twin sisters who had entered the ffolkeses' service on the same day. The other's name was Dolly and, identically pert in their identical maids' outfits, they were next to impossible to tell apart.

'Oh, me poor feet!' Iris groaned. 'They're fair killin' me!' She collapsed on to the chair next to Tomelty's.

''Ello, beautiful,' he greeted her with the uncouth coquetry he had long since patented. His was a line as subtle as semaphore and you couldn't help wondering how it ever worked. Yet it did, again and again.

'Want me to give you a massage?' he hopefully proposed.

'Cheeky monkey! Ooooooh!' she sighed ecstatically as she tipped off her shoes under the table – the heel of the left with the toe of the right, the heel of the right with the toe of the left. She started vigorously rubbing the soles of her feet. 'I've been dyin' to do that for the past hour. They're red raw!'

She let out a sigh of pleasurable anticipation.

'Tomorrow's me mornin' off and I'm goin' to set the alarm clock to six o'clock – just to remind meself I can go straight back to sleep. Bliss!'

'So what's happening up there?' asked Mrs Varley, who was shovelling the third of four spoonfuls of sugar into her tea. 'Still all in a state, are they?'

'Not 'alf. S'why they're keepin' us downstairs – cos of all the dirt that's bein' spilt. As I was leavin' the drawin'-room with the tea-tray, that actress, Cora what's-'er-face, was callin' Gentry a lyin' 'ound – "a lyin' 'ound" – them were 'er actual words an' she fair spat 'em out! I wouldn't like to meet 'er on a dark night.'

'Well, you never will, so forget it,' said Mrs Varley, who couldn't have got through the day without plentiful dippings into her kitty of stock phrases.

'It's a turn o' speech, Mrs Varley. What they call an allergy.'

'I don't hold with allergies. Plain English should be good enough for anyone.'

She thoughtfully sipped her tea, pinkie upraised in the refined manner.

'I'm surprised, though, to hear you say she was spitting mad. She always struck me as so swelte and sophisticated.'

'Swelte?' said Iris derisively. 'That stuck-up thing? Swelte, my –'

'Iris!' warned Chitty. 'Language!'

'Sorry. But I 'ad to laugh, you see, at somethin' she let slip out.'

'Who?'

'The so-called Cora Rutherford.'

'What do you mean "so-called"?'

'Well, it was like this. They was all havin' their tea, even the copper, and she – Cora Rutherford – she was tryin', you know, to brighten up the mood with one of 'er antidotes. She's got a ton o' them antidotes.'

'I don't hold with antidotes.'

'Oh, put a sock in it, Mrs Varley! Go on, Iris, what happened?'

The kitchen was all ears. Addie had come back from the coal-house and was standing as inconspicuously as possible at the garden door – she was an inconspicuous creature at the best of times – while Dolly, who had just returned from her duties upstairs, took a seat on the other side of Tomelty from Iris.

'Well,' said Iris in a stage whisper, 'she was sittin' close to the fire in that fur wrap of 'ers –'

'Isn't it somethin', though!' Dolly interrupted her with a sigh. 'I'd just die – I'd *kill* – for a mink wrap like that!'

'It's not mink, it's fox.'

'It's mink.'

'Fox!'

'Mink!'

'Girls, girls, surely it doesn't matter?'

'How right you are, Mr Farrar. It's most aggravatin' to be interrupted in an antidote 'ardly before you've started,' said Iris, glaring at her sister.

'As I was sayin' before I was so rudely interrupted,' she continued, 'she was tellin' 'em all some story about 'er bein' a little kid – it wasn't about the theatre for once – it was about 'ow she'd been misbehavin' with some local boy – no, no, not what you're thinkin', Tomelty, you Irish tink, you – you with your one-track mind! Seems 'er an' this boy 'ad been splashin' about in a mud pool together an' when she got home 'er mum was blazin' mad at the state of 'er clothes an' ticked 'er off no end – an' she,

Cora, she said this witty, rude thing back at 'er mum –
which was atcherly the point o' the antidote – but what
made everyone laugh out loud was when she repeated
what 'er mum said when she 'eard 'er say this witty thing'
– Iris switched to an uncannily convincing imitation of
Cora Rutherford's accent – '"So dear Mama turned to me
and cried, 'How dare you speak to your mother like that,
Nelly!'" Nelly!'

'I don't get it,' said Addie.

Iris burst into raucous, dirty, gravelly laughter.

'Nelly! There she was, tellin' 'er antidote an' bein' so
witty an' all, an' she got so carried away she clean forgot
'er name was supposed to be Cora. She didn't even finish
the story. She clapped 'er 'ands over 'er mouth and that
pasty face of 'ers – just like one of Mrs Varley's soda
scones, it is! – went quite *peuce*. I daresay 'er name isn't
Rutherford neither. Ramsbottom more like.'

'Now, now, Iris,' said Chitty, who realised he was fight-
ing a losing battle in defence of the decencies, 'we don't
want any of your lip in this kitchen.'

'Little Nelly Ramsbottom,' Iris went on unrepentantly,
'the queen o' the back-to-backs!'

Her chant – 'Lit-tle-Ne-lly-Rams-bo-ttom!' – was taken
up by Dolly and even, though at first circumspectly, by
Addie, the three of them beginning to dance a conga round
the kitchen table.

'Wheeesht, all of you!' an indignant Mrs Varley shouted

at them. 'What a way to behave when there's a dead body in the house!'

'Go on,' said Tomelty, 'you said yerself as 'ow Raymond Gentry was a bad lot. You're not about sheddin' tears over 'im now, are you?'

'No, I am not,' she replied. 'But it's not a pleasant thought – sharing the house with a murderer.'

'You needn't go botherin' yer 'ead about that,' he retorted with a snort. 'This murder is strictly a toffs' affair. It's a fine art for the likes o' them – a snooty sport, bit like fox-'untin'. We might feel like murderin' one o' them, but you can bet yer last farthin' they'd never dirty their manicured fingers murderin' one of us, for sure if we ain't good enough to invite to cocktails we ain't good enough to murder neither. If one o' that bunch upstairs was to kill one of us, 'e'd be oystercised all right – but you know for why? Not cos 'e'd done a murder but cos 'e'd stepped out of 'is own class!'

For all his rough-diamond exterior Tomelty could be quite eloquent.

'Can you see any o' them takin' the time or trouble to bump one of us off in the attic an' leave it lookin' like no one's come in or gone out? Some 'ope! If ever we 'ave ours comin', we'll get it the good old workin'-class way, a quick bash on the back o' the noggin outside the Dog an' Duck. 'Ave no fear, Mrs Varley, your life – aye, an' your virtue, too – is safe as 'ouses!'

'Here, you!' said Mrs Varley heatedly. 'My virtue's my business and don't you forget it! If the late Mr Varley was alive to hear what you just said, he'd be spinning in his grave!'

'Given how flippant you've all been talking about him,' remarked Chitty, 'I'd say that, if anyone's spinning in his grave at this moment, it's Raymond Gentry.'

'' 'E's not in 'is grave yet, silly,' Iris pointed out, while powdering the tip of her nose from a pink powder-puff. '' 'E's still in the attic just where they found 'im. Not decent, I call it, leavin' a dead body without coverin' it over or anythin'.'

'Oh no, Iris!' little Addie suddenly piped up. 'That's what the police tell you to do when there's a murder.'

'What?'

'Nothin'.'

'Nothin'? What you mean, nothin'?'

'You're not to do nothin' at all. I read it in a book.'

Mrs Varley performed what in the films they call a double-take.

'*You* read a book!?'

'I've read *two* books, Mrs Varley,' Addie answered gamely. 'Jessie passed 'em on to me when she 'anded in 'er notice. You remember Jessie, mum? 'Er as up an' married the 'aberdasher's son an' went to Great Yarmouth for 'er 'oneymoon.'

'Oh yes,' said Mrs Varley grimly, 'I *do* remember Jessie. I also remember we don't talk about Jessie around here. Those banns were posted a mite too hastily for my liking. And to think the Vicar allowed her to get married in white! There's such a thing as being too Christian!'

'Anyway, mum, Jessie gave me these two books of 'ers. Quite 'ighbrow they was. One was *The Vamp of the Pampas*. Ooh, was that hot stuff!'

'Language, Addie, language! This isn't Paris, you know.'

'Sorry, Mr Chitty.'

'And what was the other, dear?' he asked.

'Well, that's the funny thing. It was one o' that Miss Mount's that's one o' the Master's guests.'

'What one was it?' Dolly asked.

'Oh, Dolly, now you're askin',' said Addie. 'I think it was called *Murder* somethin' . . .'

'Well, that don't get us much forrader,' said Tomelty, his eyes swimming heavenward. 'Just about every one of 'er books 'as "Murder" in the title.'

'That's it! That's the one!'

'What one?'

'*No Murder in the Title*! It was called *No Murder in the Title* an' it was really good! The murder takes place in the first chapter – an' really gory it is, too! The victim – 'e's some kind of big businessman, Hiram Rittenhouse – Hiram *B*. Rittenhouse the Third – a Napoleon of Finance, they call 'im – an' 'e's found squeezed inside a trouser-press in 'is suit at the Dorchester.'

'You mean they put 'im inside the trouser-press, suit an' all?!' cried Iris.

'No, 'is suit. Like in one o' them big 'otels. Not just a room but a suit.'

'Gerraway! What you mean is a *sweet*!'

'No, I don't. I do so mean a suit. Anyway, all the time you're readin' the book, you remember the murder bein' done in the first chapter an' you know who done it an' you can't work out 'ow the detective – that's a woman called Alexis Baddeley – you can't work out 'ow she's goin' to save the man who's been arrested for it – he's an 'andsome, clean-cut young Yank, Mike somethin' – I don't remember 'is second name – no, no, no, call me a liar, I do so remember, it was Mike Rittenhouse, that's right, 'e was the Napoleon's penniless nephew – an' you can't work out 'ow she'll save 'im from bein' 'ung, seein' as 'ow he definitely done it cos you read about 'im doin' it before you read anythin' else.'

Having been talking, uninterrupted, for probably longer than ever before in her young life, Addie stopped to take a deep breath.

'Well, don't leave us all on tintacks, Addie,' said Mrs Varley. 'Did he do it or didn't he?'

'No, 'e didn't!' cried Addie, beaming triumphantly at everybody in turn. 'That was what was so clever about it. It's only at the very end you discover that in the first chapter 'e was at the pictures – which 'e told the police again an' again 'e was – an' what you read in that chapter is not 'im killin' 'is uncle as 'e's supposed to 'ave done but a similar-like murder 'e saw in the picture show that – what's the word? – *inspirated!* – that inspirated the real murderer. But cos it's the first thing you read, an' cos, after 'e comes out of the picture show, 'e walks along Bond Street worryin' about this terrible thing 'e's done an' you think it's the murder 'e's worryin' about – but it's atcherly cos he spent all 'is money on this loose woman 'e met at a Lyons Corner 'Ouse – an' cos you've got it in your 'ead for the rest of the book that 'e's the one that done it, it comes as ever such a surprise that it wasn't 'im as killed 'is uncle after all!'

Flushed with what she imagined had been the unqualified success of her storytelling, she'd failed to notice that an opaque expression had started to glaze her listeners' eyes.

'Blessed if I can understand it,' said Mrs Varley.

'No more can I,' said Dolly, shaking her head.

'You got the wrong end of the stick as usual, Addie, my dear,' said Chitty in what he doubtless intended to be a kindly voice.

The kitchen-maid was now close to tears.

'No, I didn't. It's a really clever idea when you think about it.'

'I don't hold with ideas,' said Mrs Varley. 'Cause of half the problems in the world, ideas are.'

'But this young Yank, this Mike, you see, everyone says 'e –'

'Now don't start all over again,' said Tomelty. 'We couldn't make 'ead or tail of it the first time and, knowing you, you'll only make things worse. Why'd you have to tell us all that anyway, I'd like to know?'

Her lower lip trembling beneath her protruding teeth like that of a child who's been scolded, Addie said, 'I just wanted to say you shouldn't touch a dead body in a murder case before the doctor tells you it really is dead. It said so in the book, so it must be true.'

'Well, that's cleared up,' said Tomelty. 'Now what's the view around the table? Who done it?'

'Are my ears deceiving me, Tomelty,' cried an aghast Mrs Varley, 'or are you asking us who *we* think murdered Gentry?'

'An' why not? They seem to be makin' a right 'ash of it upstairs.'

Mrs Varley's eyes narrowed.

'Would there be a reward, do you suppose?'

'Reward? Nah! If the 'ole 'ouse was burnin' down an' they was all a-screamin' an' a-shriekin' an' you burst in to try an' rescue them, they'd make you wipe yer feet 'fore you got 'alf-way through the bleedin' flames!'

He turned to Dolly.

'So, Dolly, tell us who you think murdered Raymond Gentry.'

Dolly stuck her forefinger in the dead centre of her brow as though to indicate, for everyone's benefit, the exact location of her hunch.

'Well, I was wonderin',' she said, 'seein' as 'ow angry 'e made 'em all with 'is insinuendoes – I mean, couldn't it be, you know, all of 'em at once?'

'All of 'em? At once?'

'You know, all of 'em in it together? Like in a jury?'

Tomelty made short work of that argument.

'There's twelve to a jury, so that won't do. Iris?'

'Well, since you ask, Tomelty,' the upstairs-maid said primly, 'I do 'ave a theory.'

'A theory, is it? All right, Miss Alberta Einstein, let's 'ave it.'

Pointedly tossing her permed curls at the chauffeur to let him know just what he could do with his vulgar shanty-Irish sarcasm, she proceeded:

'You remember 'ow in books it's always the person you don't expect?'

'Yeah?'

'Well then, it's obvious, ain't it? The murderer must be what's 'is name – Trubshawe – the copper.'

'You're potty, you are!' cried Mrs Varley, who, in spite of her misgivings at the direction the conversation had taken, was finding it impossible to resist joining in. 'Trubshawe wasn't even in the house when it happened.'

'That never stops 'em in books. For all we know, 'e might 'ave sneaked over in the middle of the –'

'Tommyrot!' said Tomelty.

'You seem to know it all, Tomelty,' said Chitty. 'What's *your* theory?'

'Well, we're lookin' for the obvious suspect, am I right?'

'Right.'

'Then, like they always say, it must 'ave been the butler what done it.'

'Here, here, what's that? You accusing *me* of murder?'

'Nah, course not, Mr Chitty. Not you. I was makin' a joke, that's all. Just a joke.'

There was a pause. And then, impeccably on cue:

'I don't hold with jokes,' said Mrs Varley.

Chapter Ten

It was a dark and stormy afternoon. Howling like a demented banshee, shaking the bony, leafless trees on either side of the drive so violently you'd swear it was their skeletons you heard rattling, an icy wind surged around the four walls of ffolkes Manor. The temperature must have been close to zero.

Stepping out of the house with Tobermory plodding ponderously in his wake, the dog's leash trailing the snow-blanketed gravel path behind him, the Colonel stopped dead on the doorstep even before he closed the front door. The sheer force of the wind had visibly taken him by surprise and he glanced up at the heavens as though wondering apprehensively whether this was such a good idea after all. Then, manfully, he buttoned his overcoat's top button and pushed its collar up till it shielded his neck both front and back.

For the moment at least, the snow had stopped falling

and now lay deep and even as far as the eye could see, in so far as, under the lowering firmament, the eye could see very much of anything at all. But what lay ahead couldn't have been further from the quaint and powdery snow of Christmas cards – the snow as nature's tinsel. There was a desert of snow stretching away in every direction, without the oasis, either near or far, of a smattering of house-lights, which would have intimated the existence of some living community, a village at the very least, to reassure you that you weren't the sole survivor of a dead world.

How often, though, had the Colonel insisted that he preferred his seasons to be properly *seasonal*. 'The four seasons,' he never tired of saying, 'are like the four courses of a meal. A diet of perpetual sunshine is like being served a meal of four puddings.' And even now, on a day so god-forsaken he might have been forgiven for having had second thoughts about the wisdom of his walk, you could still make out on his face the masochistic satisfaction a real Englishman takes in a real English winter, the sort of winter which feels like it truly is winter, the sort of winter Dickens wrote about.

His coat buttoned right to the neck, his hairy woollen scarf wound tight around its collar, he slammed the front door of ffolkes Manor. That was another of the Colonel's idiosyncrasies. You could always tell when it was he who had come in or gone out, since he was incapable of closing a door, any door, without slamming it. He even, nobody quite knew how, contrived to slam doors *open*. No matter how regularly Mary ffolkes would remind him that there wasn't a single door in the house that couldn't be pulled-to quietly, he never did remember not to slam it.

As he strode away down the drive, the Colonel turned a judgmental eye on his wife's monkey-puzzle tree, which stood directly in front of the big bay kitchen window. It was a frippery which he gruffly pretended not to approve of but which he nevertheless couldn't help interfering with and advising on and generally sticking his nose into as he would into everything else that happened in and around his own house. But the engulfing gloom was such that it must have been impossible for him to see how well it was holding its own against the ferocity of a West Country winter. So, with an almost audible sigh, he grasped his gnarled wooden stick, a genuine shepherd's crook which he'd brought back with him from his American sojourn, whistled to Tobermory, who ambled up out of nowhere to join him, and set out on his constitutional across the moor.

Walking briskly to keep himself as warm as was humanly possible, if not so briskly as to risk leaving Tobermory behind – walking, so one imagined, his own memories along with the dog and maybe even using the dog as an excuse to permit him to walk those memories undetected – he cut an oddly vulnerable figure silhouetted against the white shadows of the desolate lunar landscape.

Every so often, coming to a brief standstill, he'd test the

ground ahead of him with his stick to make sure he wasn't unwittingly about to insert his foot into one of the tiny but treacherous gullies, now deceptively ironed out by the snow, with which, as he knew, the moors were pockmarked, for he was as familiar with them as with the back of his own hand. And every step he took was accompanied, mechanically, almost automatically, almost as though he himself were unaware of what he was doing, like a labourer whistling while he worked, by an affectionate halloo to Tobermory.

'Come on, Tober!' he'd cry out, without even troubling to turn his head, and 'Here, boy!' and 'That's it, try to keep up with me!' and 'Yes, yes, you're a plucky old mutt, that you are!' And because, apparently, not another denizen of Dartmoor, neither human nor animal, had ventured outdoors on such a forbidding Boxing Day, the distinctively squiggly pattern of his footprints stood out so vividly on the otherwise pristine terrain you could, in an absolutely literal sense, follow in his footsteps.

It was, after fifteen minutes or thereabouts at a steady pace, when he had left ffolkes Manor pretty far behind – the house-lights were still visible but they had become far too small, anonymous and untwinkly to be any longer describable as 'warm' – it was then that Tobermory started to appear vaguely restless.

Not that he failed to continue trudging along after the nice man who, he seemed to comprehend, was understudying his real master. From time to time, though, painfully cranking up his fossilised neck muscles, he would turn his head to sneak a look back over the terrain which they'd already covered. Yet he never once barked or even growled, and the Colonel, his breath as visible as cigar smoke, never once took notice of the creature's growing unease.

Then, as unexpected as it was brief, a sickly mist-enhaloed sun appeared from behind a low-lying bank of clouds and the entire landscape momentarily softened. Just at that moment Tober turned again – and this time he did bark. His barking sounded, from a distance, like nothing so much as the phlegmy wheezing of an asthmatic old codger, but it was enough to stop the Colonel in his tracks.

Shielding his features from the wind, he looked back at the dog, whose vocal exertions were causing not only his tail but his whole ramshackle frame to wag.

'What is it, Tober? You smell something, boy? A rabbit? A goat? Surely not?'

Cupping a palm over his brow, the Colonel peered back in the direction in which the dog was still barking.

'But you're right, there *is* something – or somebody. Good boy, Tober, good boy! You may be at death's door, but you've still got some of your wits about you.'

For a few seconds he said nothing. Instead, he stared straight ahead of him, alert, certainly, though less anxious than just plain curious.

Then, gradually, what had at first been uncaptioned curiosity did begin to turn into a nagging anxiety after all.

He called out, 'Hello there!'

Then, after a lengthy pause:

'Hello!! Why don't you answer?'

And then, after a much shorter pause:

'Who *is* that? Come closer where I can see you!'

The instant the shot rang out, he fell like a stone.

Chapter Eleven

'Depends. Depends.'

Trubshawe was speaking. He stood with his broad, bull-necked back to the fireplace, but at an oblique angle to it, concerned as he was to avoid blocking its warmth from the drawing-room's other occupants. In contrast to the glowing fire, the pipe that permanently dangled from his lips was also, so far as anyone could recall, permanently unlit, to the point where you began to wonder if you'd ever actually seen it emitting smoke. Like many a man of his age, he *wore* that pipe rather than smoked it, and it had become as indispensable an accessory to his self-presentation as the Vicar's dog-collar or Cora Rutherford's tonitruous tangle of bangles.

Who knows what comment, or whose, prompted so typically cautious a response from him? 'Depends. Depends.' It could have been his motto, his 'legend', as the French affect to call it.

He had spent his whole career being dependable. It was

obvious, even to those who had only fleetingly crossed his path in the line of duty, that he'd never been one of the Force's star detectives, that no tabloid reporter had ever dubbed him 'Trubshawe of the Yard'. But he was what the Great British Police Establishment is most comfortable with – the type of investigator who arrives at the solution to a problem (he himself would instinctively have avoided the word 'mystery') not through some ostentatious lightning-flash of inspiration or even imagination but by simply, doggedly depending on others to point him, often without their actually realising they were doing so, in the right direction.

He would pose a question, listen politely and patiently to the answer, then listen a little more, then still a little more – oh, he had all the time in the world! – until the hapless suspect, intimidated by the prolonged silence, even feeling obscurely responsible for it, proceeded to blurt out all sorts of things he never intended to reveal. And it's then, one imagines, that this temperamentally slow and, yes, plodding man would pounce – in his fashion. He would move in for the kill, just as patiently and politely as, earlier, he had laid the ground and set the trap.

Sherlock Holmes he therefore was not. Yet in his stolid, even boring way, he had probably nabbed many more criminals than any number of glittering practitioners of the venerable craft of detection.

As for the ffolkeses' guests, having spent the last forty-five minutes or so resting in their rooms, they were now seated comfortably at the fireplace again, increasingly engrossed, from the sound of it, in their own humdrum affairs.

'Oh, there you are, Farrar. Everything quite satisfactory downstairs?'

'Yes, Mrs ffolkes. The servants seem to be bearing up rather well considering.'

'Considering?'

'Considering the state they were in when the body was first discovered.'

'Oh. Oh yes. Yes, of course. They *were* in a state, weren't they?'

There was something not altogether natural about Mary ffolkes's voice. Resembling nothing so much as an elderly butterfly, if such a creature can be said to exist, she had always been a fussy, fluttery woman, ever terrified of the Colonel's 'moods', those vocal and too often public exhalations of his famous fiery temper. If there was one thing she dreaded in life, it was a 'scene', though in her case such a 'scene' might amount to no more than a couple of raised voices at the dinner-table. But now, when she spoke, a hoarseness of articulation combined with an unusually hesitant delivery suggested she was labouring under some more extreme strain.

She stood near the tall french window, noticeably apart from her friends, and even from the far end of the room she could be observed agitatedly toying with one of the knotted tassels with which the heavy drawn curtains were fringed. Every so often, too, when she thought no one was looking in her direction, she would tweak the curtains apart and steal a swift glance out on to the moors. Then she would just as swiftly draw them to again and, sporting a brave smile, turn cheerfully – just a tiny bit too cheerfully – to face the company.

After a moment she spoke again:

'Sorry, Farrar, but would you happen to . . .?' she started to ask.

'Yes, Mrs ffolkes?'

'Would you happen to know if my husband has returned?'

'Uh, no.'

'Ah. Well, thank you anyway.'

Then, pretending she'd had a belated afterthought, she added, 'Oh, and Farrar . . .'

'Yes?'

'Did you mean – sorry – but did you mean he *hasn't* returned or did you mean you don't happen to *know* if he has?'

'Well, he may be changing, of course, but it's not likely he could have come in without anyone hearing him. His being with Tobermory and all. And, you know, the way – well, the way he has of always slamming the door.'

'Yes, yes, of course. You're right, of course. Just my foolishness.'

And yet she couldn't prevent herself, not nearly as furtively this time, once more tweaking the curtains open and staring blankly at the empty, desolate landscape which stretched away from the house.

It was hard to credit that no one else had noticed the gradual alteration in her demeanour, that no one else had sensed the hysteria locked up inside her like a genie trapped in a bottle. But then, even at the height of a crisis, normally constituted human beings appear to require next to no excuse to revert to their natural state of self-absorption, as witness the fragments of chit-chat which were drifting round the drawing-room and from which it could be gathered that, in the absence of anything to be urgently debated, any collective decision to be taken, the ffolkeses' house-party had all gratefully subsided into the pre-murder routine of their various quotidian rounds.

The Vicar and his wife, for example, were huddled together in a private confab. For all one knew, they were discussing how they were ever going to confront the future under the cloud which the events of the last twenty-four hours had cast over their reputations. Or they could just as well have been sticking mental pins into a mental effigy of the terrible Mrs de Cazalis.

Those two wicked witches of the West End, Cora Rutherford and Evadne Mount, were having a high old time puncturing the pretensions of mutual acquaintances in the interconnected worlds of plays and books. From time to time a *mot* from one or the other would make itself piercingly heard above the general babble – 'Yes, he was short, the little runt, but not as short as the shrift I gave him!' (that was the novelist) – 'Her own hair? Not bl**dy likely! By the look of it, it wasn't even her own wig!' (that was the actress) – followed by a cascade of tinny tee-hees from Cora Rutherford and booming haw-haws from Evadne Mount.

Then there were the Rolfes. They were seated side by side on the sofa nearest the fire, next to a collection of carved wooden figurines, about a quarter life-size, all of them representing darkies in fezes and topees – postmen, stationmasters and other minor colonial dogsbodies – which the Colonel had brought back home from one of his African trips. When he was not distractedly fingering one or other of these peculiar statues as though greeting a dep-utation of pygmies, Henry Rolfe would squeeze his wife's hand tight in his own, while she could be seen raising a fin-ger to her eye – was she actually brushing away a tear?

So their apparent reconciliation meant that the tragedy of ffolkes Manor was to have at least one positive conse-quence. It had paradoxically saved a marriage that might have died had Raymond Gentry not. For the Rolfes, the word 'tender' for too many years had meant something akin to 'raw' and 'bruised'. Now it really looked as though there was a chance it could once again come to mean 'soft' and 'romantic'.

One positive consequence – or two? For, last but not least, we arrive at our pair of young lovers. Selina and Don were snuggled up on the smaller of the two sofas. And though they were whispering, or imagined they were whispering, communicating in a language too intimate to be spoken aloud, the fact that virtually everybody else was conversing in low voices made it impossible to avoid overhearing what they were saying.

'Oh, Don darling,' said Selina, peering with such undivided attention into the depths of the young American's eyes you'd have thought he would either have to close them or turn aside from her field of vision, 'was I awfully cruel to you? I didn't mean to be, really I didn't. It's just that – I suppose I let myself get carried away.'

Even if Don had been listening to every word she had uttered, it was obvious from what he himself said next that only one of those words had truly registered.

'Selina,' he whispered, 'you called me –'

'"Darling"? Yes, I did. Do you mind?'

'Mind? You're asking me if I *mind*? Darling, darling, darling Selina, I'll mind only if you *don't* call me darling! From now on, I'll expect every sentence you say to me, every single question you ask me, to end in darling! I won't ever be content with just Don. Matter of fact, I never, *ever* want to hear you pronounce my name again. From now on, for you, I've only got one name – darling.'

Selina laughed, a high, bright, tinkly laugh, like someone

grinning aloud. It was the first time she'd laughed since the body had been discovered. Maybe even the first time since her arrival at the house.

'Why, Don – I mean, darling! darling! – how eloquent you've become.'

'Now you're making fun of me.'

'No, no, really I'm not. I thought that was a very poetic little speech.'

'Oh, if you take me at all, Selina, you'll have to take me as I am. I don't kid myself I'm any kinda poet.'

'Darling, please stop running yourself down. My – well, my infatuation, I suppose I have to call it, with Ray – it wasn't really him, you know – to be honest, I'm no longer all that sure I ever actually liked him – it was the world he represented.'

She perused the semi-circle formed by her parents' guests.

'You see the sort of milieu I come from. I do adore every one of them. Most of all Mummy and Daddy, naturally, but also Evie and Cora and the Vicar and Cynthia and . . . Goshsakes, they're all frightfully sweet and everything, but they're so much older, so much more *settled*, than I am. I was beginning to feel I was a prisoner in this house. I craved life and experience and adventure, and Ray opened doors for me, doors into worlds whose existence I knew about only from books and mags and films.'

'You do realise, my darling,' said Don, comically solemn

in his youthful ardour, 'that *I* can't open those doors for you. They're just as closed to me as they were to you. And seeing what effect they had on you – like your using the word "milieu", that's such a Raymondish word! – I mean to keep them closed.'

'I do realise it. And it's because of that I love you, not in spite of it. That's what you've got to understand.'

'Oh, I know I'm a colourless character, a bit of a cookie cut-out figure.'

'What are you talking about? You have absolute oodles of It.'

'It? What's It?'

'Haven't you read your Elinor Glyn?'

'Why, no, I –'

'What? You never read *It*? It's a modern classic.'

'I'm not really the bookish type, you know, Selina.'

'It means sex appeal, you egregious darling!'

Don's eyes opened wide enough to swallow up the whole visible world.

'Hot dog! You – you think I've got sex appeal?'

'I'm telling you, oodles of it, you clod, you mad, wonderful clod!'

It was all too much for him.

'Oh gee – oh gee!' he stuttered, overwhelmed by the speed at which his luck seemed to have turned. 'And I always thought I was just, you know, tall, dark and one-dimensional. My only excuse was that that's how I was made by my Creator.'

'And He did a wonderful job. He,' she repeated, before adding archly, 'or She.'

'She?' Don jovially echoed her. 'A female God, eh? Should I take that to mean you've become a – a – whaddya call 'em?'

'What do you call what?'

'You know, those harpies who chain themselves to the Parliament gates and wave their umbrellas in the air and proclaim emancipation for women?'

'Feminists?'

'Feminists, yeah! So you're a feminist now, are you?'

'That's for me to know and you to find out,' said Selina, a roguish smile playing on her lips.

'Well, don't worry, I'll soon cure you of that nonsense. There's only one person who's gonna be allowed to wear the pants in our marriage and I promise you it ain't going to be the little wifey!'

'But, Don, women already have the vote.'

'Not in my home they don't! Besides, you're too beautiful to be a feminist.'

'Oh, you dope, you darling, you sweet, sweet peachereno!' giggled Selina. 'I never realised you could be so masterful!'

'Hot dog!' Don cried again.

This time, however, he truly did cry out, causing everybody in the room to interrupt their own conversations and stare at him in amusement.

He blushed to the roots of his hair.

'Sorry, I –' he began to say in an embarrassed voice.

But he never did manage to complete his apology. Suddenly, at the french window, Mary ffolkes buried her face in her hands and burst into loud, heaving sobs.

Everybody looked at one another – which is another way of saying that nobody knew where to look.

Selina was the first to respond. Followed close behind by Dr Rolfe, she rushed over to the window.

'Why, Mummy, what is it?' she cried out. 'What's the matter with you?'

As Selina cradled her, Mary ffolkes tried to speak, but hiccoughing sobs were shaking her whole frame.

'Now, now, Mary, my dear,' murmured Rolfe in his dulcet bedside voice, deftly unpinning the Cairngorm brooch which held the collar of her taffeta dress in a secure clasp, 'you must try to remain calm.'

Sliding a protective arm around her shoulders, he whispered softly to Selina:

'Let's get her over to the sofa. She needs to lie down for a few minutes. I'm afraid what's happened has been just too much for her. I might have known the strain would tell. She's not as young as she used to be. Her heart, you know . . .'

Together, propping her up, they began to walk across the room. Already half-way, however, the Colonel's wife had not only steadied herself but was attempting to tidy up the strands of hair that were flopping over her forehead, a nervous tic familiar to everybody who knew her well.

'Thank you, but I'm really all right,' she mumbled almost inaudibly. 'Do please forgive me, I'm being such a silly-billy.'

When they reached the sofa, Selina hurriedly plumped up a cushion and rested her mother's head against it, while Rolfe, stretching her two legs out lengthwise, removed her shoes.

'Feeling better now?' asked Selina, anxiously scrutinising the reddened, tear-streaked features.

'Much better, thank you. I'm going to be fine. Just let me catch my breath.'

While he almost surreptitiously pressed his thumb on his patient's wrist to take her pulse, Rolfe said, 'Now, Mary dear, may I ask if something – I mean to say, something specific – brought on this little attack?'

'It's – well, to tell the truth, it's Roger. I'm so worried.'

'Worried, Mummy?' asked Selina, puzzled. 'What do you mean?'

In Mary ffolkes's reply there could be detected an uncharacteristic trace of bitterness.

'You see – you *haven't* noticed. You've all become so preoccupied again with your own affairs. And why not? I can't blame you for that. But not one of you seems to have noticed that Roger has been outside for a long time – really a lot longer than is good for him, particularly in weather like this. It's started snowing again, quite heavily. I'm a born worrier, I know, but . . . Oh, forgive me for being so foolish!'

Trubshawe immediately trained his gimlet eye on the grandfather clock. It was one-forty.

'At exactly what time did he leave?' he asked Mary ffolkes.

'But that's just it,' she mumbled, wiping away her tears with a lacy handkerchief which she drew from the sleeve of her cardigan – her cardie, as she invariably called it. 'That's what's so frustrating. I don't know. I just don't know. It was just Roger off on one of his constitutionals. He's taken a walk at least once every day of his life. Except – except it seems to me this time he's been out much longer than usual. I'm sure I'm getting into a dither for nothing, but we women do have our instincts, you know . . .'

'Anyone else note what time the Colonel left?'

'Well, sir –'

'Yes, Farrar?'

'You recall, he wanted someone to pop down to the kitchen to check up on the servants?'

'Yes?'

'Well, one of the kitchen walls has a large bay window and, if you stand beside it listening to all the below-stairs gabbing –'

'Yes, yes, get on.'

'Well, it enables you to see anybody leaving the house.

And after about fifteen minutes the Colonel did walk past the window, just by the monkey-puzzle tree, with your dog Tobermory trotting along behind him – and it was exactly twelve-twenty by the kitchen clock.'

'Twelve-twenty, eh?' Trubshawe paused for a moment of reflection. 'That would mean he's been on the moors for quite a bit above an hour.'

He turned again to Mary ffolkes.

'I'm sorry, Mrs ffolkes, but you understand I'm not what you would call conversant with your husband's ambulatory habits. Is that a normal length of time for his walk? Or too long? Or what?'

'Oh dear, Inspector, I really couldn't say. Obviously, it's never occurred to me to time one of Roger's walks. What can I tell you? I just feel in my bones he's been away too long.'

'Now, Mary,' Evadne Mount said to her cheerfully, 'you really are worrying about nothing at all, you know. I'm certain Roger's out there taking a long, vigorous walk to clear his head and, what's more, enjoying every blessed minute of it. I also believe he'll literally laugh his head off when he learns how alarmed you were. I can almost hear that laugh of his now.'

'For once I'm in agreement with Miss Mount,' Trubshawe nodded sagely. 'It's perfectly understandable you should be prey to all sorts of anxieties, what with everything that's taken place here in the last couple of days. And you probably think your husband's been absent longer than usual for no better reason than that you yourself have been looking out for him. Aren't you forgetting the proverbial kettle?'

Mary ffolkes blinked.

'The proverbial kettle?'

'I mean, about watching it boil,' Trubshawe explained.

'Oh yes. Of course. When you put it like that . . .' she added doubtfully.

'But that said and done,' he went on, 'I would like to see you have your mind put to rest. So this is what I propose. A small group of us men – you, Don, if you would, Farrar and me – Rolfe here will stay behind in case you have any further need of him, Mrs ffolkes – we'll collect some torch-lights and go out looking for the Colonel. Farrar ought to have some idea of the direction in which he tends to take his walks, so I'm pretty confident we'll meet him on his way back, possibly even strolling up the driveway as we open the front door. Whatever – at least you'll have the satisfaction of knowing he's no longer out there on his own. Now how does that sound?'

'Oh thank you, Inspector,' said Mary ffolkes, smiling palely. 'I know I'm being needlessly alarmist, but – yes, I would be awfully grateful.'

'Good, good,' replied Trubshawe. 'Then shall we get going, men – Don, Farrar?'

'I'm coming with you,' Evadne Mount declared.

The Chief-Inspector instantly negatived this suggestion.

'I won't hear of it, Miss Mount. This is a man's job, and your place is here with the other ladies.'

'There you go again! And it's all pish-posh. I'm as much a man as you are, Trubshawe. Besides, there's nothing for me to do here – Cora could tell her stories to the back of the Clapham omnibus and never know the difference. No, no, no, you can like it or you can lump it, but I'm coming with you.'

And she did.

Chapter Twelve

The landscape appeared even less inviting than when the Colonel had set out on his constitutional. In fact, it looked as though God had taken a giant eraser to the horizon and simply rubbed it out like a blackboard – or whiteboard. It was now snowing heavily again, and the only sound to be heard, except for the whine of the ebbing wind, was a powdery creaking underfoot. Nothing, however, could have left a less Christmassy impression than the eerily virginal moorland that afternoon. Its whiteness was the whiteness of death, its pallor the hideous pallor of a cadaver.

Even the torchlights which cast their yellow haloes at everyone's feet illuminated only the stark fact that there *was* nothing to illuminate. You half-expected the startled eyes of some feral creature to be trapped blinking in their beams – but no. Nothing. There was no such creature to be seen.

Nor – and this was a thought which had no doubt already crossed the mind of everyone in the search party, though no one had shown any readiness to put it into words – nor was the Colonel to be seen. Trubshawe's parting reassurance to Mary ffolkes, that he might well encounter her husband walking back up the driveway of ffolkes Manor on his way home, had proved, after no more than a few minutes, to have been hopelessly optimistic. Only under the shelter of the monkey-puzzle tree were Roger ffolkes's unobliterated footprints, preceding Tobermory's by a couple of yards, visible to the naked eye. But there was only one set of his prints and they were headed in only one direction – away from the house.

It was the Chief-Inspector who eventually broke the silence.

'The cold getting to you, Miss Mount?'

The authoress was attired in a ratty, moth-eaten tweed coat, one that had seen many better days, a thick woollen scarf wound several times about her neck and the matelot's tricorne hat which had become her trademark in London's literary world. This outré ensemble assuredly kept the freezing temperature at bay, but it also gave her a troubling resemblance to one of those madwomen who can be found peddling boxes of matches on the forecourt of Charing Cross Station. Not that she gave a fig about that.

'Not at all, not at all!' she protested in a muffled voice still loud enough to echo over the moors. 'I like the cold.'

'You *like* the cold?'

'You heard me. And please don't give me one of those

condescendingly incredulous looks of yours that we've all had to get used to. I know I'm an author and therefore, for someone like you, an eccentric. But there are lots of us who simply hate the sun, who hate being drenched in sweat. Yes, sweat. I call it sweat because that's what it is. I can't speak for you, Chief-Inspector, but *I* sweat. I don't perspire.'

'Well, well, well. So it's true what they always say. There's nowt so queer as folk.'

Don, enveloped in the racoon coat which had caused a minor sensation when he first arrived at ffolkes Manor, turned, mystified, to the Chief-Inspector.

'Sorry, I didn't get that – what you just said.'

'What I just said? Ah, yes, of course. Well, I don't wonder you didn't get it. It's an old English expression. You can bet your bottom dollar it dates back to Chaucer, just as all those old expressions seem to do, even the smutty ones. "Nowt so queer as folk" – it means there's nothing in the world as strange as people themselves.'

'Oh, I see. You mean, like Miss Mount preferring cold to heat?'

'That's right. I love the sun myself. With the missus – God rest her soul – I used to go caravanning every August in Torbay. I'd just soak it up. How about you?'

'Oh yeah, me too. But then, you see, I'm from California.'

'California? Is that so?'

'Yeah. Los Angeles. Nice little town. Full of orange groves and movie studios. Ever been there?'

'Furthest I've been is Dieppe. Day trip. Couldn't see what all the hubbub was about.'

'You, Miss Mount?' asked Don.

'Evadne, dear. Please call me Evadne.'

'Evadne.'

'That wasn't too difficult, was it?' she said sweetly. 'Now, what is it you'd like to know?'

'Los Angeles. Have you ever visited it?'

'No, I never have. Though, as it happens, I did set one of my whodunits there. I genned up on the place by reading Dashiell Hammett. You familiar with his stories? Not my cup of tea, as you might expect, but he knows his stuff all right.'

The pause that followed was motivated less by any reluctance on Don's part to enquire about the plot of the whodunit in question than by his expectation that a précis of that plot was going to be volunteered anyway, whether he solicited it or not.

For once, though, the précis was unforthcoming, so he finally said:

'I'd be interested to hear what it's about. Your whodunit, I mean.'

'We-ell, I don't know,' answered Evadne Mount, glancing at the Chief-Inspector. 'I have the distinct impression our friend from Scotland Yard finds me a bit too style-cramping whenever I talk about my work.'

'Oh, please. Don't mind me,' said Trubshawe, batting his two gloved hands together while striding onwards over the snow. 'You never have before. Besides, it'll help to pass the time.'

'Right you are,' she said, needing no further encouragement. 'Well, the book was called *Murder Murder on the Wall* and its central character was an aged, loony silent film actress loosely based on Theda Bara – you remember, the star of *A Fool There Was*? – well, *you* won't remember, Don, you're not nearly old enough, but she'll certainly have set off a palpitation or two in the Inspector's manly young breast.'

'Couldn't have been easy for you to create a *silent* character,' Trubshawe, not missing a beat, slyly interposed.

'This film star,' she continued, declining to rise to his bait, 'lives a reclusive existence inside a deliriously creaky Bel Air mansion with only her incontinent Pekinese dog for company. Because she can no longer bear to contemplate the ravages of her own physical decline, she's had all the mirrors in the house turned to the wall and even has a cleaning lady, what we in England call a char, come in every day to dust the furniture – though not the way you think. In fact, the cleaner's job is to coat with *extra dust* any shiny surface in which there's still a chance of her mistress's appearance being reflected.

'The thing is that, even though she's on her uppers, and has been for as long as anyone can remember, it's common knowledge on the Hollywood grapevine that there's one valuable she's never pawned, a fabulous ruby offered her many years before by the Maharajah of Udaipur.

'Then, one morning, her brutally murdered body is discovered by the cleaner. She duly rings up the police, who can find no trace of the ruby, and the sole clue to the killer's identity are the letters LAPD which the actress was able to scrawl on her bedroom wall, in her own blood, before she expired.

'Naturally, suspicion arises that she must have been trying to "point the finger", as Hammett would put it, at some member of the LAPD itself – you know, the Los Angeles Police Department. That is, until Alexis Baddeley happens to come along. Nosing around in her usual incorrigible fashion, she interprets those four letters as being, instead, the dying woman's abortive attempt to spell out the word "lapdog" and eventually finds the ruby concealed inside a cheap cameo brooch attached to the Peke's collar.'

'Oh gee, wow, that's really clever,' said Don. 'I'd really like to read that.'

Trubshawe cupped his hands and blew into them.

'Dashed if I can see the point any longer,' he said. 'Now that you've been served the whole plot up on a plate.'

'Not so fast, Chief-Inspector, not so fast,' Evadne Mount sniffily expostulated. 'You'll note that I didn't give away the identity of the real murderer.'

'Pooh, that's no brain-teaser. It was obviously the char.'

The novelist let out a cry of triumph.

'Hah! That's just what I was counting on the reader to think! Actually, the murderer turns out to be a police officer after all, a "crooked cop", as the Yanks call them. It's a double twist, you see. Those letters LAPD meant exactly what everybody originally assumed they meant and had nothing to do with the Peke. In her death throes the film star was genuinely trying to communicate who the killer was. So that, even when Alexis Baddeley gets it wrong, she still gets it right! Eh, Trubshawe, what have you to say to that? Trubshawe? Are you listening?'

Surprised at not receiving any response, she suddenly noticed that the Chief-Inspector had fallen several paces behind her before coming to a complete halt. Arching his hand over his brow, in unnervingly the same gesture as the Colonel's just an hour before, he was trying to make out something or somebody in the distance ahead of him.

An ominous silence descended on the party. Everyone strained to see for themselves what could have attracted the Chief-Inspector's attention. At first there was nothing. Then, amid the restless play of shadows, a dark and amorphous form, like a mound of cast-off clothes unceremoniously dumped on the horizon, rose out of the snow. And no sooner had one's eyes encompassed its contours, they were irresistibly drawn to a second, smaller mound a few feet away.

'What the – ?' said Trubshawe, doffing his tartan cloth cap and scratching his scalp.

'Why,' said Evadne Mount, 'I – I – I'm positive –'

Swallowing the rest of her sentence with a gulp, she exclaimed, 'Great Scott-Moncrieff!'

'What? What is it?' cried the policeman. 'My eyesight isn't what it used to be – one of these days I'm going to have to fork out for a pair of specs – and this torchlight is dazzling my eyes.'

For a few agonising seconds Evadne Mount chose not to speak. Then:

'Trubshawe,' she finally said, 'I can't yet see what the larger of the two mounds is, though,' she added grimly, 'I can guess. But I'm afraid, I'm very much afraid, the smaller one is – is Tobermory.'

With lips set so tight around his pipe that he came close to biting its stem in half, Trubshawe made his way, half-walking, half-running, towards the two matchingly sinister shadows.

Tobermory's was the first of the bodies to be bathed in the harsh yellow beam of his torchlight. The dog was lying on his side and, if it hadn't been for his foam-flecked mouth, his smashed-up rib-cage and the blood which polka-dotted the blankness of the snow, he could almost have been asleep. He wasn't asleep, though, he was dead. Yet the breath of life had quit his body so recently, and with such haste, that his nostrils, if no longer quivering, were still moist.

No one dared to speculate on Trubshawe's feelings as he contemplated his dead companion. At last, though, he turned his torch on the larger of the two shapeless masses. There was, of course, no suspense whatever as to its identity. It was, as everyone knew it could only be, the Colonel.

'Oh, Jesus!' said Don in a whisper.

'This is truly vile!' gasped Evadne Mount. 'Ray Gentry was vermin – but Roger? Why would anyone want to murder Roger?'

The Chief-Inspector wasted no time venting either grief or fury. He bent over the body like a terrier poised at a rat-hole and laid his head sideways on the Colonel's chest. Then, gazing up at the cluster of faces circled about his own, he cried out:

'He's alive! He's still alive!'

At first sight the Colonel had seemed just as dead as Tobermory. But when a light was trained directly on to his face, both his eyelids began to twitch – independently of one another, a strange and rather horrible sight – and, every five seconds or so, a convulsively jerky little quaver would shake each of his shoulders in turn.

'What's happening to him?'

'I think he may be in some sort of a coma, Farrar – possibly he's had an internal haemorrhage – not impossible he's even had a stroke. Rolfe will be able to make a proper diagnosis. But he's definitely alive. Look here.' The police-man directed his index finger at a bloodied rip in the

Colonel's overcoat. 'The murderer was obviously aiming at the heart, but, see, the bullet went in much too high, through the shoulder and out again.'

Quickly taking in the surrounding waste-land, he muttered, 'No point in looking for the bullet in this weather. Or for footprints. They'll all have long since been buried under the snow.'

Once more he looked down at the unconscious man.

'I'm no doctor,' he said, 'but in my time I've had to deal with a good number of men who've just been shot and I'm convinced he can be saved.'

'But what are we going to do?' asked Don. 'Don't they always say you should never move a wounded body?'

'Yes, I daresay they do, but I'm less worried about the wound, which seems to be a relatively superficial one, than about a possible psychological reaction setting in. No, I certainly don't recommend leaving the old boy here on the ground while one of us runs back to the house to fetch Rolfe. In this case, we don't have a choice. We've got to carry him back ourselves.'

'Yeah, you're right, of course.'

Don at once peeled off his racoon coat and said to Trubshawe:

'Here. We can use this to support him. You know, like on a stretcher?'

'We-ell, but that's a pretty flimsy jumper you have on. Aren't you afraid you'll freeze out here?'

'Don't worry about me, I'll be okay.'

'Good lad,' said Trubshawe approvingly. 'You've got what it takes.'

Then Evadne Mount spoke up.

'And Tobermory?'

'I know, I know . . . For the moment, though, the only thing that matters is to get the Colonel home. Don't think I've forgotten old Tober. I haven't and I never shall. But we're going to have to abandon him for now. I'll come out here later and – well, I'll make sure he's given a decent burial. Thank you, anyway, for asking.'

'Why gun down a poor old blind animal?' said Don. 'It's just crazy.'

Again Trubshawe gazed at the lifeless creature who had once been his most faithful and, at the end, his best friend, and for a few seconds his natural unflappability was tempered by a very real and visible emotion.

'No, son, whatever it was, it wasn't crazy,' he quietly replied. 'Tober may have been blind, but they do say a blind man's surviving senses – specially his sense of smell – are sharpened by the loss of his sight and I imagine that's just as true of a dog. P'raps truer. Tobermory was a witness, a dumb witness, so he had to be silenced. Dogs, even blind dogs, know right from wrong, and they remember, too, who did right and who did wrong. He would have snarled and growled at the murderer for ever afterwards.'

'Inspector, I couldn't be sorrier.'

'Thanks, but this is no time for sentiment. Now, men,' he said, gauging the strength of each one, 'if we follow Don's suggestion and use his coat as a stretcher, I think we can get the Colonel back home without worsening his condition. Farrar, help me roll him over – softly, softly does it – *softly*, I say. Don, you look as though you're the strongest of the three of us, so why don't you pick up your coat from the other end? That's right – good, good – but take care you keep it from swinging too much. It's not a hammock. Farrar, you and I will take him from this end.'

'What about me?' asked Evadne Mount. 'What can I do?'

'You? You're going to be our guide. We'll really need a guide, so keep your mind and your eyes focused on the way ahead. Here – take my torchlight as well as your own and direct them both at your feet. If you observe any hump, any bump, any ridge, any kind of concavity, anything at all we should look out for, make whatever detour you have to and we'll follow suit. Understood?'

'Understood.'

'Now. Everyone knows what he's got to do? Okay. One – two – three – all together!'

Then, with a wave of his hand, like the boss of a wagon train, he cried out:

'Lead on, Evadne Mount!'

So it was that our dolorous little procession forged its slow and solemn path across the snow-mantled moors.

Chapter Thirteen

It seems that Mary ffolkes had chosen to ignore Dr
Rolfe's recommendation that she remain in a reclining
position until the search party's arrival home. Or else,
more likely, knowing her, she had at the very last minute
been alarmed by a cry from Selina – who at her mother's
request had stationed herself at the french window in
order to catch the earliest possible glimpse of the
Colonel's return – and then leapt up to discover what had
occasioned it. Whichever it was, the poor woman must
have witnessed the funereal spectacle of her husband
being borne across the moors on an improvised stretcher
and, having assumed the worst, as loved ones inevitably
do, simply fainted away. For, when the Colonel was finally
transported into the drawing-room and his comatose
body eased on to the sofa, Rolfe was already in the process of administering the smelling-salts.

Realising that nothing could more quickly and effectively
snap her out of her fit than to be told that her husband's

condition wasn't as terminal as she believed, Trubshawe all but elbowed Rolfe aside to give her the glad news.

'Mrs ffolkes, can you hear me? I say, can you hear me, Mrs ffolkes?'

Half-raising her eyelids, baring eyes that were filmy with shock and grief, Mary ffolkes peered into his rough and ready features.

'Roger? Is he . . .?'

'No, Mrs ffolkes. He isn't dead, if that's what you were going to ask me. I won't keep it from you. He's in pretty bad shape. But he isn't dead and he isn't about to die.'

The effect was instantaneous. Her eyes appeared suddenly alive again, as though re-energised by a surge of electricity, and she even tried to sit up, though she was gently prevented in that by the policeman.

'So he's going to be all right?' she murmured.

'Yes, Mrs ffolkes, he's going to be all right,' said Trubshawe, lighting his pipe for the first time in anybody's memory as he bent over her. He took a deep puff and exhaled the smoke with a pleasure all the purer for having been so long delayed. 'That's why I want to make sure you'll be all right too – for his sake. He's going to need you now more than he's ever needed you.'

'But I don't understand. You tell me he's in a bad way. What's happened to him? What happened out there?'

The apprehension etched on Trubshawe's face no doubt reflected the internal dialogue he was now conducting with himself. Should he tell her or not? Did this good, simple, God-fearing woman have the physical and mental stamina to learn about the cause of the Colonel's condition? Or would it be better for her state of mind if he concealed from her (but for how long?) the fact that some as yet unknown individual's desire to be forever rid of her husband had actually prompted him or her to commit the very worst of crimes?

He took the plunge.

'Well, Mrs ffolkes, it's also my regretful duty to inform you – but, if I do, it's because I've a shrewd hunch you're a strong enough woman to hear this – that someone tried to murder the Colonel.'

Mary ffolkes sat up with a start. So much so, she had to be held back by Cynthia Wattis, who had been dabbing at her friend's fevered brow with a handkerchief.

'What? Someone murder Roger? Oh no, no, no! It can't be! You must be mistaken!'

'I'm afraid not. It was no accident. He was shot at.'

'Oh, my God!'

'Fortunately, his assailant wasn't the shot he imagined he was. Or the distance was just too great. Or p'raps there was too much doom and gloom out there on the moors for him to take proper aim at his target. In any event, the bullet passed through your husband's shoulder and, thank God, there's no obvious sign that any lasting damage has been done.'

'But we've got to get him to a doctor! Immediately!'

'You're forgetting, Mrs ffolkes. We have a doctor among us. Dr Rolfe here. He's with your husband as we speak, and I'm sure he'll know what has to be done.'

Throughout their exchange the Doctor had indeed been examining the still-unconscious Roger ffolkes, placing an ear to his heart, as Trubshawe had already done, while simultaneously taking his pulse. And once his diagnosis was complete, he came across the room and stood at the Chief-Inspector's side.

'Well?' said Trubshawe.

'Well,' replied Rolfe, 'even if none of the important organs was touched, he's had a terrific shock to his system. A man of his age, you know . . . But, Mary, do let me assure you. Roger had the – I mean, has – Roger *has* the constitution of an ox and – well, as you know, I ruined my life on account of one stupid, tragic blunder, but I can promise you now, I can absolutely promise you, he's going to pull through.'

'Thank heaven for that! And thank you, Chief-Inspector, and you other men too, Don, Farrar, Evie, for having brought him back to me safe and sound. Well, anyway' – and if for no more than an instant, her distress was tempered by one of those half-apologetic half-smiles of hers, the only ones she ever half-permitted herself – 'if not as sound as he might be, then at least safe. I shall be eternally grateful.'

'Oh, Mary,' cried Cynthia Wattis, 'how very courageous you are, refusing to crack! But then, that's the sort of person you've always been.'

'Don't delude yourself, Cyn,' answered the Colonel's wife. 'I'm anything but courageous. To tell the truth, I'm actually shedding buckets of tears. If you can't see them, it's because, a long, long time ago, I learned how to channel those tears down the inside of my cheeks. It's an art we women have to master.'

'My dear,' said Evadne Mount, 'in my book, crying on the inside is the very definition of courage!'

Whereupon the novelist turned to the Chief-Inspector and, like a quick-change artiste, abruptly switched both style and subject-matter.

'I say, Trubshawe,' she boomed, 'since I'm not needed here, you wouldn't have any objection to my popping up to my bedroom to change? I'll catch my death if I don't get into some warm indoor clothes.'

'No, no – go, do. Take your time,' the Chief-Inspector carelessly replied, not a little relieved to be delivered, even temporarily, from the inhibitive presence of his brilliant but provoking rival.

'Tell me, Doctor,' he then asked, 'what's to be done with the Colonel? Dare we move him into his own bed? I mean, until the weather lets up and we can get him to a hospital.'

'I'd certainly prefer to see him in a proper bed if possible. Mary,' said Rolfe to the Colonel's wife, 'I presume you've got a fire going in your bedroom?'

'Oh yes. By now it ought to be quite toasty warm.'

'Then I propose we carry him up, undress him and put him to bed. After I patch him up, I'll give him a shot which should knock him out. What he needs now is calm and lots of undisturbed sleep.'

Trubshawe gave the Doctor a meaningful look.

'A shot, you say, Rolfe?'

'That's right.'

'Precisely what sort of a shot?'

'Oh, a small dose of morphine. I always have some on me. It's perfectly harmless. Just enough to –'

But before Rolfe could say another word, the Chief-Inspector had turned his unfinished sentence into an unfinished question. The change was one of intonation only, but the implication was radically different.

'Just enough to . . .?'

Rolfe visibly bristled.

'Just enough to put him to sleep for several hours, was what I was going to say. But, look here, Trubshawe, why are you asking me these questions? What is it you're insinuating?'

'Am I insinuating something?'

'I would say you are. I would say you're insinuating that I'm not competent to tend to Roger.'

'Not at all. I have as much faith as anyone in your medical skills.'

'Then what is the meaning of this unwarranted questioning

of my methods and – and, specifically, of the medication I wish to prescribe?'

For the first time since arriving at ffolkes Manor, the man from Scotland Yard seemed to be caught short for a suitable riposte. He puffed two or three times on his pipe before answering his interlocutor.

'Rolfe,' he said in a guarded tone, 'I'm here, as you know, in an unofficial capacity. I'm here, basically, because you all requested me to be here. You yourself, moreover, were the person who came to fetch me. Informal as my investigation has necessarily had to be, I did insist from the beginning that, if it was to be conducted at all, it would have to be conducted in accordance with the – well, with what I like to think of as the immemorial practices in application at the Yard.

'Now, it's a fact – a fact you've all had to come to terms with – that almost all of you are potential suspects in the murder of Raymond Gentry. In the light of what's just occurred, however, the case has taken on a whole new dimension, one whose significance none of you seems so far to have grasped.'

'A new dimension?' said Cora Rutherford.

'Well, Miss, just think about it. Since, as far as I can surmise, the attempt on the Colonel's life took place when all of you were in your rooms – and, yes, you don't have to remind me, I know quite well that, for what it's worth, you married couples all can and doubtless all will vouch for each other's presence during that period – but since, as I say, it took place when you were all out of sight, then almost all of you must equally be considered suspects in the attempted murder of Roger ffolkes.'

'But that's preposterous, quite preposterous!' exploded Rolfe. 'What is it you're suggesting? That one of us toddled up to our bedroom then at once slipped out of the house again in the howling snowstorm and took a potshot at the Colonel?'

'Somebody, Doctor, *somebody* took a potshot at the Colonel. Surely you would agree it could hardly have been other than the same somebody, the same fiendishly clever somebody, who took a potshot at Raymond Gentry inside a locked attic room?'

Since nobody seemed to have any plausible counter-argument to offer, he took their silence as meaning that they did all agree and continued:

'Now – to come back to what's to be done about the Colonel's present condition. Here we have you, Rolfe, one of the potential suspects – no more, I grant you, but also no less than anybody else in this room – here we have you telling me, cool as you please, that you'd like to have him carried up to his bedroom, where you would then give him an injection. That of course sounds all very right and proper, except that, as you must see, it would scarcely be advisable for me, even under circumstances as extraordinary as these, to let one of the suspects in a murder case inject some unknown fluid into the body of one of the murderer's victims. Especially as the very first question I shall naturally want to put to the Colonel when he regains consciousness is whether he *saw* and, more to the point, *recognised* his assailant.

'Answer me, Doctor,' he said imperiously. 'In your opinion as a professional man, just as I am in my own field, am I being unreasonable?'

Rolfe appeared initially to be on the point of making a protest. But when he did reply, it was in his usual cold, calm voice.

'No, Trubshawe, you aren't being unreasonable, save in a single respect.'

'And what is that?'

'You yourself have just described the person who murdered Gentry and – we must assume – also tried to murder the Colonel as a fiendishly clever fellow. Right?'

'Right.'

'Now, I ask you, how clever would it be of me to announce to all of you here – including a retired Scotland Yard detective – that I was going to give Roger a harmless injection then actually proceed to give him a lethal one? If anything were then to happen to the Colonel, as surely you can see, instead of a nice, juicy array of suspects, there'd be only one – yours truly.'

'Quite so,' said Trubshawe, 'quite so. That's exactly what I expected you to say. And it's a line of argumentation I have just one problem with.

'Not being a medical man myself, I would never be able to prove – to *prove*, Dr Rolfe, for where the law is concerned suspicion is nothing without proof – that such an injection was in fact responsible for inducing the – well, let's say the seeming heart attack to which the Colonel might later succumb.

'If a fatal heart attack *were* the outcome, it would of course look very bad for you. But, I repeat, I myself don't know enough about these matters to be sure that such an effect could positively and conclusively be traced back to such a cause. And, frankly, I don't fancy finding myself in that position, even though I'm here in an informal capacity. My duty hasn't changed, and I'd be derelict in that duty if I simply said to you, yes, go ahead, give him the shot, do as you think best. I'm sorry, but you must see the position I find myself in.'

Rolfe pondered this for a few minutes, glanced over at the Colonel lying stretched out on the couch, insensible to the argument which was raging about him, then once more addressed the Chief-Inspector.

'Yes, that all makes sense. But I too find myself in an awkward position. Whatever may be your doubts and misgivings, Trubshawe, I know what's right for my patient, and Roger is, and has been for many years, my patient, not yours. He must – I repeat, he *must* – be given morphine at once. If not, I cannot answer for the consequences. There might at the very least be a dangerously prolonged reaction to the physiological *and* psychological shock he's already suffered.'

He turned to Mary ffolkes, who had been intently following the debate.

'Mary, my dear,' he said, 'I'm going to have to leave the decision in your hands.'

'My hands?'

'The question is – do you trust me?'

'Trust you? Well, I . . . well, of course . . . Of course I trust you, Henry. You know I do.'

'No,' said Rolfe unexpectedly.

'No? But I just said yes.'

'No, Mary, I'm afraid that, in this case, that kind of hesitantly polite nod of approval isn't enough.'

'Oh dear, why must everything be so complicated?'

'Answer me yes or no, Mary,' said Rolfe. 'Do you trust me to give Roger the injection I'm convinced he needs if we hope to prevent an adverse metabolic reaction?'

Even though the look Mary ffolkes afforded him, one born of a long friendship, had already soundlessly answered his question, she also said in a voice designed to dispel any further doubt:

'Yes, of course I do, Henry. Please give Roger your full attention.'

While Madge Rolfe discreetly squeezed her wrist in thanks, the Colonel's wife now spoke to Trubshawe.

'Chief-Inspector, I do understand your caution – indeed,

I'm grateful for it – but I've known Henry Rolfe for many years both as a doctor and as a friend and I have no hesitation in entrusting my husband to his care. You will please allow him to go ahead.'

The policeman knew when he was beaten.

'Very well, Mrs ffolkes, I bow to you in this instance. It goes against all my professional instincts, but so be it. Your husband's health must come first.

'So,' he then said to Rolfe, 'now that that's settled, what's to be done?'

'First thing,' said Rolfe, 'is for one of you women to boil water – and plenty of it!'

'Boil water?' exclaimed Cora Rutherford. 'You know, Henry, I've often wondered why, whatever the ailment, you doctors always insist on having water boiled. What on earth do you get up to with the stuff?'

'Oh, for God's sake!' cried an exasperated Rolfe. 'Can't you just do what you're told to do and stop asking imbecilic questions!'

He turned to his wife.

'Madge? You I can rely on, can't I? Well, hot water – at once.'

Then to Trubshawe:

'We men, meanwhile, have to get Roger into his bed. Perhaps you and Don could help me carry him up to the bedroom?'

'Right. Let's get started, Don.'

Mary ffolkes endeavoured to raise herself to her feet.

'No, no,' said Trubshawe, wagging a finger at her, 'this time, Mrs ffolkes, you're following my orders. You've had a shock, you know, and you need as much rest as the Colonel does. And – and, well, I may as well tell you this now – there's something else I'm going to have to insist on.'

'You frighten me, Mr Trubshawe,' said Mary ffolkes feebly.

'There's no cause for that. All I was going to say was that, once your husband is comfortably settled, once he's had the, er, the knock-out potion, which should put him out for – for how long, Rolfe?'

'Oh, a good five or six hours.'

'Once he's out, I shall have to insist on locking the bedroom door.'

'I say, Inspector,' said the Vicar, 'that seems rather a drastic measure. Is it really necessary?'

'I think it is,' replied Trubshawe. 'After all, everybody's still a suspect and somebody has tried to kill the Colonel once already and I just don't believe his room should be left open to all comers.'

'But,' cried Mary ffolkes, 'locking poor Roger in! How awful! What if he should wake up and find he can't open the door?'

'Any chance of his prematurely coming to, Rolfe?'

'None at all.'

The Doctor took Mary's hand in his.

'You'll have to trust me in this too, Mary dear. I can

guarantee that Roger will sleep soundly for several hours. But if you're really worried, Trubshawe and I will look in on him every half-hour or so to make sure nothing's amiss. To be honest, it's a needless precaution but, if it reassures you, we'll be glad to take it. Now, Trubshawe, Don, let's get him into his bedroom.'

'Doctor?'

'Yes?'

'Anything else you need done?'

'If you'd really like to make yourself useful, Farrar, what you could do is go down to the kitchen and have Mrs Varley prepare some consommé for Mary.'

'Consommé?'

'Yes. Very thin and very hot.'

'Right.'

'Farrar?'

'Yes, Chief-Inspector?'

'I don't think it would be helpful for the servants to know what's just happened. With this second crime following so close on the first, there's a risk of them really getting the wind up. The last thing we need is a gaggle of sniffling, snivelling, moronic maids threatening to give notice.'

'Understood, sir. No mention of anything they shouldn't know about.'

'Good. Well, boys, let's get going. And again – right, Rolfe? – the word is *gently*.'

Half-an-hour later, after the Colonel's wound had been attended to, after he had been given his shot and lapsed into a peaceful slumber, Evadne Mount, who had now come back downstairs from her bedroom, took the opportunity of a moment's pregnant silence to arrest everyone's attention with just three words. Three Latin words.

'*Lux facta est.*'

'And what in heaven's name is that supposed to mean?' enquired Cora Rutherford.

'"*Lux facta est*"? Your Latin not up to scratch, Cora?'

'Never mind my Latin. Just answer the question.'

'It means "Light is shed". From *Oedipus Rex*. Sophocles, you know.'

'Thank you, dearie. But, yes, I do know who wrote *Oedipus Rex*.'

'Ah, but have you forgotten I rewrote it? With calamitous results! It was my very first play, *Oedipus vs. Rex*, and what I tried to do was retell the myth as a conventional courtroom drama. The defending counsel was Tiresias, the sightless seer – I was thinking of Max Carrados, you know, Ernest Bramah's blind detective? No? Anyway, it was he who proved, solely by his powers of deduction, that "the Oedipus case", as it was referred to throughout the play, was in reality a travesty of justice.

'The climactic twist, you see, was that Oedipus had been framed by his political enemies, who hadn't just spread the rumour that Jocasta was his mother but had themselves killed Laius, his alleged father. Then they substituted some hapless double to be murdered by Oedipus when they met each other at the crossroads of Daulis and Delphi.

'Well, what a dud, what a stinkeroony, what a pile of horse manure! The whole thing was done in masks and, if I'd had any sense, I'd have worn a mask myself! Poor "Boo" Laye – Evelyn Laye, you know, heavenly in intimate revue but, typically, fancied herself as a great dramatic actress – why won't they stick to the one talent they do have? – well, "Boo" Laye played Jocasta – rhymes with "disaster", I used to quip! – and when the audience began to boo us all at the curtain call, the poor, addlepated darling believed they wanted her to take a separate bow. I thought I'd die!'

'But why,' the actress persisted, 'has light been shed, as you so gnomically put it?'

The novelist fell suddenly serious.

'Why?' she said. 'I'll tell you why. Thanks to a chance remark made in this very room not upward of two hours ago, a bulb flashed on in my rapidly dimming old brain and I saw – I saw as though it had been illuminated by a bolt of lightning – exactly what has been happening here these past thirty-six hours.'

There was a silence while everyone absorbed this startling claim.

Then the Chief-Inspector, who had reverted to sucking on the stem of his unlit pipe, said:

'Let me get this straight. Just so there's no chance we're talking at cross-purposes, do I take it you're referring to Gentry's murder?'

'I am.'

'As well as the Colonel's attempted murder?'

'That too. Actually, it was the attempt on Roger's life which provided me with the very last piece of the jigsaw puzzle. A giant piece. Now I know the whole plot.'

'The whole plot, you say?'

'Even its twist. For, unless I'm mistaken, just like my Oedipus plot, this one does indeed have a climactic twist. I've been doing quite a bit of sniffing about, more than any of you realise, and, as I say, I now believe I'm in a position to lay the entire case out in front of you all.'

'Look here, Miss Mount,' grunted Trubshawe, 'if you do indeed possess certain facts – or theories – about this business, facts or theories of which we all ought to be apprised, me in particular, then let's have them. No more monkeying about, please. In your opinion – I repeat, in your *opinion*, for it is only an opinion – and I repeat yet again, with a different but no less relevant emphasis, in *your* opinion, for it is only yours – who killed Raymond Gentry and who tried to kill the Colonel?'

'Forgive me, Trubshawe, but I'm not ready to tell you yet.'

'What!'

'Oh, just let me explain. I'm not simply being a tease, you know. It all has to do with the difference between what you might call proposing and exposing. Don't you see, if I were baldly to announce who I believe did it, it would be like a maths teacher *proposing* a problem to his students, then instantly giving them the solution without in the meantime *exposing* any of the connective tissue which enabled him to arrive at that solution, connective tissue which would also enable those students of his to understand why it was the only solution possible.

'I want you all to understand why the person who I believe killed Gentry and tried to kill Roger could only be that person *and no other* – and to do that I've got to let the whole story unfold as I myself gradually came to understand it.'

'Well – well, all right,' replied Trubshawe with surprisingly good grace, 'I suppose that's fair enough. But just when *do* you intend to tell us?'

'Oh, now. At once. Immediately. But what I'd like is for all of us to gather again in the library. A criminal, so they say, always returns to the scene of the crime. So why shouldn't a detective – if I may flatter myself by appropriating such a label – not return to the scene of the investigation?'

For a few moments nobody said anything. Some of those present plainly thought the novelist had finally taken leave of the little that was still left of her senses. As for the others, though they would never willingly have owned up to it, even to themselves, they were perhaps obscurely tempted by the prospect of participating in a real-life rehearsal of the last – more accurately, last-but-one – chapter of a classic whodunit.

Then, finally, the Chief-Inspector gave his response to the proposal.

'There's one thing you seem to have forgotten,' he said. 'I haven't yet finished my own investigation.'

'Yes, you have,' retorted Evadne Mount. 'You've questioned all of us. All of us, that is, except Mary here, but I can't imagine you suspect her of trying to kill her own husband.'

'No, you're wrong.'

'What!' cried a horrified Mary ffolkes.

'Please, please, Mrs ffolkes, you misunderstand me. All I meant was that I haven't interviewed any of the servants.'

The novelist snorted.

'Speaking as someone who has just solved the mystery,' she said airily, 'I can unhesitatingly assure you that there wouldn't be the slightest use in your questioning them now.'

'We-ell,' said Trubshawe, still doubtful, 'if you really do believe you're in possession of all the facts . . .?'

'Actually, I don't believe it,' came the confident reply. 'I know it.'

Chapter Fourteen

Inside the library Evadne Mount faced the assembled company while everyone, even Trubshawe, still sucking on that long since extinct pipe of his, waited for her to start presenting her evidence. But when she finally did speak, what she had to say wasn't at all what anyone had expected to hear.

She turned to the Doctor's wife, who was unwrapping a new packet of Player's, and asked, 'Can I cadge, Madge?'

Madge Rolfe stared at her.

'What?'

'Can I cadge one of your nicotine lollies?'

'One of my . . .?'

'Your ciggies, dear, your ciggies.'

'I didn't know you smoked.'

'I don't,' answered the novelist.

She opened the packet which had been tossed into her lap and drew out a cigarette. Then, lighting up and taking what looked very much like a beginner's puff, she began.

'You must forgive me if I start off on a personal note,' she said with the complacent tone of someone who doesn't care a jot whether she's forgiven or not. 'But if there's one thing in this world I flatter myself I know how to do well, it's tell a story, and, assuming none of you minds, I'd like to tell this remarkable story of ours in my own words, at my own pace and without omitting any of my own – rare – misjudgments.

'It really has been the weirdest experience in my life, an experience that, had it not involved two brutal crimes, one of them committed against a close friend, I might even have enjoyed. Just think! Here we are, a group of suspects gathered together in the library to hear how and why a murder was perpetrated! It's a scene I've written so many times in my novels. Yet if any of you had told me that one day I myself wouldn't just be present at such a scene but would actually be playing the role of presiding sleuth, I'd have said you wanted your head examined!

'Of course,' she went on, directing her gaze on each of her listeners in turn to ensure that not one of them was paying her less than the attention she believed she deserved, 'like my own fictional detective, Alexis Baddeley, I'm no more than an amateur. And, as I don't have to remind you, I've never once had Alexis solve a locked-room crime. I like my whodunits to keep at least one foot on *terra firma*.

'I've never had any truck with murder methods involving ropes and ladders and pulleys and doorkeys yanked through keyholes on strings which somehow succeed in combusting of their own accord and murder victims found stabbed in the middle of the desert with nary a footprint in the sand, coming or going, or else hanging from a beam in a padlocked garret with no sign of a chair or a table or any item of furniture they could have climbed up on and not even a damp patch on the floorboards to suggest the murderer had used a block of ice which had since melted. I can't be doing with such contrivances. For me they're too darned *fangled*, to borrow the Colonel's delightful coinage.

'Anyway, John Dickson Carr has cornered that particular market and what I say is, if somebody's unbeatable, why bother trying to beat him?

'Sorry, I'm getting a bit carried away here, and I know you all think I'm a ghoulish old pussy, but I am coming to the point. And that point is that we were all so hypnotised by the *method* of Raymond's murder – a method none of us dreamt could ever exist outside a book – we just couldn't see the larger picture.

'Locked-room murders, you know, aren't unlike chess end-games. What I mean by that is that they bear about as much relation to real murders, murders committed by real people in the real world, as those end-games in the illustrated magazines – you know, a Knight and Pawn versus an unprotected Bishop to mate in five moves – well, as much as those end-games bear to the real strategies and configurations of a real game of chess. It's something my dear friend Gilbert has always understood, which is why he's the nonpareil genius he is.'

From the blank expressions that flitted from one face to another like a contagious yawn, it was clear nobody knew which Gilbert she was referring to. And since it was equally clear nobody liked to say so, she explained:

'Gilbert Chesterton. What makes his Father Brown stories so unique is precisely that they *are* end-games and they don't pretend to be anything but. By confining his clever little narratives to a dozen pages, he avoids having to articulate all that laborious plotline padding that a novelist like me needs to justify the dénouement. And his readers have the satisfying impression of being whisked straight to the climax of a full-length whodunit – the only part of it, to be honest, that really interests them – without having had to plough through the tedious exposition.

'The point, Miss Mount,' said Trubshawe, 'the point!'

'As I've said many times before in this very house,' she went on, conspicuously ignoring his interruption, 'if you really want to kill somebody and walk away scot-free, then just do it. Do it by pushing your victim off a cliff or else stabbing him in the back on a pitch-black night and burying the knife under a tree, any tree, any one of a thousand trees. Don't forget to wear gloves and be sure not to leave any incriminating traces of your presence behind you. Above all, eschew the fancy stuff. Keep it simple, boring and perfect. It may be all too simple, boring and perfect for us writers of mystery fiction, but it's the kind of crime whose perpetrator is likeliest to get away with it.'

'That's all very enlightening, I'm sure,' Trubshawe interrupted her again in a voice that was both suave and gruff. 'But when we agreed to join you in the library, it wasn't to hear your opinions on the difference between factual and fictional murders – opinions which, as you yourself have admitted, you've already voiced many times. Just where is this leading to?'

Evadne Mount frowned.

'Do learn to be patient with me, Chief-Inspector,' she replied gravely. 'I shall get there. I invariably do.'

She took another, more confident puff on her cigarette.

'So there we were – there *I* was – confronted with two murders, each of which was very different from the other in its method. One was, as the Chief-Inspector would put it, a "fictional" murder, patently committed by somebody who'd read a lot of whodunits – though not, I repeat, any of mine. And the other was a "real" murder, an attempt at a real murder, the kind of murder which is committed every day in the real world.

'For the first murder, Raymond Gentry's, there were almost too many motives. Apart from Selina here, everybody in our little party was secretly, and in some instances not in the least secretly, relieved to see him put out of commission once and for all.

'And the initial mistake I made was to persuade myself

236

that even among such a wide and motley range of suspects there were distinctions to be drawn. Nearly all of us had been the object of Gentry's malicious little smears. (There were exceptions and I'll come to these in a minute.) Which implied that, theoretically, nearly all of us had a good reason for wishing him dead. Nevertheless, what struck me initially, I repeat, was the existence, as I saw it, of two separate categories of suspects.

'There were those, on the one hand, for whom Raymond's revelations would have been utterly catastrophic were they to have turned up in *The Trombone*. Cora, for instance. As she herself was honest enough to point out to us, her career would be ruined if word, instead of mere rumour, began to circulate about her dependency on . . . on, shall we say, certain substances.

'Now, now, Cora, you don't have to look daggers at me, I fancy I know what you're itching to reply. Yes, it's perfectly so, there was one other such suspect, and that was me. My books, I unblushingly confess, have a vast readership, and even though they're all about murder and greed and hatred and revenge they're really rather genteel fictions read mostly by rather genteel people. If these genteel readers of mine were suddenly to find out that – well, I'd prefer to pass over in silence something you already all know about me – but, yes, I can imagine what effect that would have on my sales.'

Having manfully grasped the nettle of her own past sins, she was ready to launch herself back into the fray.

'There were also those, however, who, distressing as it must have been to hear once private squalors publicly aired, had nothing to fear from *The Trombone*. You, Clem, for one.

'It's true, unfortunately, that you played fast-and-loose with the facts of your wartime experience, and this has unquestionably been a Christmas you'll want to forget, and want all of us likewise to forget. Yet you yourself, if I remember aright, actually acknowledged that, whatever warped amusement Raymond Gentry took in distilling his poison, the yellow press was never going to give a tinker's curse for the white – or off-white – lies of a clergyman in an extremely modest living on Dartmoor.

'Then we come to our friends the Rolfes. It can't have been pleasant for either of you to see years and years of pretending to shrug off all those whispers as to what precisely transpired between Madge and some swarthy gigolo in Monte Carlo or how Henry botched what ought to have been a routine operation, curtailing not only a baby's life but his own career along with it. It can't have been pleasant, I say, to have all your face-saving efforts brought to naught in one fell swoop by Gentry's hateful muckspreading. But, again, like the Wattises, you were never prominent enough, and you're not prominent enough now, to interest the type of individual who'd read a piece of toilet paper like *The Trombone*.'

If, so far, all those present had listened more or less uncomplainingly to Evadne Mount argue her case, it wasn't that they were now serenely at ease with the notion that the most ignominious facts of their lives had become public knowledge. Each time she mentioned one of their names, there was a start, an audible gasp, even, on Mrs Wattis's part, a stifled tear. But the argument was so lucidly presented that, despite the renewed humiliations it brought in its wake, it felt like not only a duty but almost a pleasure to hear it out. What's more, the tension that had been screwed up so tight over the preceding thirty-six hours had had to find a release, and release of a kind was what she was slowly but surely giving her fellow guests.

'So you might have supposed, as I did at first,' she went on, 'that the only two legitimate suspects were Cora and myself. Who, after all, would commit a murder just because some dog-eared old dirt was going to be dished up in a village of a hundred or so inhabitants?

'Well, my answer to that would be – just about anybody! Oh, I saw the horror in your faces when Gentry started firing his lethal little darts, not just horror but homicidal loathing! And I soon realised how wrong I'd been in assuming that the craving for vengeance had to be commensurate with the degree of exposure.

'Frankly, it was a mistake I of all people should never have made. If I've set several of my books in a Home Counties village, it's because it offers the writer of whodunits a more fertile breeding-ground for murder than the most insalubrious back alley in Limehouse! You want to know what a sink of iniquity really looks like? I'll tell you. It has picturesque thatched cottages and Ye Olde Tea Shoppes and Women's Institutes and Conservative Associations and Bring-and-Buy Sales and Morris Dancing on the village green and Charity Fêtes in the Vicarage garden –'

'Oh come, Evadne,' the Vicar pooh-poohed mutinously, 'there you do exaggerate . . .'

'Sorry again, old bean, but I'm afraid that's bilge. You'll find this hard to credit, but I've actually had a bad review or two – there was one in the *Daily Clarion* I won't forget in a hurry,' she snarled, baring her fangish false teeth, 'yet not once has a reviewer criticised one of my novels for painting too dark and malignant a picture of rural life.

'Then there's my fan mail. Most of it's not from paying customers, who evidently believe that, having forked out seven-and-six for a book, they have no further obligation to its author, but from readers in villages who obtain my whodunits from their local circulating-library. I should let you read that fan mail. I recall one letter. It was from a little old lady in some idyllic hamlet in the Cotswolds telling me how she suspected the district nurse of slowly poisoning her crippled husband, and the sole basis of her accusation was that she'd chanced to catch the poor woman borrowing a copy of *The Proof of the Pudding*, which has exactly the same premise. And there was another, from somebody who'd read *The Timing of the Stew* and who was persuaded the stationmaster had read it as well, since his wife had vanished, supposedly run off with the coalman, but she, my fan, she knew better, she knew he'd buried both of them under the station's ornamental rockery.

'In the Detection Club we once coined a name for this sort of macabre village – Mayhem Parva. Well, I seriously doubt there's a single village in England's green and pleasant land that isn't a potential Mayhem Parva!

'So, Vicar, no, I don't exaggerate. I'm taking your case only as a general example, you understand, but it's my belief that a mild-mannered man of the cloth, as I know you to be, would be just as likely to commit murder to prevent his name from being besmirched at the local British Legion dinner-dance as a film star would be to prevent his or hers from being splashed across the front page of some nationally distributed scandal mag.

'And what that meant, of course, was that I immediately found myself right back where I started. I was obliged to regard nearly everybody present as equally suspect.

'Now for the exceptions. There was Selina, first of all, the only one of us to mourn Raymond's passing. She may have seen the light now – let's not forget the row they had in the attic – but I don't think any of us would have questioned the feelings she formerly had for the man. I ruled her out at once. She, it seemed to me, couldn't conceivably have killed him.

'Nor, I state without fear of contradiction, could her mother. I say that not only because she's one of my oldest and dearest and truest friends but because I know she's incapable of harming a fly. She's certainly incapable of harming a fly by trapping it in a locked room, swatting it to death, then managing to get out of said locked room again without opening either its door or its window!'

She beadily scanned her audience.

'To be sure, given the uncanny similarity between Raymond's murder and the kinds of murders that are routinely committed in whodunits, the very fact that Selina and Mary ffolkes were the least likely suspects may have caused some of you to wonder privately if perhaps one of them did it after all. Not me. As far as I was concerned, they really were the least likely suspects. They do exist.

'Donald, now. A different case, Donald. True, as far as any of us are aware, no skeletons lie lurking in the cupboard of his young life. Here, though, a more traditional motive raised its head. Jealousy. Don was in love with Selina – *is* in love with Selina – and he was visibly jealous of his rival. We all remember how they almost came to blows.

'Nor have we forgotten that Don actually threatened to kill Gentry. "I'll murder you, you swine, I swear I'll murder you!" We all heard him shout these words. Even if we sympathised with him and told ourselves that that's all they were, just words, the fact remains that, as the Chief-Inspector reminded us all, he swore to end the life of somebody who was indeed subsequently shot through the heart.

'Then poor Roger himself was shot and all of these

splendid theories of mine were thrown into confusion. For there seemed to be no motive at all for murdering him.'

She settled herself more comfily in her chair.

'In a whodunit, of course, there would have been at least one obvious motive – that Roger had discovered some crucial clue to the identity of Raymond's murderer and had to be put to death himself before he had a chance to share his knowledge with the authorities. But the circumstances of this case were so very special. Because Henry suggested we all be present throughout the Chief-Inspector's interrogation, everything said about the events leading up to Gentry's death was said in everybody's presence. I cannot recall a single occasion, prior to his taking his constitutional, when the Colonel was alone with one of us and might unknowingly have let slip some idle remark that put the murderer on his mettle.

'Yes, there were those twenty minutes or so which he spent with Mary, when we all retired to our bedrooms to dress and freshen up. But really, I don't think we need entertain for a second the notion that it was to his own wife that he passed on some damning item of evidence and that it was his own wife who later felt compelled to do away with him.'

Horrified that such a grisly conjecture had even momentarily crossed her friend's mind, Mary ffolkes looked up in reproachful surprise.

'Why, Evie,' she cried, 'how could you think such a thing!'

'Now, now, Mary love,' replied the novelist soothingly, 'I said exactly the opposite. I said I *didn't* think such a thing. You've already been told I don't suspect you. All I'm doing is hypothesising, ticking off one possibility after another, no matter how improbable.'

With a grimace of distaste, she stubbed her half-smoked cigarette into the ashtray as though squeezing the life out of an insect, muttered, 'Don't know what you see in 'em,' to Madge Rolfe and once more picked up the threads of her thesis.

'Well then, since the first murder had too many motives and the second no apparent motive at all, I was flummoxed. And that was when I decided instead to apply my "little grey cells" – if I may filch a conceit from one of my so-called rivals – to apply my "little grey cells" to the respective *methods* employed, in the hope that they might tell me something about the murderer's psychology.

'Concerning the first of these methods, the locked room, we all tended to make the same assumption, and who could blame us? We all took it for granted that Raymond's murder had been premeditated to the least detail. Which was, considering how fantastical it seemed, a fair assumption on our part.

'But there was one detail of that murder which, it suddenly occurred to me, could have been altered at any minute, even right up to the very last minute, without in any way compromising the whole diabolical scheme. *The identity of the victim.*'

Having talked non-stop, she needed to take another deep breath and, as she did, Trubshawe could be heard musing, 'H'm, yes, I think I begin to see what you're getting at.'

At this late stage of the proceedings, though, Evadne Mount was in no mood to share even a scintilla of limelight with anyone else. She continued more vigorously than ever:

'The other assumption that all of us made was that the second crime, so crude and clumsy in its execution, was in the nature of an afterthought, or at the very least something the murderer hadn't originally planned on. We all assumed, in other words, that the Colonel's shooting on the moors was an unforeseen consequence of Gentry's shooting in the attic.

'Then I had quite the brain-wave. What, I found myself thinking, *what if Gentry's murder, not the Colonel's, had been the afterthought?*

Now the whole library erupted.

'Oh, that's silly!'

'Well, but really! When the crime was so meticulously worked out!'

'This time, Evie, you've gone too far!'

'I said all along it was absurd to –'

'Oh, just hear me out, won't you!' she cried, silencing them with a single bark, like an infant blowing out all the candles on a birthday cake with a single puff.

'Look, all of you. Just suppose, for the sake of the argument, that it was the intention of somebody in this house to murder Raymond Gentry. Well, he pulled it off, didn't he? He got clean away with it. Raymond *was* murdered, and none of us, not excluding the Chief-Inspector here, had the slightest notion by whom. The criminal – I think, from now on, I'm going to call him, or of course her, X – the criminal, X, had achieved what he'd presumably set out to achieve.

'Why, then, did he or she next try to murder the Colonel? It doesn't add up. Especially as you all agree, don't you, that at no time did Roger drop any remark that might have made X decide he would have to die too. True, it was the Colonel who discovered Raymond's body. But Don was there, too, and no one has attempted to murder him.

'As for the idea that the two crimes might not be connected at all, well, I don't suppose any of us ever took that seriously. I know coincidences exist – if they didn't, we wouldn't need a word for them – but it's really too much to ask of the Law of Probability that the two men were both shot, within a mile or so of each other, within a few hours of each other, by two different murderers with two totally different motives!

'So why was the Colonel shot at? The more I mulled over the mystery, the harder it was for me to conceive of any logical reason why Raymond's murderer should *afterwards* want to kill Roger. At the same time, I gradually did begin to see at least one reason why Roger's murderer might have found himself tempted *in advance* to kill Raymond. I began to wonder, in short, whether it was Roger, not Raymond, who had always been X's destined victim.'

She gave her disturbing new twist to the plot a few seconds to sink in.

'And this suspicion of mine was actually strengthened by the page of notes that the Chief-Inspector found in the pocket of Gentry's bathrobe, notes, remember, which had been typed out on the Colonel's own typewriter.

'What everybody assumed was that these notes demonstrated beyond doubt that we were up against a blackmailer. As an author of whodunits, though, I was unimpressed from the outset by a clue left so nonchalantly for the police to put their hands on. If Raymond really had planned to blackmail us all, would he have sashayed about the house with the evidence of his villainy so handily poking out of his bathrobe pocket? And was it really necessary to compose such skimpy little notes on a typewriter? On Roger's typewriter to boot? Surely it would have been both simpler and safer to jot them down by hand? Unless, of course, and this was the crucial point, unless you were concerned *that your handwriting might be identified*. I wondered about all of that the moment those notes first turned up.

'Then Trubshawe let us all take a look at them.

'You may remember that, when I read them over a couple of times, something nagged at me for a good while afterwards that all was not as it should have been.

'Well, suddenly – thanks to Don here – I got it. I realised that I had seen something in the notes which confirmed what I was coming more and more to suspect – that it wasn't in fact Gentry who had typed them.'

'What did you see?' asked Trubshawe.

'What did I see? To be absolutely literal, it's what I didn't see which put me on the *qui vive*.'

'Oh, all right, Miss Mount,' said the policeman with the weary sigh of a parent agreeing to humour a child for the very last time. 'I'll play along with you. What *didn't* you see?'

'*I didn't see you*,' said Evadne Mount.

The Chief-Inspector gaped at her.

'Just what do you mean by that grotesque statement?' he growled.

'Pardon me,' answered the novelist, 'that was my whimsical side peeping out. I'll try to keep it under control. What I meant,' she said more soberly, 'was that I didn't see *u*. The letter *u*?'

Everyone looked at her in mystification.

'You all remember those notes. They weren't in shorthand, but in a kind of journalistic telegraphese. I recognised the style because I've been interviewed many, many times in my life and once or twice I've taken a peek at my interviewer's notepad.

'Well, consider what was written about Madge here. If you remember, it read "MR" – obviously Madge Rolfe –

248

then a dash – then the words (I'll omit the scurrilous adjective, which isn't relevant to my point) – then the words "misbehavior in MC" – "MC" standing naturally for Monte Carlo. Well, what finally dawned on me was that the word "misbehavior" was spelt without the letter *u*. That's what I meant when I said it wasn't what I saw in Raymond's notes that made me suspect the truth, it's what I didn't see. I didn't see *u*.'

Now she was almost grinning at her own artfulness.

'It's a very common misconception that having a blind spot necessarily consists of *not* seeing something that's in front of you. Sometimes, you know, it consists of seeing something that's *not* in front of you. We all saw that letter *u* because we all expected to see it, and it was only when Selina took so long to reappear from her bedroom and I heard Don say to her, "We've all been missing you" – *missing you* – the missing *u*? – that I finally understood what it was that had troubled me.

'Once I did understand it, however, I instantly realised what it meant. That's how "behaviour" is spelt by the Americans, without a *u*. Rotter that he was, Ray Gentry was also a journalist, and words were the tools of his trade. To me it was unthinkable he would ever have spelt the word that way.

'Those of you who've seen my play *The Wrong Voice* will know how significant language and its misuse can be in a whodunit. If you recall, the murder victim is a schoolteacher whose dying words, after he swallows a whisky-and-soda laced with arsenic, are "But it was the wrong voice . . ." Now everybody assumes, naturally, that what startled him was the *identity* of the speaker whose voice he'd just heard. Only Alexis Baddeley realises that, as an English master, he is in reality alluding to his *grammar*.

'While cradling the victim in his arms, that speaker had cried out, "My God, he has been taking ill!" Where a genuine Englishman would have used the passive voice – "he has been *taken* ill" – he used the active voice, thereby revealing that he wasn't a genuine Englishman, which was what he was pretending to be, and that he was ultimately the murderer.'

There ensued a momentary silence. Then, of all people, Don spoke – Don, who hadn't yet uttered a syllable, even when Evadne Mount had reminded everyone of his threat to kill Raymond Gentry. Which is why, when he now did choose to speak up, his voice, almost unrecognisably raspy with resentment, shattered the silence like a gunshot.

'Yeah, the murderer. Like me, you mean?'

The novelist stared at him. A web had formed on his forehead of tiny patches of nervous dampness.

'What's that you say, Don?'

'Oh come on, ma'am, you know what –'

'Evadne,' said the novelist softly, 'Evadne.'

'Evadne . . .'

Not himself for the moment, he pronounced her name as awkwardly as though it were a tongue-twister.

'You don't have to deny what you're thinking, what you're all thinking. Only an American could have written those notes and I'm the only American here.'

'Don darling, nobody thinks you wrote them!' cried Selina, giving his thigh an affectionate squeeze. 'Tell him, Evadne. Tell Don you don't suspect him.'

'Oh yes she does,' he said sullenly. 'You all do. I can see it in your faces.'

'Don?' said Evadne Mount.

'Yeah?'

'Are you a reader of whodunits?'

'What?'

'Are you a reader of whodunits?'

'Heck, no,' he answered after a few seconds. 'Frankly, I can't stand 'em. I mean, who cares who killed –'

'All right, all right,' the novelist testily cut him off. 'You've made your point.'

'Sorry, but you did ask,' said Don. Then, perhaps emboldened by the realisation that he had found a chink in her hitherto impregnable armour, he added, 'Say, why *did* you ask? What's *your* point?'

'My point is this. If you *were* a reader of whodunits, you'd know enough to give the matter a little more thought before accusing me of accusing you. And if you *had* given the matter a little more thought, you would soon have realised you aren't the only suspect just because you're the only American.'

'I don't get you. How come?'

'Well, Cora, for instance –'

'You know, Evie darling,' drawled the actress, 'it would be terribly, terribly sweet if, just once, I wasn't the first "for instance" to pop into your head.'

'Where these crimes are concerned, Cora, we've all had to get used to being "for instances". Anyway, as I was about to say, after taking London by storm in the stage version of *The Mystery of the Green Penguin*, Cora was snapped up – I believe that's the expression – was snapped up by Metro-Goldwyn-Mayer and lived for the next two years in Hollywood. Unfortunately, as Raymond reminded us with his usual gallantry, she didn't quite rise to the occasion' – now she held up her right hand like a traffic policeman to prevent her friend from interrupting again, as was all too visibly her intention.

'But even if things failed to work out for her altogether satisfactorily,' she went on, 'during those two years it may well have become second nature to her to spell as the Yanks do.

'Then there are the Rolfes, who lived for several months in Canada before Henry's misadventure in the operating-theatre brought him and Madge back, via the Riviera, to dear old England. Now correct me if I'm wrong, but I've always understood that the Canadians spell the American way, not the British.

'Nor,' she said, 'if we're going to be absolutely logical, can we even rule out Clem.'

'Me?' cried the Vicar. 'Why, I – I've never been to America in my life!'

'No, Clem, but you did admit that you couldn't spell for toffee. Well, it's not impossible, I'm sure you'll agree, that the word "misbehaviour" was misspelt for no other reason than that it was typed by someone who simply didn't know how to spell.

'So you see, Don, dear – that missing *u* doesn't significantly reduce the number of suspects.'

'Now just a godd**n minute, Evie!' Cora Rutherford suddenly shouted at her. 'I wish you'd stop treating us all as though we were in one of your cheap novelettes. I did very, very well in Hollywood, very respectably – what am I saying, more than respectably, much more than respectably! I was in *Our Dancing Daughters* with Joan Crawford and *The Last of Mrs Cheyney* with lovely, lovely Norma Shearer.'

'Yes, Cora, I know you were. All I meant was –'

'Anyway, who's to say you didn't write those notes yourself? Who's to say you didn't deliberately spell "misbehaviour" without the *u*, just to throw the rest of us off the scent? Your cardboard characters get up to that sort of fakery-pokery all the time!'

'Bravo, Cora!' cried the novelist, clapping her hands. 'Congratulations!'

'Congratulations?' the actress warily echoed the word. 'Why do I always get a teensy bit suspicious when somebody like you congratulates somebody like me?'

'You shouldn't. I intended it sincerely. For you're spot on. I might well have done just that. I didn't, of course, I didn't do any such thing. But, yes, the possibility that I might have done it keeps me up there as one of the suspects.'

'All right, ladies,' said Trubshawe. 'Now that both of you have had your say, could we please return to the matter at hand?'

'Certainly, Chief-Inspector, certainly,' Evadne Mount acquiesced with a grace that might have been mock but might also have been authentic.

'Where was I? Oh yes. The planting of those bogus notes in Raymond's pocket not only confirmed for me that there was something extremely fishy about the whole business but reinforced my growing conviction that X's true objective was the Colonel's death.

'Then, finally, it came to me.

'It had, I believed, been X's plan all along to kill the Colonel by luring him into the attic and shooting him there. And he would have carried out that plan to the letter if Selina hadn't, at the eleventh hour, invited home a piece of human slime – forgive me, my dear,' she put it gently to Selina ffolkes, 'but I think you know he was – a piece of human slime who, on that unforgettably horrid Christmas Night of ours, managed in just a few hours to turn everybody in the house against him.

'We all felt like murdering Raymond – I know I did – but, at some stage in the evening, X must have realised that he alone had not one but *two* reasons for murdering him. Don't forget – if I'm right, he had already plotted the Colonel's murder to the last detail. But what, I imagine him saying to himself, *what if I were to switch victims?* What if I were to murder Raymond *instead of* the Colonel? Or rather, what if I were to murder Raymond *and then* the Colonel?

'Not only would the police assume that the first of these two murders, Raymond's, was also the first in a more profound sense, the more significant murder, the really relevant one, the one on which all the ensuing investigations would focus. But, and this must have been for our killer the "clincher", as they say, Raymond's murder would also generate *a whole new set of potential suspects* – suspects *and* motives – unlike the Colonel's murder, for which there was likely to be only one suspect and one motive.'

There was no question, and she knew it, that Evadne Mount had her circle of listeners where she wanted them. They were literally hanging on her every word, held under the spell of her personality, and she would have been something less than human if she hadn't gloated just a little.

'Think of it,' she said with an impudently undisguised air of self-congratulation. 'X, whose ultimate intention it is to kill the Colonel, decides to commit another murder first, a murder designed to cast the shadow of suspicion away from himself and on to a half-dozen entirely new suspects, virtually all of whom had a motive for doing away with Raymond Gentry. Suspects, I might add, so classic, so traditional, they could all have come straight out of, or indeed gone straight into, a typical Mayhem Parva whodunit.

'Just try to imagine X's glee at finding himself presented with such a perfect collection of red herrings. The Author. The Actress. The Doctor. The Doctor's Wife, who naturally has a Past. The Vicar, who also has a Past. Or rather, unfortunately for him, who *doesn't* have a Past. The Colonel. The Colonel's Wife. And finally, bringing up the rear, the Romantic Young Beau, who, like all Romantic Young Beaux, is head-over-heels in love with the Colonel's Daughter.

'And, yes, I say red herrings and I mean red herrings. For that, I'm afraid, is exactly what we all were – pure flim-flam, as irrelevant to what was really afoot as one of those utterly pointless ground-plans which some of my rivals insist on having at the beginning of their whodunits and which only the most naïve of readers would ever think of consulting.'

Evadne Mount stopped, for a fraction of a second, to catch her breath again.

'However,' she continued, 'convinced as I was that I'd hit upon the truth, I knew that my hunch could not hope to be more than that, a mere hunch, unless and until I was able to corroborate it with real factual evidence. So I decided at last to re-direct those perhaps not-so-little grey cells of mine to the problem that had baffled us all from the start –

the question of exactly how Gentry's murder was done the way it was done.

'In *The Hollow Man* John Dickson Carr actually interrupts the narrative of his novel to lecture his readers on all the principal categories of locked-room murders. Since I couldn't call to mind off-hand what these were, I came looking for the book in this very library. Roger, alas, has never been an aficionado of detective fiction and, apart from a complete collection of my own efforts, all gifts from me, all unread, I'm certain, there was nothing. No Dickson Carr, no Chesterton, no Dorothy Sayers, no Tony Berkeley, no Ronnie Knox, no Margery Allingham, no Ngaio Marsh, not even Conan Doyle! Quite, quite scandalous!

'I racked my brains and racked my brains, but the only two locked-room stories whose solutions I myself remembered, Israel Zangwill's *The Big Bow Mystery* and Gaston Leroux's *The Mystery of the Yellow Room*, had recourse to the selfsame trick, which was to have the murderer barge into a locked room – and then, *and only then*, before anybody else has arrived, have him stab the victim, who was alive up to that very instant.

'Well, that was no help at all. Roger did indeed barge into the attic, but Don was at his side. Each saw what the other saw and unless, most implausibly, they were in cahoots – what, by the way, *is* a cahoot? – neither could have killed Gentry on the spot.

'I was resolved, though, not to let myself be led astray by

the outlandish circumstances of the crime. A man lay dead inside a locked room. There was no magic, no voodoo, no hocus-pocus about it. The thing had been done and hence it could be undone. And the only way left for me to undo it, I realised, was to indulge in a little personal sleuthing at the scene of the crime.

'So earlier, you recall, when I asked the Chief-Inspector if I might have leave to go to my bedroom and change out of my wet clothes, what I actually did first was sneak up to the attic.'

The instant she made this brazen admission, nobody could resist stealing a glance at Trubshawe, who was plainly torn between admiration for his rival's deductive powers and aggravation at her self-confessed indifference to one of the most widely publicised ground-rules governing any criminal investigation.

'Miss Mount,' he said, shaking his head in disbelief, 'I really am rather disturbed to hear you make such a statement. You knew very well that, till the local police arrived and a proper forensic examination had been carried out, nobody, not even the bestselling author of I don't know and I don't care how many whodunits, had permission to enter that attic room.'

'I did know that,' she calmly replied, 'and I apologise. Notwithstanding my public legend as the Dowager Duchess of Crime, I'm an extremely timorous soul when it comes to breaking the law.

'My fear, however, was that before the police turned up

– and what with the snow-storm and all, none of us had any idea how long that was going to be – the attic could very easily be tampered with. Remember, I was convinced the murderer was among us. What was to stop him or her taking advantage of some lull in the proceedings, just as I did, and slipping upstairs to remove a piece of hitherto unnoticed evidence?'

'What! Well, I . . .' Trubshawe fulminated. 'So you admit that's what you did do?'

'I admit nothing of the kind. I did not remove a single object from the room. All I meant was that the ease with which I – an innocent party, I do assure you – the ease with which I got in and out of it could also have been exploited by the murderer himself.'

'I give up!' said the Chief-Inspector helplessly. 'At least can I assume you didn't touch anything?'

'No-o-o,' said the novelist. Then she added coyly, 'Not much.'

'Not much!'

'Oh, hold on to your corset, Trubshawe. When you learn what I found out, you'll agree it was well worth it.'

She turned to address the entire company.

'Now the one thing everybody said about that attic room was that it was empty. An empty room, that's what the Colonel said, what Don said, what everybody said. But it wasn't empty at all, it was by no means bare. There was a wooden table with two drawers, a rickety upright chair – the plain cane-bottomed type that always makes me think of Van Gogh – and a ragged old armchair. It also had a window and a door and bars on the window and a key in the keyhole of the door. So though it was pretty austere – and made even more sinister, I can tell you, by the presence of Gentry's dead body – there was still some scrawny meat for me to gnaw on.

'And I really *worried* at that room! I examined absolutely everything in it, even things I suspected weren't worth examining.

'First, I examined the floor more thoroughly than I'd been able to do this morning, and I noted once more how dust-free it was for a room which had supposedly been unused for months. Remember, Trubshawe, that was the minor oddity I tried to direct your attention to?

'Then I examined the door itself to see whether it could have been removed from its hinges and, after the murder, hinged back on again. But that, I soon realised, was ridiculously impractical. Even if the door was hanging half off those hinges, thanks to the combined strength of Don and the Colonel, it was obvious it had never, ever been removed.

'Then I examined the bars on the window to see whether maybe *they* could have been removed. Quite out of the question. They were caked with rust, both of them. I seriously doubt they've been tampered with since they were originally installed.

'Then I examined the table. Not a sausage. Nothing in either drawer. No hidden partitions. It was just an ordinary wooden table, scratched and chipped, like a thousand others in a thousand other lumber rooms.

'Then, when I was about to pack it in, I sat down in the armchair to take the weight off my feet – and that's when it hit me, when it literally hit me!' she boomed out, startling everybody with one of those deafening guffaws of hers.

'Are you telling us,' said the Chief-Inspector, 'you know how the crime was committed?'

'Not only how it was committed but who committed it. In this case, if you know how, you know who.'

'Well, for God's sake, will you let the rest of us in on it!' Madge Rolfe all but screamed at her. 'Why must you leave us dangling like this? It's really intolerable!'

'Sorry, Madge,' replied the novelist. 'I've grown so accustomed, as a writer of mystery fiction, to spinning out the suspense that here I am doing it for real. You see, we've arrived at the first of those pages of a whodunit when the reader, who, I hope, will already be keyed-up, starts to get downright edgy. After all, he has invested a good deal of time and energy in the plot and he just can't bear the thought that the ending might be a let-down, either because it's not clever enough or else it's too clever by half. At the same time, he has to remind himself not to let his eye stray too far ahead for fear of inadvertently catching sight of the murderer's name before he reaches the sentence in which it's revealed by the detective.

'Actually,' she dreamily elaborated on her favourite theme, unmindful of the agonised impatience of her listeners, 'to turn the screw even tighter, I used to reorganise my pagination with the printers. It drove my publishers crazy, but I'd add a couple of paragraphs here or else delete a couple of lines there, just so that the detective's declaration "And the murderer is . . ." would sit at the very foot of a page and the reader would have to turn that page before he was able to discover, at the top of the next one, who the murderer actually was.

'But then, you know, new editions are brought out – my books generally run into many editions – the original layout goes to pot – and all my time and trouble –'

'I swear,' Cora Rutherford hissed at her, 'I swear on my dear old mum's eternal soul that if you don't get back on track, Evadne Mount, there'll be a second murder inside this house! And, as I'm certain Trubshawe here will back me up, no jury would ever convict me!'

'Very well, but I do insist you let me go on in my own inimitable fashion.

'Take your minds back to early this morning. On some pretext or other, probably by dangling a choice morsel of gossip before him, X entices Raymond Gentry into the attic and shoots him at point-blank range through the heart. The Colonel, who's running his bath, hears the shot, as we all do, followed by a blood-curdling scream. On his way up to investigate, he runs into Don, whose bedroom is situated nearest the stairs. Because the room is locked – bizarrely, from the inside – they stand in front of it for a little while uncertain what to do. And it's then the Colonel notices a trickle of blood oozing out of the attic on to the landing. So they realise they've just got to get in.

'Putting their shoulders to the door, they eventually succeed in opening it – and the first thing they see is Raymond's dead body. Yet, horror-stricken as they are at the sight of the corpse, they do have the presence of mind to give the whole room a good examination. Nothing. Or rather, nobody. It's a very small room containing next to no furniture and both of them swear it was unoccupied. Am I right, Don?'

'Yeah, that's how it was.'

'So what do they do next? Because they can already hear the household starting to stir, and because they're both determined to prevent Selina from even so much as glimpsing Raymond's body, they rush back down into the hallway, where we're all shambling about in our dressing-gowns wondering what in heaven's name is going on. Which is when the Colonel, as you all remember, broke the terrible news to Selina as humanely as he knew how.

'That, you agree, is what was happening in the hallway. What meanwhile was happening inside the attic?

'For the very last time I invite you to review the scene. The Colonel and Don have both retreated downstairs. The attic door is hanging half off its hinges. Raymond's body is still shoved up tight against the door, still oozing blood. The only other objects in the room are the table, the upright chair and the armchair.'

Her voice dropped to a husky whisper.

'What I venture to suggest happened next is that – if I can phrase it this way – *the armchair suddenly stood up on its hind legs.*'

Everybody in the library gasped in unison. It was almost as though she had *spoken* in italics, almost as though they could feel the hairs stand up on the napes of their necks, almost as though those hairs, too, were in italics.

As for Chief-Inspector Trubshawe, he was scrutinising the novelist with a queer expression on his face, an expression intimating that his irritation at her unorthodox methods, as also at the torrential verbosity with which she had been exposing them, had now capitulated to unconditional admiration for the results they had produced.

'You don't mean . . . ?' he said.

'I do mean,' she replied calmly. 'The murderer had concealed himself or herself *inside* the armchair. That's undoubtedly why Gentry's body had been pushed up against the door – to make it even harder for anyone to break in and so gain for X a few more valuable seconds in which to conceal himself.

'Hunched inside that armchair, having already committed the murder, it was X, don't you see, not Raymond, who was responsible for the blood-curdling scream we all heard. For his plan to work, it was essential to call our immediate attention to the crime.

'Then, as soon as the coast was clear, Roger and Don having quit the attic to let us know what they'd discovered, he – or, I repeat yet again, she – quickly and quietly clambered out of the chair, patted everything back into place, stepped over Gentry's body and nipped down to the hallway.

'Given the pandaemonium reigning in that hallway, it would have been child's play for him or her to mingle unobserved with the rest of us. *Et voilà!*

There was the briefest of pauses. Then Trubshawe spoke again.

'May we know,' he asked, 'how you arrived at that – I do have to say – very persuasive conclusion?'

'Easy,' said Evadne Mount. 'I told you that I sat down on the armchair. I also told you that that was when it hit me. I even added, to be extra-helpful, the word "literally".

'The fact is, when I did sit down, the bottom of the chair instantly gave way under me – so much so that my own rear end hit the floor with an embarrassingly hefty thud. But even as I was feeling a very foolish old biddy indeed, my two stockinged legs slicing the air like a pair of scissors, I knew I'd found the solution. And once I'd managed to extricate myself, I set to examining the insides of that chair. As I expected, the whole thing had been hollowed out so that, like some monstrous glove puppet, it could actually accommodate a crouching human body. And that, I realised, was how and where the murderer was concealed.'

'Very neat,' murmured the Chief-Inspector. 'Very, very neat.'

'Do you mean X for having devised such a method,' enquired Evadne Mount, 'or me for having discovered it?'

Trubshawe smiled.

'Both, I guess. But hold on,' he added, a new idea occurring to him. 'You said that the instant you knew how it was done, you also knew who'd done it. What did you mean by that?'

'Oh, Inspector, now there you do disappoint me. I really believed you at least would understand the most significant implication of my discovery.'

'Well,' he answered, 'I must be stupid – I *am* retired, you know – but I don't.'

In the ensuing silence a clear young voice rang out.

'I think I do,' said Selina.

'Then why don't you share your thoughts with us, my dear?' the novelist said benignly.

'We-ell . . . it strikes me this way. We – I mean, Mummy and Daddy's house-party – we all got here only two days ago, Ray, Don and I last of all. If what you say is correct, then none of us could have been the murderer because none of us would have had either the time or the opportunity to scoop out that armchair or whatever it was the murderer did to it.'

Evadne Mount beamed at her with the gratified air of a school-mistress congratulating an especially smart pupil.

'Right first time, Selina!' she cried. 'Yes, it's absolutely true. Once I realised how incredibly well prepared Gentry's murder must have been, how far in advance it had to be set up, I knew that not one of you – I should say, not one of *us* – could have committed the crime.

'No, the only person who could have done it was some-body who was here already. Somebody who saw and heard everything yet said nothing or next to nothing. Somebody who is among us now yet not among us. Somebody who is present yet almost transparent.'

Her eyes narrowed behind the glinting pince-nez. Then, in what can only be described as an eerily *silent* voice, she said:

'You know who you are. Why don't you speak up for yourself?'

On hearing that question, I decided, without an instant's hesitation, to do what she asked. For I understood – indeed I think I'd understood ever since I'd failed to kill the Colonel – that it was all over for me.

Chapter Fifteen

'Farrar!?' Mary ffolkes half-whispered, half-shrieked.

It's amazing how foolish you feel, standing in front of a group of people, people you're personally acquainted with, clenching a revolver in your fist and forcing yourself to cry 'Hands up!' or some-such corny line as though you were in a third-rate play or picture-show. From the moment I rose from my chair in the library it was as much as I could do to keep from giggling.

Mary ffolkes continued to stare at me in disbelief, her hands twitching, her eyelids flickering nervously.

'You, Farrar? You tried to kill Roger?'

I no longer had any reason to hold back. It came as an immense relief to be able to open up at last. It felt good to speak in the first person again. If I'd said so little during the past twelve hours, it wasn't that I'm the taciturn type by nature, just that I'd had to be exceptionally careful not to give myself away.

'Yes, Mrs ffolkes,' I replied, 'I tried to kill Roger.'

I strained to keep my voice as matter-of-fact as possible.

'You see,' I explained, 'the advantage of my position in your household was that, if I wasn't upstairs, everyone assumed I must be downstairs, and vice versa. So no one ever really missed me. When your husband sent me down to find out what was happening in the kitchen, I hung about for ten minutes or so, standing at the big bay window and pretending to listen to the servants' chatter. Then I saw the Colonel walk past the monkey-puzzle tree. I slipped out of the house, caught up with him, shot him and returned before anyone, upstairs or downstairs, had time to notice I'd been gone.'

I now addressed Trubshawe.

'I'm truly sorry, old man, about Tobermory, but you yourself realised I couldn't allow him to live. When the Colonel fell, he set up such a howling . . .'

'But I don't understand,' said Mary ffolkes. 'I don't understand.'

The poor uncomprehending woman looked at Selina, at Evadne Mount, at the Rolfes, at seemingly everyone but me, as though the solution to the mystery might be reflected on their faces instead of mine. She reminded me of the one guest at a dinner party who hasn't 'got' an off-colour joke which has everyone else splitting their sides and is hoping that, if she peers into their eyes for long enough, it's bound to dawn on her at last.

'Roger and I were always so kind to you. We never, ever

treated you as one of the servants. You were almost like the son we never had.'

This was the scene I'd feared. The Colonel had deserved to die, in that I'd never wavered, but his wife didn't really deserve to find out why.

'It's strange,' I replied almost wistfully, though still clutching my revolver. 'They say vengeance is a dish best eaten cold. I'm not so sure. I've been so hungry for vengeance all my adult life, year after year of it, that there were times my mouth would literally water at the prospect of exacting it. Yet now, all these years later, when I have exacted it, more or less, I can't claim that – that I've *gorged* on it as I expected I would. And I don't just mean because I didn't succeed in killing the Colonel.

'Mrs ffolkes, the longer I stayed in your husband's service, the fonder I got to be of the old guy and the more I had to remind myself he was the man who did me wrong so many years ago. I'm even finding it hard to regret I didn't kill him. And if you find that just as hard to believe, don't forget I've got a set of duplicate keys to every door in the house. I could easily have snuck into his bedroom and finished him off before he'd a chance to give Trubshawe a few interesting facts about his life in America, facts that would have led the police directly to me. Yet I chose not to.

'As for Raymond Gentry,' I added, 'well, that's a different story. No one will convince me I didn't do the world a service by removing him from it.'

I could see that the Chief-Inspector was champing at the bit to give me the usual party piece about my being under no obligation to make a statement but anything I did say – well, you know the rest. But I was set on having my own say first. I meant to be heard. I'd kept silent for too long.

As it happens, we were both of us pipped at the post by Evadne Mount.

'So you do have a voice, young man,' she said, 'as well as a pretty turn of phrase. You know, I've had my eye on you for some time. Not that I realised right from the beginning you'd done it or anything like that. It was just that I found you – well, really rather fascinating.'

'Me? Fascinating?' I won't deny I was flattered. 'Why?'

'You're something I never thought to encounter. The perfect factotum. You were always there when you were needed and never when you weren't. Everywhere yet nowhere, present yet anonymous, omniscient yet invisible. Attentive to everything that was going on, everything that was said and done, as though you were recording it, taking it all down, mentally taking it all in. Your eyes never met any of ours and you almost never spoke – and even when you did, *not once*, unless I'm very much mistaken, in the first person. You missed nothing and you contributed nothing. You practically never intervened and you absolutely never interfered. As for your – with respect – your utterly nondescript features, and your even more nondescript clothes, well, they made you, as I say, almost transparent. If I weren't afraid of outraging the Vicar, I'd be tempted to compare you to God.'

'Like God I never lied,' I said.

'Come now,' she murmured. 'Once, surely?'

'Once?'

'Your name. Since your motive was vengeance, and since vengeance, if my experience is anything to go by, inevitably necessitates some form of subterfuge, I'll lay ten to one it isn't Farrar.'

She was uncanny. I couldn't help smiling at her.

'Bravo, Miss Mount. No, it isn't Farrar.'

'May we know what it is?'

'I *want* you to know what it is. Otherwise what I've done would become meaningless.'

I took a deep breath.

'My name is Murgatroyd. Roger Murgatroyd.'

Mary ffolkes gazed at me in astonishment.

'Roger? Why, Roger's the same name as . . . as Roger . . .'

'I was named after him. Your husband was – I mean, he is – my godfather.'

'You were named after him? And yet you . . .'

She buried her face in her hands and burst into convulsive sobs. For her it seemed it was my attempt to kill someone whose name I shared that was the truly heinous crime. And because I was starting to feel sincerely sorry for her I didn't care to remind her that, even though he may have treated me like a son, it had never occurred to the Colonel to address me other than by my – pseudonymous – surname. Or show the slightest interest in my family or my background, which of course suited me fine as his future murderer – or would-be murderer – yet, I can't deny, obscurely offended me as a human being.

'No,' I continued, 'my name isn't Farrar. But then, your husband's name isn't ffolkes and he's as much a Colonel as the Vicar was an Army padre.'

Trubshawe was now clearly feeling it ever more incumbent on himself to reclaim the authority that was rightly his in a criminal matter.

'Look here, Murgatroyd,' he said to me in what he must have hoped was the ineffably reasonable voice of British officialdom, 'we can surely talk this over without the gun – which is, I assume, the murder weapon. You're not going anywhere with it, are you, so you may as well put it down.'

'I don't think so,' I replied. 'Not for the moment. Not until I've decided what to do next.'

'Now listen,' he went on, 'I won't insult your intelligence by pretending you're not up for the chop. I know it and you know it. But from the way you've been talking, you don't strike me as – well, as a natural-born killer. So what's the use of behaving as though you were? Eh? Aren't I right?'

I looked down at the loaded gun.

'You know why I'm not going to put down this revolver?' I said after a while. 'Because it guarantees me an uninterrupted hearing. It acts like a microphone. Except that, instead of magnifying *my* voice, it forces you to lower *yours*.

'So, just for now, I'll go on speaking through it and I suggest you all go on sitting where you are and not moving more than you have to.'

'I was right!' cried Evadne Mount. '"To speak through a revolver" – you *do* have a pretty turn of phrase. Young man, you could have been a writer.'

'Thanks. Matter of fact, I am a writer. Or let's say I was a writer.'

'*Who are you, Roger Murgatroyd?*'

It was Mary ffolkes who shot the question at me, without warning but now also without a trace of agitation in her voice.

'Let me give you a clue, Mrs ffolkes,' I answered. 'My father was Miles Murgatroyd. That name mean anything to you?'

'Why, no,' she said, confused once more. 'I'm – I'm afraid I never heard it before. It's a very unusual, very distinctive name. I'm sure I would have remembered it if I had.'

I found myself believing her.

'It doesn't surprise me. What I have to tell you happened a long, long time ago. You'd never even met the self-styled Colonel.'

'The self-styled . . .' she began. Then her voice trailed off into nothingness and she fell tremulously silent again.

'There's no polite way of putting this, Mrs ffolkes. You've got to know that, in his younger days, your husband was what they call a confidence man.'

'That's a lie!' screamed Selina.

'I'm sorry, Miss Selina,' I said as gently as I could, for I'd always had a soft spot for her. 'But it's God's truth, I swear. Your father's real name wasn't Roger ffolkes, it was Roger Kydd. He started his career, if that's the word I'm looking for, playing dominoes for cash on the London-to-Brighton train line. Then he graduated to the three-shell scam on Bournemouth Pier and, when my father met him, he'd just done a two-year prison stretch for forging cheques – a stretch in Dartmoor, ironically enough – and he was eking out a miserable living trying to pick the pockets of toffs waiting for cabs in front of the Ritz. My father had stopped in Piccadilly to light his Woodbine, he put his hand in his pocket for a match and he found Kydd's hand already in there. Instead of turning him in, though, my father, who I think was something of a soft touch, decided to take him under his wing.

'Remember,' I said to the Chief-Inspector, 'when you and the Colonel had your private little chat in this very room, he mentioned that there was a Priest's Hole in the house. Well, I had actually concealed myself inside that Priest's Hole, and when I heard him go on to talk about what he'd gotten up to in his youth and I realised he was on the point of revealing his true name, I immediately ran out of the secret passage into the corridor and interrupted him by knocking at the door. Fortunately, I was already dressed, like the rest of the staff, so I hadn't had to go to my bedroom to change.

'I wanted to silence him temporarily before I got the chance to silence him once and for all. If Scotland Yard ever learned who he really was, it would have been the easiest thing in the world for them to trace his connection to Miles Murgatroyd, which I naturally couldn't let happen.

'You see,' I went on, 'after the two of them had managed to patch over the awkward business of Roger Kydd trying to pick his pocket, my father decided to throw in his lot with him and they left Britain together to make their fortune in the States. For five years they prospected the Alaskan gold fields, five long, hard years when they lived on bacon and baked beans and became the closest of pals. Naturally, when my father got married, Kydd was his best man. And naturally, when I was born, he became my godfather.

'Then, just when everything seemed to be going right at last, it actually all started to go wrong.'

'What do you mean by that?' Trubshawe asked.

'I mean that my father and "the Colonel" – I guess it would be simpler if I just went on calling him that – my father and the Colonel finally hit pay-dirt. A deep seam of riverbed gold in a valley in north-west Alaska. I have this memory of my mother clutching a telegraph in her hands and shouting at me that we were going to be rich!

'Except that we hadn't reckoned on the Colonel's chicanery and greed. I am sorry, so very sorry, Mrs ffolkes – Miss Selina – but I swear on my blessed mother's grave I'm telling you exactly how it was. Just forty-eight hours after that first telegraph arrived we received a second one. It turned out that my father had plunged headlong into a ravine and broken his back.

'Maybe it was an accident and maybe it wasn't. To this day I don't know and I'm not accusing anyone. What I do know is that, while Miles Murgatroyd was being transported to a filthy, vermin-infested hospital tent near Nome, Roger Kydd had already filed a claim to the gold-mine in his name alone. He then sold that claim on to some big mining outfit, pocketed the proceeds and vanished off the face of the earth.'

'What did your father do then?' asked Selina.

I paused for a few moments before speaking again.

'What did he do then? He died. He died not because his back was broken but because his spirit was broken. Oh, he was no spring chicken. He'd been globe-trotting for nigh on quarter of a century and he knew the kind of place the world was and the kind of people who lived in it. But he and the Colonel had become inseparable. That's what killed him.'

'And then . . . ?' said Evadne Mount.

'My mother did what she could to claw back her rights – our rights. But she discovered that, in the US of A, if you don't have money you also don't have rights. Over there, rights are something you buy, and they don't come cheap.

'So, since she'd married "beneath her", in the horrible expression, and she'd been disinherited by her bigoted Baptist pastor of a father, she had to bring me up on her own. She embroidered smocks in a Frisco sweatshop till her eyeballs were as raw as sandpaper. Then, when she couldn't do that any more, she took in other people's laundry. Then, when she couldn't do that either, we ended up in the poorhouse. And you have to know that, in the California of those days, the poorhouse wasn't just a metaphor. It's where the two of us really lived for three years. Till she died.

'I was dumped in an orphanage, I lit out, I was caught, I was brought back, I lit out a second time and that time nobody bothered to try and catch me. So I mooched my way across the country. I worked as a carpenter in an Omaha saw-mill, I signed up for a stint aboard an oil tanker off the Gulf of Mexico, I served hash in a Fort Worth hash-house, I was a professional card-sharp on a Mississippi riverboat. You name it, I did it.

'I finally got myself a job as an actor, touring in barnstorming mellers – that's melodramas to you. Because of my father's nationality I could do a snooty British accent and I'd get typecast as a Brit.

'Then we were left stranded when the company manager ran off with the female juve – along with the box-office takings – and I was out of work again. So I started riding the freight trains. And during those hot nights under the stars I'd tell the other hobos the gold-rush stories my father had told me and they ate them up and said I should write them down.

'I did write one down and sold it to a pulp magazine – *The Argosy*, its name was. I got twenty dollars for it and that twenty-dollar bill made me a writer. I'd have kept it and framed it, except that I needed it to feed me while I wrote the next one.

'Eventually I'd scraped the bottom of my father's kitty of stories and I had to make up my own and I discovered I was good at that too. Good at the kind of detective stories that were all the rage, stories about grifters, gamblers, blackmailers, showgirls and those single-minded, double-crossing bitches who are as hard as the nails they never stop polishing. Way too hard-boiled for you,' I added, referring to Evadne Mount.

'H'm, yes,' she replied, 'I belong to what I daresay your lot would regard as the runny soft-boiled school. But, you know, Mr . . . Mr Murgatroyd, when I think about how you murdered Raymond, I find it hard to credit you never tried your hand at a locked-room whodunit.'

'It's funny you should say that. I could imitate just about any style, and I actually did once have this idea for a locked-room story with all the traditional trimmings. But none of the pulp rags would buy it. Thought it was too prissy, too Limey. What they were looking for was the rough, tough stuff taken straight from the headlines and breadlines. And by that time I'd become a pro. Whatever they wanted, I gave them.

'Then, when I was finally beginning to pull in some real dough, I hired a private detective, a Pinkerton agent, to find out what had happened to Roger Kydd. I suspected he'd returned to England with all the loot he'd stashed away, and I hadn't a hope of tracking him down myself.

'For a while there I thought it was money wasted, just flushed down the drain. In the end, though, my man did come up trumps. He reported back to me that Kydd had bought this – this "pile", I think you say, on Dartmoor and set himself up as Colonel ffolkes. With two small *f*s, if you please.

'If he'd still been based in the States, I guess I'd have taken my revenge the American way. I'd have gunned him down in some back alley and been done with it. But when I realised he'd transformed himself into an English gentleman, well, I decided to show you Brits that we Yanks could also commit – what did you call it, Miss Mount? A Mayhem Parva murder? I decided to test my locked-room plot in the real world. I liked the irony of it, his trying so hard to be English all over again.

'I came over on the *Aquitania* and booked myself a room at The Heavenly Hound in Postbridge. Most evenings the Colonel would have a tankard or three in the bar and I had no trouble getting him chatting, especially when he learned we had a mutual passion for philately. He brought me back here a couple of times to show off his stamp collection, and the rest was a breeze. He was looking for someone to run the estate and I told him I was looking for a job, so he offered me the post of manager. That was nearly four years ago.'

'Why did you wait so long before taking your revenge?' asked Trubshawe.

'Those four years were to be my alibi.'

'Your alibi?'

'I knew that, once I'd murdered the Colonel in the attic, I'd have no real alibi and so I'd be a prime suspect. And I thought that, if Mrs ffolkes could inform the police that I'd been in her husband's employ for as long as four years, that would help to avert suspicion from me.

'Also, I realised I'd need time to repair the armchair. So, before I made my move, I waited as patiently as I knew how for a really severe winter – the kind of winter the ffolkeses had told me about, the kind of winter that meant the house would be so isolated the police wouldn't be able to come snooping around for three or four days, which would give me the time I needed to do such a good repair job on the chair no one would ever know it had been tampered with. But, of course, I hadn't counted on a retired Scotland Yard Inspector living just a few miles away.'

Then I added – 'ruefully' is the adverb I suppose I would have used if this had been one of my own stories – 'I also hadn't counted on Her Grace the Dowager Duchess of Crime being of the party.'

I made a little mock-bow – rueful again – in Evadne Mount's direction.

'Thank you, young man,' she said, returning the bow. 'So my exposé of how and why you committed the two crimes was accurate?'

'Ha! Accurate isn't the word,' I replied with a mirthless laugh. 'For me it was almost creepy having to listen to you tell the story, my story, listen to you tell it as though you'd written it yourself and I was just a character in one of your books. I couldn't even help admiring the way you picked up on that missing *u* in "behaviour". Now that was a dumb mistake.'

'It was indeed,' she agreed. 'But, you know, I always say it's the cleverest crooks who make the dumbest mistakes. I might even borrow yours for my next whodunit. The few readers capable of picking up on it, as you put it, will most likely assume it's a printer's literal. God knows, there are enough of those about nowadays.

'Anyway,' she continued, 'it *is* gratifying to realise that, in the midst of tragedy, my instincts remained intact.'

'Well – maybe less than you think,' I said.

'Oh? What makes you say that?'

'Only that the one thing you don't seem to have cottoned on to is *your* responsibility in the murder of Raymond Gentry.'

'My responsibility! *My* responsibility! Why, I – I never heard of such a –'

'Yes, your responsibility. You were absolutely right when you suggested that the Colonel had been the victim I originally singled out for my locked-room murder. And you guessed right, too, when you said that, after Miss Selina arrived at the last minute with Gentry, I chose to murder him instead – promising to give him some piece of bogus dirt about the Colonel and persuading him to meet me in the attic before the rest of the house was up and about. And you were also right about why I changed my plans – so there'd be a whole new set of suspects and motives.'

I turned to Trubshawe.

'You were puzzled, remember, at not finding the murder weapon inside the attic? What you didn't understand was that I'd deliberately taken the gun away with me – for the simple reason that I didn't want Gentry's death to be thought of as a suicide. For my plan to work, it had to be seen for what it was: a murder. Only not one committed by me.

'And what *you* didn't understand' – I turned once more to Evadne Mount – 'is that, if I decided to switch victims, it was partly because I'd heard you holding forth again and again about how much safer and more effective it was to murder someone by just shooting him or knifing him and then burying the knife or the gun. What was it you said? Eschew the fancy stuff? Well, you're the expert. So that's what I did. I decided to eschew the fancy stuff and just gun the Colonel down while he was out walking Tobermory, poor old Tobermory, on the moors.'

Shaken by the turn of events, Evadne Mount was, for once, speechless. It was Selina ffolkes who spoke up instead.

'But don't you see, Evie,' she said, 'it means you saved Daddy's life!'

'Eh? What's that you – ?'

I cut her short.

'Miss Selina's speaking the plain truth,' I said. 'If I'd stuck to my original plan, I'd surely have succeeded in killing the Colonel in the attic, just as I succeeded in killing Gentry there. But your theories were responsible for making me change that plan and, as it turned out, it was because of those theories that I botched the Colonel's murder. For you know, my dear Miss Mount, those theories of yours, all those fine theories of the Dowager Duchess of Crime? Frankly, they stink. You just have a go yourself and you'll discover as I did it's not so easy committing a murder that's simple, boring and perfect.'

The novelist instantly cheered up.

'Well, thank God for that!' she exclaimed. 'So it seems that, just like Alexis Baddeley, I'm right even when I'm wrong! I trust, Trubshawe, you won't forget that, if ever we should combine forces on another case.'

Silently, though quite visibly, mouthing, 'Heaven forfend!', the Chief-Inspector then leaned forward and spoke to me in his soberest voice.

'Murgatroyd, you do know that by killing Gentry, however worthless an individual he was, you were causing the shadow of suspicion to be cast on a number of wholly innocent people?'

'Yes,' I answered, 'but the fact that just about everyone had a motive meant it was very unlikely any one suspect would be arrested. My grievance was with the Colonel. I didn't want to see anyone else hurt.'

'But have you thought about this? That if things *had* turned out the way you wanted, if you *had* got away with it, *no one would ever have known.* I mean, no one would ever have known which of the ffolkeses' guests the real murderer was. That shadow would have remained over all of them alike. *For ever . . .*'

I shrugged my shoulders.

'People forget – sooner than you expect. And I was prepared to place my trust in English law. As I understand it, in your legal system there's no such thing as a miscarriage of justice.'

'You're right there,' agreed Trubshawe. 'But what about Gentry? What had he ever done to you?'

'Gentry? He had it coming. I have no regrets.'

'Well, I'm sorry, but in this country we don't hold with people taking the law into their own hands. You killed one man and you tried to kill another. You'll have to pay for that.'

'I don't think so. Aren't you forgetting I'm armed and you're not?'

'Listen to me, man. You're obviously no fool. You must know you're done for. You can't murder us all and it would be senseless to try to escape across the moors in this weather.'

There was a pause when neither of us spoke. Then:

'I *am* going to escape,' I countered in a voice that sounded alien even to me. 'Though not across the moors.'

I tightened my grip on the revolver.

As I did, I heard Evadne Mount shout, 'Stop him! Stop him! He's going to kill himself!'

What a woman. She was right again.